THE LAST DANCE OF MARY KELLY

E. David Brown

ISBN: 9781998270057

Published by Tumbleweed Press

Cover design by Tatiana Sayig

Printed in Canada

"We are our own devil, and we make this world our hell"

Oscar Wilde

Contents

Author's Note

Devotees of the Whitechapel Murders will scour every sentence in this novel to assess its historical accuracy. I acknowledge that I am guilty of distorting the incidents, time frames and facts. Some of the statements made by historical figures appearing in this book are actual quotes attributed to them. I did extensive research while writing *The Last Dance of Mary Kelly*, so extensive that I chose to jettison the majority of facts of what was in preference to what might have been. As Mark Twain said, "Get your facts first, then you can distort them as much as you please." Which I confess I have done.

Chapter 1

The rifleman sitting inside the bell tower of the Coffeyville Methodist Church fired one shot. Grat Dalton pitched forward, leaving a bloody smear on the cantle of his saddle. The back of his head vanished, but his face remained intact, capturing his outrage at being killed with nothing to show for it. Bryson Ward spurred his mount to race out of the crosshairs of the deputies and vigilantes determined to kill every one of the outlaws who dared to rob their bank. Bryson's horse pulled up short at a wagon blocking his escape. Tumbling end-over-end, he landed in the dusty street on his back, out cold. The gun battle lasted twelve minutes, long enough for three more of the infamous Dalton gang and four citizens to die.

Bryson came to when he felt a stream of warm liquid on his face. He opened his eyes. A large man wearing a shiny star urinated on him.

"This one's alive," the man shouted, then kicked him in his ribs. "Get up."

"Can't you see I'm hurt?" Bryson pleaded.

"Can't you see I don't give a rat's ass?"

The man jerked Bryson to his feet, almost wrenching his arm out of its shoulder socket.

"This one's alive too, Sheriff."

Bryson turned his head and saw two deputies dragging Emmett

Dalton down the street by his legs.

"Keep them that way until we hang 'em," the sheriff said.

Bryson screamed as they kicked and punched him all the way to the jail.

"Wait a minute, boys. You got it wrong. I'm not with them. I'm a reporter."

It took the three of them to force Bryson into a cell. He grasped the outer bars of the door and held on. It was a mistake. The sheriff took one step back and kicked the door, clanging it shut on Bryson's thumb. Bryson looked in disbelief as his severed thumb fell to the floor. The sheriff picked it up and held it at Bryson's eye level. He tossed it into the feed bowl of a vicious-looking Bluetick Coonhound that was better at preventing escapes than twenty deputies combined. The dog arched its back as it rose from its pallet of straw to sniff the unexpected treat in his bowl. He liked what he smelled and gulped it down in one swallow.

"Jesus Christ," Bryson screamed, waving his mangled hand around the cage. Blood splattered the walls.

"Either shoot him or let him go," Emmett shouted from the adjacent cell.

"Is that any way to talk about your partner," the sheriff said.

"Fuck you Calvin. He ain't no partner of mine."

"What do you call him then?"

"A hostage, I brought him along in case things went south."

"Nice try, but he's gonna swing alongside you."

Bryson tore a strip of cloth from his shirttail and wrapped it around the bloody stub. "Listen to him. I'm not one of them; I'm a reporter."

"Mister, you better figure out how you're going to report your own hanging."

"Calvin, you honestly think that I'd let a chickenshit like him ride with me? I've seen geldings with more balls than he has."

"What would you have done with him once you got through using him as a hostage?"

"I wouldn't waste no water on him if that's what you mean."

The sheriff came over to Bryson's cell and looked through the bars for what seemed eons before saying, "Okay then, what paper do you write for?"

Bryson was growing woozy from the pain and loss of blood. "The Manhattan Tribune."

"Ain't that the paper that Stephen Crane writes for?"

The mere mention of the rising star of the boy journalist kindled Bryson's jealousy. "Yeah."

"Hell of a writer that Crane is. I'll wire your paper to see if you're on the level. Hope that your boss wires back before the trial."

Bryson pressed his face against the bars. "Why?"

"Thing is, we don't postpone justice waiting for telegraphs to come in."

"He means hangings."

"Ain't it the same thing, Emmett?"

"Round here it is I guess."

"Quit joking," Bryson screeched. "My life is at stake!"

"Either send the telegraph or kill him on the spot. I can't stomach listening to his whining while I'm waiting to do the drop."

The sheriff nodded and walked out of the holding area.

"Thanks for telling him I'm not one of your gang."

"Don't thank me. I was fixing to use you as a shield and get rid of your sorry yellow ass later."

"Thanks anyway."

"Shut up," the last of the Dalton gang said before Bryson passed out.

*

Two days later, Sheriff Calvin Hanks walked into the jail waving a Western Union telegraph. He unlocked the cell door. "Looks like you're on the level. Sorry about the thumb, but it'll give you something to write about."

"So long, Shakespeare," Emmett said as Bryson staggered out of his cell.

Bryson Ward kept his lips pressed as tightly as a freshly embalmed corpse. He walked behind the fat lawman. He fixed his eyes on the rack of rifles and shotguns in Calvin's office. He wished that he had the courage to take one down and blow the legs off the tin star who had mutilated his hand.

"Here, these belong to you." Clavin Hanks handed Bryson a pair of saddlebags. "Leastwise they was on the horse that throwed you."

The sheriff stared at Bryson's damaged hand a moment. "What the hell. I can't let you leave without giving you something for your troubles." He went over to a cabinet and took out a smooth leather holster and gun belt. He handed it to Bryson. Burned into the back of the belt was Emmett Dalton's name. "This here goes with it." He pushed a black barrelled Colt 45 into the holster.

"I can't take these."

"Sure you can. He ain't going to need them where he's headed. Ain't that right Emmett," he shouted into the holding area.

"I wouldn't count on it," Dalton answered. "Write something good about me leastwise, something as good as you can write about a bad man."

Chapter 2

The sun threaded its rays through the hand-hewn niches that served as the windows of the fieldstone house. A man wearing a collarless shirt tucked into trousers held up by a rope drew aside a curtain dividing the inside of the dwelling. He hid a package wrapped in butcher's paper behind his back. A young woman bending over a carpetbag lying on top of a straw tick glanced over her shoulder. She frowned at the tattered cap pulled down over the man's eyes. "It's bad luck to wear a hat in-house, Da," she said and returned to stuffing the bag with clothes.

He sat down on a three-legged stool next to a chamber pot. "Bad luck is something we have enough of without bringing more down on our heads, Mary." The man rubbed his callused palms across the stubble of his beard.

The girl picked up a tortoiseshell hairbrush and turned it over in her hands.

"That was the only thing your màthair had to show after sixteen years with me."

"It was enough," she answered, tossed the brush into the bag, and snapped it closed. "If you ask me, I won't go, Da."

Her father shook his head. He reached into his pocket and took out a cold pipe. "There's nothing for you here. Leastwise over there the mills are hiring." He clamped his teeth around the stem of his pipe and stood up. "Here," he bent his head and shoved the package he had been concealing at her.

She placed it on the bed and tugged at the twine tied around the bundle. She folded back the paper and picked up a simple blue dress. At the bottom of the package was a pair of ankle-high lace-up boots. "They're beautiful." She knew that the dress and shoes had set her father back three months' wages.

"Maggie O'Shea helped choose 'em for me. She was a good friend of your máthair."

"London's not that far, Da." She folded the dress and rewrapped it in the butcher paper. "It's not as though I'm going off to Canada."

He cleared his throat. "Thank the Lord for that. Once you cross the ocean, you're gone forever."

"It's for the best. I'll be able to send something to pay the grazing fees. Once things are better over here, I'll be back."

"That's what Francis said." He reached into his back pocket and removed a handkerchief, and wiped his nose. He had lost his brother during the 1867 uprising. Though Mary had heard the story a thousand times, it still brought the angry taste of metal to her tongue.

"He wasn't a Fenian. His only crime was to set out with some lads from the village to tear down fences the English were putting up around the commons. It was meant as a lark. It were a strange night, full orange moon and raining, when two soldiers appeared at our door. I walked to their wagon. One of the soldiers pulled back a tarpaulin. They pitched the lifeless body of my brother, Francis Kelly, over the edge of the wagon. He landed face-down in a puddle of muddy water. It's a shame, Mary, a bleeding waste. If he'd only asked me before going off and doing something rash, I would have told him that this sorry bit of land's not worth fighting for. Either you die for all of Ireland or none of it."

Patrick Kelly had said nothing when his daughter told him she was crossing the water to England. Forced to pay for the right to graze his sheep on what was once public land, he had to take a job nearly twelve miles away, sorting rags in a local pulp mill.

"With you gone, Mary, aside from me, there's no one to tend the flock. I used to question why God saw fit to bless us with only one child. I don't ask questions anymore. I've seen families of ten starve trying to get by on what I brought home for a household of three." He stared out the open doorway. "I mean two." His eyes were dry. The tears left in him had been shed burying his wife five years before. "Count your blessings, Mary Kelly. That's what your máthair would say. Remember this? I had no shoes and wept until I met a man who had no feet."

"I remember," Mary whispered.

Her father stood up, walked over to the bed, and lifted the carpetbag off the straw mattress. "We best get going if you're to make a new life for yourself."

Mary Jeanette Kelly waved at her Da through the soot-covered window of the train as it pulled away from the platform. He did not return her goodbye. Her father had aged a hundred years.

It took Mary an hour to walk from the train station to the docks, where a ferry would take her to Liverpool. From there, she would have to endure another long rail ride to London. Mary waited as an RIC opened every bag of the people standing in line before herding them up the gangplank and into the bottom of the boat reserved for lower-class passengers.

Get your skirt moving." The constable prodded her between her breasts with the baton he carried like a sceptre. She batted away his arm and pressed her carpetbag against her chest. His face turned red. A fleeting smile stretched on his pasty face to the bottom of his grey muttonchops. "Take no offence, Miss. I meant nothing by it. Please open your bag for inspection."

Mary opened her bag and allowed him to root through it with his baton. "It's standard procedure, Miss. Can't be too careful, what with all the radicals trying to bring the rebellion to England."

"I'm not used to travelling," she replied, holding back the urge to call him an arse-kissing lackey of the British.

"First trip, eh?" He took the bag from Mary and walked up the gangplank with her. "Where are you bound for?"

"Whitechapel, a man came to my village and told me there was work there for those who want it."

The RIC stopped midway up the ramp. He shook his head. "Don't take me wrong, Miss. But, if I were you, I'd turn around right now and go back home. London's got enough pot wallopers."

Mary grabbed the bag from the Irish constable's hand. "I've

secured myself a position at Hollens Textile Mill. I got a letter of introduction from the man who came to my village to prove it."

He placed his hand on Mary's shoulder. "I have a daughter about your age, and I'm telling you this as a father: go home, girl."

Mary threw her head back and pushed her way past him. "I have a position, I told you. The man gave me a paper to present when I get to Whitechapel."

"I can see you're too stubborn to listen to good advice. At any rate, let me tell you before you go, the only position I know of from which a girl the likes of you can make a living in Whitechapel is on her back. Get along with you now. You're holding up the line."

An elderly gentleman dressed in a black suit and wearing a fedora nudged his way through the crowd and in front of Mary. He presented the purser at the top of the gangway with his boarding pass. "First class," the purser remarked after inspecting the man's ticket. "You should have boarded over there to avoid mingling with this lot." He pointed at another gangway at the mid-section of the ferry. The elderly gentleman tipped his hat to Mary and scurried up the flight of stairs leading to the upper deck. The purser snatched Mary's pass from her hand and pointed at another set of stairs leading to the lowest level of the ferry. "Go on, be quick about it. Get down there with the rest of your kind."

Mary hesitated. "When I arrived, I saw them loading pigs and sheep down there."

The purser pushed back his white cap. "If the pigs don't mind your company, why should you mind theirs?"

Mary forgot she had promised her father she would try to keep her temper under control. She inherited her flash point from her mother's side of the family along with her blonde hair, full bosom and wide hips.

"You're right. I shouldn't complain. If the swine don't mind being carried across the channel on the same ship with a pudding-faced dung heap like you, why should I care?" Mary marched across the steel deck of the ferry and down the stairs without looking back.

The stench of animal excrement mingled with the odour of the people crammed into the lower level turned Mary's stomach. She shoved her way through the crowd and leaned over the guardrail to gulp in a breath of fresh air. It was apparent the owners of the vessel saw no need to instruct its crew to wash down the animal's pens after each journey. She hung over the rail for the eight hours it took to cross the body of water separating Ireland from England.

When the ship entered port in Liverpool, she staggered down the gangway. She boarded a train waiting alongside the docks to load its cargo of livestock and human beings. The train steamed away and cut across the heartland of Britain. Mary thought that the countryside was no less green than her homeland. Her opinion changed as the train travelled south. Immense smokestacks spewed coal dust and sulphur into a sky-stained pewter with the vomit of progress. A small boy who got on the train by himself sat next to Mary. The clacking of the train's wheels against the iron rails soon lulled the boy to sleep. He squirmed on the wooden bench and rested his head on Mary's lap. A sign was strung around his neck, which read, "Can't afford to keep him. Please take him in."

Mary pulled down the blind over the filthy window and covered the boy with the shawl she wore around her shoulders. Her mother, in honour of Mary's first communion, gave it to her. She smiled and soon joined the boy in sleep, knowing that despite everything, her parents had done as well for her as they could.

Chapter 3

"Don't look at me like that, Morris. I'm not going anywhere the locals are itching to pop a Yanqui." Bryson Ward turned his face away from the man sitting behind a massive oak desk who blew a cloud of cigar smoke in his direction.

The fat man snorted. He pushed himself away from his desk with his stomach. "Haven't heard myself ask you to cover no damn tamale revolution. Besides, I gave that assignment to Crane."

"Crane? That kid knows as much about reporting as..."

"As you don't." Morris rasped. He spit a glob of brown juice into the spittoon next to his chair. "The kid may be wet behind the ears, but he's got a real way with words."

"How the hell can you chew and smoke at the same time?" Bryson screwed up his face in disgust.

"It's a talent." Morris emptied a shot glass full of phlegm from his lungs. Although he was only twelve years older than Bryson, he could have passed for his grandfather. "So what you're saying is that you don't want this or any other assignment that is a bit dangerous."

Coming from anyone else, these words would have triggered a knockdown, but Morris Breck had served his time in the boiler room. No one could deny that. Before Stephen Crane was even gas in his mother's stomach, Morris was wading through the muddy fields of Shilo soaked with the blood and guts of his countrymen. After throwing back a few jars with Bryson and the boys, Morris would remark that if it had been possible for Alexander Gardner to take his daguerreotypes of the dead in colour, Americans would never entertain the thought of fighting another war. Though a pacifist, Morris was foremost a newsman, always on the prowl for some murder or disaster that he could capture, complete with graphic descriptions of the carnage and words of anguish from the victim's loved ones for the public's edification.

Bryson waved his arms. "You might as well quit looking at me. I've had my fill of bullets and bad guys. That stint in the Cherokee territory sealed it for me."

Morris lifted the lid of his humidor. He pulled out two cigars and offered one to Bryson. "Okay, I won't ask you to go to where you might dirty your spats. I'll give you an easy one this time, something I should be handing over to the society page. But seeing as how you're so exhausted, I'll send you to London instead."

Bryson stashed the cigar in his vest pocket. "What gives?"

"Does the name Henry Stanley ring a bell? How about Doctor Livingstone?"

The reporter shook his head. Morris wagged his cigar at Bryson like a schoolmarm scolding her students. "Christ, don't you ever read the newspapers?"

"I've got too much respect for myself to read them. I know the class of bums who write for them."

Morris suckled the end of his cigar, wrapping his lips around it like a pacifier. "I know some guys who were with Stanley at the Herald." He blew a grey doughnut of smoke and coughed. The flap of fat on his neck waggled back and forth. "They said he was a strange piece of work. They told me that if the bastard had as much talent as he had ambition, he would have gone far in this business. As it was, he turned in his notepad for a Bible and a mission, and he's been abusing the natives in Africa ever since."

Bryson glanced down and stroked the stub of his missing thumb through the black glove he always wore. "So what's Stanley got to do with me?"

"Ever hear of Eduard Schnitzer?" Morris didn't wait for an answer. "Course you haven't. He wouldn't amount to turkey shit if he hadn't gone and got trapped in a tribal uprising. It would serve his ass right if the natives popped him into a pot and had him for dinner." Morris blanketed Bryson in a cloud of smoke. "Schnitzer's is a personal friend of Sir Henry Morton Stanley. The Kraut is probably the only man I know of who has a bigger ego than Stanley. Changed his name to Emin Pasha. Means the faithful one in Turkish. Seems this cabbage head is another one of those loons with an obsession to explore the Nile."

"Let me take a guess. Stanley is going to make like the cavalry and go to his rescue." Bryson adjusted the black leather glove on his damaged hand. A cork filled the space where his thumb should have been.

"More like Custer if I had my way. Personally, I don't give a sack of warm cow chips whether Stanley ever comes back. I've had it up to my ears with that clown's white man's burden routine. I want you to go to London to find out what the British public thinks about all this crap. You know, get the common man's point of view and play it out against those lavender-scented dandy's sherry and armchair talk."

"Boss, if Stanley finds Pasha, it'll be the story of the year. But if it turns out to be a wild goose chase the owners of this rag will screw you to the wall for wasting their money."

Morris rolled his eyes and chewed on the end of his cigar. Flakes of wet tobacco stuck to his front teeth. "I don't care how the story comes out so long as we come out defending both sides. My father taught me you will never be wrong if you take both sides. He hired men to fight in the war on the South and North sides. The Union won, and we won. There was no way we could lose. That's the philosophy every journalist should follow. Never commit yourself to any point of view until the game has been decided."

In Bryson's ten-year association with his boss, he had come to accept that Morris was basically an unethical bastard with principles. He took great pleasure in pointing it out to his editor whenever the opportunity arose. Perhaps that is why he got all the crummiest assignments.

Morris grunted. He grasped both arms of his chair and hoisted his body out of it. Rivulets of sweat appeared on his forehead while he caught his breath. Twenty years of sitting behind a desk had turned his legs into jelly, barely able to support the three hundred pounds of his upper body. "Here's your boarding pass. Be at the dock by ten sharp."

Bryson looked at the ticket and frowned. The senior editor made his way around the desk and dropped one of his orangutang arms around his reporter's neck. "Something wrong with the accommodations?"

"You're damn right there's something wrong. What's the big idea of booking me in steerage? The only thing lower than this is riding in the hold with all the corpses of pickled Paddies headed back to Ireland to be planted in the sacred sod."

"Sorry pal, it's the best I could do. We all have to pull together in hard times."

Bryson tossed the boarding pass on a mound of papers precariously balanced at the edge of Morris's desk. "Forget it." He started for the door. Before touching the knob he pivoted on his heel. "Don't think I've forgotten that KKK meeting you sent me to cover in Georgia."

"It was a mix-up. You were supposed to be incognito."

"Incognito my ass, I almost got lynched"

Morris threw his arms over his head in exasperation. "Outside of that slight incident, things have gone pretty smoothly for you. The Tribune has always been there to bail you out when you got into trouble, hasn't it?"

Bryson walked back into the centre of the room. "Until I started working for you, I had two thumbs."

“Whoa there, don’t blame me for that.”

“It seems like a pretty damn good place to lay the blame. It was you who sent me to the Cherokee Territory to interview the Daltons.”

“Another mix-up. I didn’t know the Territorial Governor would rescind his offer of amnesty.”

“Morris, you knew three weeks before I stepped off the stage in Tulsa that the Daltons’ had robbed a bank in Lubbock and killed a teller.”

“Complaints, complaints, I’m getting a little tired of your bellyaching. There are reporters who would sell their grandmothers for a chance to be in on the capture of an infamous outlaw gang.”

“A dog ate my thumb.”

“The long and short of it is that you’re a malcontent,” Morris growled. He lumbered around his desk and sat down. He picked up the boarding pass and fanned himself with it. His face resembled an overripe tomato ready to burst. “I’ve given you two of the best scoops of this decade, and all you can do is whine, ‘It’s too dangerous, boss. I might get hurt.’ ”

“Don’t push it, Morris.”

“Hell, Bryson, I got twenty reporters ready to jump on a story like this one. I could have given this assignment to Bret Harte. He’s already over there and knows the ropes.”

“Gimme a break. What would Bret Harte want to do with our rag? The man was a U.S. Consul in Germany and Scotland.”

“I haven’t got the time to sit here begging you. Do you want the assignment, or don't you?" The springs of the chair groaned as Morris leaned forward and held out the ticket. He belched before dangling the carrot in front of his favourite reporter. "I got authorization from the big muck-a-mucks to give you, within reason, of course, an expense account for six months."

Bryson stretched out his arm and took the boarding pass. He popped it against the palm of his hand. "Quantify within reason."

"Hold it to about seven hundred beans."

"What if I spend less than that?"

"The paper will be grateful if you can keep it below the allotted expense authorization." Morris's collar was wet. He always perspired when money was the subject of conversation.

"Come on, Moe. Don't play coy with me. You know what I'm driving at."

"Okay, anything you manage to save out of it is yours." Morris leaned back in his chair and stared at the plaster swirls on the ceiling as if pleading for forgiveness from that big editor in the sky.

Bryson smiled. "It's sweet but not sweet enough."

"What do you want from me, blood?"

"Nah, all I want is a better class of passage. I'm no Vanderbilt, mind you. Just book me above the waterline, and I'm yours."

"The extra fare comes out of your pocket." Morris barked.

"Sorry, either the Tribune picks up the tab all the way or it's no go."

Morris slumped in his chair in defeat and waved Bryson away

from his desk.

The reporter folded the boarding pass in half and slipped it into the lining pocket of his jacket. "There is one other thing."

The pedestal of Morris's chair creaked as he shifted his full weight to the side. "It better be good."

"Boss, you'll like this one. I want our agreement in writing."

Morris tore a piece of paper off of his writing pad and scribbled down something. He swore as he folded the note in half and placed it in an envelope. "Son-of-a-bitch, twenty years ago, if you'd tried to highjack me like this, I'd have snapped your neck." He dabbed the flap with glue and sealed it before giving it to Bryson. The reporter nodded and rocked back and forth on his heels as he waited for his boss to look up at him. "Is there something else you want before I kick your ass out of my office?"

"Just a word of encouragement," Bryson grinned and ducked as the paperweight on Morris's desk went sailing past his head.

"Don't come back from England until I send for you."

"Moe, why don't you just come clean from the beginning of handing out an assignment and spare us both a lot of grief."

"What, and deprive myself of the exercise? Now get out of here. You've wasted enough time. I got a real story coming in from Philadelphia. Seems like some lunatic is going around carving up nuns in the city of Brotherly Love."

Chapter 4

The sensation of warm water cascading down Mary's legs awoke her as the train entered a long tunnel. She curled her lip and sniffed the air. Her hand came to rest on her soaking-wet dress. The boy, who had used Mary as a bolster, sat up and turned his face away. The dirty windowpane of the train captured his expression of humiliation.

Mary laid her hands on his shoulders and forced him to look at her. "Well, what do you have to say for yourself?"

"I'm truly sorry, Miss. It was the train, you know. It stirred me up. I didn't feel it coming until it was done."

The boy seemed to shrink and disappear as shame devoured him. Mary ran her hand over his close-cropped head. "All is forgiven. I have other dresses in my bag. As for this one, it needed a wash anyway."

"You're not putting me off?"

"I didn't say that. But what's over is over. And since it can be mended, there's no harm done." Before the boy replied, he and Mary were pitched forward as the train pulled into the station. Mary returned to a seated position. Steam billowed up from under the train.

A hog-faced man entered the car. He stood in the aisle with his arms behind his back. His jowls shook as he turned his head. "Get up, move on with you." His stomach strained to escape the jacket stretched around his barrel torso. “We got to clean this sty before it leaves.” He kept one arm behind his back and pointed with the other. He shook a set of keys dangling from a metal ring attached to a short iron bar. “What are you waiting for, an invite from Queen Victoria herself?”

Mary remained seated. The other passengers slowly rose from the wooden benches they had been glued to for several hours. She waited for them to gather their belongings and file down the aisle like sheep being led to the shearing pen. Out the window Mary saw a man dressed in the identical uniform as the porker man place a small step-stool at the exit platform of the car ahead of hers. Well-dressed gentlemen and women of quality, as Mary’s mother called them, exited the luxury coaches. Mary wondered how many birds had to die to furnish the plumes that decorated the fancy hats the women wore. The uniformed man offered his hand to each person as they detrained. As the ladies brushed by him, he tipped his hat without receiving so much as a nod in acknowledgment of his service.

“You there,” the voice preceded the man as he bulled his way through the crowd exiting the 3rd class car. The veins on the side of his neck throbbed. The keys on his ring clanked violently together when he shook them in front of Mary’s face. “Are you deaf as well as Irish?”

Mary grasped the edge of her seat and glared at him. His breath was as foul as the dung heap outside of her father’s barn. “There’s no need for you to talk like that.” She held her temper. “I was waiting for the crowd to go by before getting up."

"Christ, you Paddies are all alike." He grabbed her by her arm and started to pull her to her feet. "If I have to, I'll drag you and that whelp of yours off this train." The conductor's face screwed up in pain when a hand dropped onto his shoulder and dug its fingers into his muscle. Confronted by a young man towering a good two heads above him, he released Mary and backed away.

The young man's head was bowed, his cap pulled down to the bridge of his nose, obscuring his features. He lifted his head and pushed back his cap. A twist of red hair tumbled across his forehead. His pale green eyes captured the anxiety of the conductor. He held out a paper sack. "Take one. They're good for what ails you." He reached into the bag and removed a toffee.

The conductor's voice cracked. "I'd advise you not to go looking for trouble here, lad, or you'll get more of it than you bargained for."

The young man slipped a toffee into the breast pocket of the conductor's tunic. "Enjoy it, mate. It may be the last time you have a full set of equipment with which to chew."

The conductor glanced behind him. A bearded man and his bald companion walked up and stood on either side of him. On their jackets, they wore the same button as the young man, a red fist on a white background with 1848 stitched underneath. "Got a problem here, Darcy?" The bald man inquired.

The young man shook his head. "No trouble, Caleb; I was just about to ask this gent to call his chum outside to bring up the stool."

He gestured with his thumb at an ancient woman on the seat behind him. “This here grandmother can barely stand, much less make it to the front of the car and jump to the platform.” From the scarf around her head to her shoes, she was dressed in black. She appeared to be asleep. Her head was tilted forward. Her chin rested on her breastbone.

Darcy looked at Mary. “Hello there.” He smiled. “While you’re at it, you might help this lass and her wayne with their luggage.” The eligible bachelors in her village, Mary thought, would count themselves blessed to possess a full set of teeth as white and perfect as the young man’s.

“He’s not my child,” Mary said.

“I don’t care whose brat he is.” The conductor held up his clenched fists. His knuckles were white, drained of blood. “No Irish trash is going to tell me what to do on my run. Get this whore, her bastard, and that hag behind you out of here before I call for help.”

“I was giving you a chance to do something Christian for once in your measly life. The choice was yours, and you missed it.” Darcy retreated, brought up his arms and squared off.

The sharp click of the doors opening at both ends of the car brought a look of relief to the face of the conductor. “Looks like the odds have changed a bit, eh, Paddy?” Two trios of burly railroad yard workers wielding pipe wrenches blocked the exits.

Darcy’s hand slipped under his coat flap. When it reappeared he grasped a club with sawed off nails embedded in its knobby head.

"Chew that toffee now. You'll be on soft food after this."

Mary sprang to her feet. She inserted herself between the two groups. The boy began to cry. "Enough of this!" She shoved the young Irishman. "You should be ashamed. Can't you see there are women and a child here?"

The young man hesitated a moment and lowered his arm. "Never let it be said that Darcy Darnell failed to respect the wishes of a lady." He reached into the rack above his head and took down Mary's carpetbag. He led the way down the aisle to the exit door. Mary followed closely behind him. She turned to look at the conductor.

"What do you want from me, a thank you?" He growled. "If it wasn't for you, none of this would have happened."

Darcy pointed his club at the conductor. "Be bloody well grateful she was here. Things stand as they are for now. But take my word the people will have their day, and your sort will be washed out to sea." One of the yard workers opened the door for Darcy and discreetly patted him on his back. "I'm with you, brother." Darcy nodded and jumped to the platform below. He held out his hand to Mary. She picked up the boy and lowered him into Darnell's open arms. The boy wriggled in his arms like a freshly caught fish and broke loose. He hit the ground running and was swallowed by the mass of people entering the train station. Mary saw his head pop through the bodies surrounding him as he briefly paused to wave goodbye. "You must have a way with children," Darcy said and walked away with Mary's bag.

Mary trailed after him. The archway leading into the building was flanked on either side by lions. Above the archway stood a statue of Britannia, her sword raised in a menacing gesture of welcome. Mary froze when she stepped into the cavernous train station. The granite walls rose sixty feet from the floor and closed in on her. Shafts of sunlight poured through the windows, trapping dust motes in their rays. Mary maneuvered through the mass of people scurrying throughout the station like rats abandoning a burning slaughterhouse. The marble floors, worn to glass smoothness by a million feet, groaned as trains rumbled in and out of the station without pause. Noise, voices without form, lost in a mélange of accents and tongues melted into one desperate howl. She saw the young man. He stopped in front of a bench where a derelict was sleeping. The man on the bench pulled the newspapers covering him like a blanket over his head. Mary dashed toward the young man. She snatched her grip from him and said, “We can’t leave now.”

“Why not?”

“The old woman. We left her back there.”

“She isn’t in need of our’s or anyone’s help now. She dozed off for eternity.”

Mary’s lips went pale as she crossed herself. “We have to notify someone.”

“That would serve no purpose. When the inspectors discover her, they’ll be obliged to take care of her. So, let’s not deprive the old mother of a funeral at the crown's expense."

"You think you're clever, don't you?"

"Clever enough to know when to stand my ground, clever enough to understand the difference between a just cause and lost cause."

"I'd rather not share the pleasure of your company anymore, sir."

"Is it something I said?"

"Because of your misplaced sense of chivalry, you came within a fingernail of shedding blood."

"Miss, you're as green they come. You couldn't have left the old sod more than a day ago and already you see fit to tell me how one should conduct one's self in the big city. Until you understand the rules of survival here, don't be so presumptuous as to offer your milkmaid opinions to one in the game. If I had let that bloke have his way, he'd have bullied us all the way down the aisle and charged us full pence to disembark from his bloody train."

"I'd have paid the pence to avoid trouble. I've seen the results of such false courage. The churchyard back home is full of boys who refused to give an inch."

Darcy tilted back his head and laughed. The derelict on the bench moaned and turned to face the wall. Darcy put his finger up to his lips, "Shush, mustn't disturb the best of the Empire."

"I don't have the time or inclination to continue our conversation."

"Before you go, tell me miss are you one of the many trying to escape the poverty, and shame back home or one of the few who have seen fit to bring the battle to them?"

A chill travelled up Mary's spine. She pressed her bag to her chest and nervously scanned the faces of the people nearby for their reaction to the young man's declaration. "Are you daft? Someone might overhear you and take you for a Fenian."

"Me?" Darcy brought up a laugh from the pit of his stomach. I ain't no Hugh O'Neill. My battle is on the floor of Hollens Mill. All I want is a piece of the pie instead of the crumbs the owners flick our way."

Mary dropped her guard on hearing him mention Hollens Mill. "You work at Hollens?"

"Aye, I'm a top-rate machinist. It's my job to ensure the engines of that damn hell hole sing like the heavenly host day-in-day-out."

Mary slipped her hand into her carpetbag and fumbled around for something. She withdrew a yellow piece of paper folded in half. "This is a letter of introduction to a Mr. Hollens. A man came to my village seeking girls to work at his textile mill."

Darcy plucked the piece of paper from Mary and held it up to the light. The faint trace of the watermark in the shape of a unicorn revealed itself. "When my mum came over in 65, they weren't giving out invitations. A man pounded on our door after my Da died saying that as the farm was lost anyway, why not seek our fame and fortune in England. So she buried my pa and carried me and my brothers and sister over to the land of plenty. When she got here it didn't take her long to realize that the milk and honey actually tasted like piss and vinegar."

"If you hate it so much, why not go back home?"

"I have no home, miss. I didn't catch your name."

"That's because I didn't toss it your way. But if you must know, I'm called Mary Jeanette Kelly."

Darcy grabbed her hand and pumped it like he was drawing water. "Mary Kelly, most recently of Ireland, my name is Darcy Darnell, not so recently of Sligo."

The derelict on the bench lifted his head. "Now that you two have been properly introduced, get the hell away from here."

Darcy took Mary by her hand. The street in front of the building was bustling with activity. The throngs of people escaping the train station split into all directions of the compass. Carriage drivers shouted at well-heeled passers-by to take their cabs and save shoe leather. Lorries, loaded beyond their capacity, swayed side-to-side as they sped down the road, ignoring the pedestrians who crossed in front of them. Hucksters congregated in the square outside the entrance of the station, peddling everything from hair restorer to fruit. They broke off their banter only long enough to chase off the occasional panhandler who tried to tap their potential customers for a bit of loose coin.

Mary was amazed to see how many newspaper stands there were, more than she recalled seeing in her entire life. As Darcy walked past one of the stands, he released Mary's hand when a paper vendor announced, "News of the day. Murder in Whitechapel. Queen says prayer in remembrance of the third anniversary of Khartoum uprising. No word from Stanley."

"Do you know how to read?" Darcy asked Mary before dipping into his pocket to pull out a coin.

"My Da made sure I got through primary. He told me a person who can't read or write is a victim of their own ignorance."

"Seeing as you have the necessary skills." Darcy handed Mary the paper. "Find the bit on the murder and tell me what it says." He led her over to an old fountain, dry and in disrepair. They sat down on its ledge. The front page was dominated by the news of the memorial service held for General Gordon. Mary read aloud the first paragraph.

Darcy shrugged. "That's one we ought to thank the Moors for. My uncle served in that bastard's regiment in China. He lost his leg just so the Empire could maintain its right to sell those people opium and keep them bowing before the Union Jack. Can you believe it, half the Tommies over there were Irish." A pigeon landed at Darcy's feet. He took aim and nailed its head with a projectile of spit. "Chinese Gordon," he muttered the name like a curse. "Never mind that, read me about the murder."

Hunting for the article, Mary flipped through the paper twice. It was sandwiched between a notice for land for sale in Australia and an advertisement for Doctor Mollock's Cure for Male Inadequacy. Next to the block relating the story of the murder was a column that told of the expedition of Sir Henry Morton Stanley to rescue someone called the Emin Pasha. "There's not much here on the murder," Mary said.

"Read what there is."

Mary read slowly, pronouncing each word on its own. "The mutilated body of a man, 20 to 30 years of age, was discovered Tuesday morning in Whitechapel." She paused and looked at Darcy. He nodded for her to continue. "The victim, Gerry Connolly, is well known to police as a member of the International Workers Movement and Irish Republican Brotherhood. His common-law wife, Martha Turner, identified Mr. Connolly's remains. The police are withholding the details of the murder from the public pending further investigation. Sir Charles Warren, Metropolitan Police Commissioner, speculates that the nature of the death is consistent with the punishment and warning that anarchist groups deal out to disloyal members."

Darcy bit his lower lip and sighed. "Warren's smooth. Not only does he know who the real assassins are, but he also finds a way of covering their tracks. First, he accuses us of destroying the moral fabric of society, and now he succeeds in laying his cronies' crimes at our doorstep."

Mary folded the paper. "Did you know Connolly?"

"As well as one can know a brother. He was in the movement."

"The movement?"

"The less you know of that business, the better off you are." He stood up and helped Mary to her feet. “He worked at the mill with me. Poor sod told me he’d found a good skirt and was on his way to reforming her.”

“Reform her from what?”

“Never mind. Learn your trade in the mills, lass, because the only other trade available outside the mills in Whitechapel, as so many other green girls have found, is not worth the shame.” Darcy threw his shoulders back and stood erect. “Enough of that. Where are you off to? Do you have a place to stay?”

“My Da has arranged three months room and board at a Mother Cantons boarding house.”

“I know the place. It’s only a few corners from the mill. I’d take you there myself, but I have a meeting.”

“No need to bother. Just point me in the right direction.”

“I think a hansom would be the way to go. By the time you manage to find your path through the maze of streets of London, it’ll be Judgment Day.”

“I can’t go spending money on such luxuries as that.”

“Take this, little sister.” Darcy forced a note into Mary’s hand. “Find a driver and tell him to drop you off directly in front of your boarding house. Until you learn the streets, it’s not advisable to go wandering about Whitechapel on your own.”

“It’s not proper to take a stranger’s money,” Mary protested while thinking at the same time how grand it was to arrive in a country where people became friends in a matter of minutes.

"Consider it a loan until you get yourself established. Who knows by that time maybe you won't think of me as stranger." Darcy walked away before Mary could protest. She tried to follow him down the street but lost him in the chaos of the city.

A profound fear came over her. She felt the crush of people around her. She was alone in a city of over a million individuals. She looked at the note curled in her fist, swallowed her pride, and made her way toward a hansom parked at a corner. The driver's back faced Mary as he groomed his horse. Mary wondered how he kept from dying of the summer heat in the ankle-length black coat and stove pipe hat that he wore as a mark of his profession.

"Excuse me." She tapped the driver's shoulder. When he turned around, Mary handed him the money and the piece of paper bearing the address of Mother Cantons rooming house. "Do you know how to get to here?"

The driver rolled his tongue inside his cheek and looked Mary up and down. "Looks like you got lucky, darling," he said and stuffed the money into his pocket. "Go on get in," he ordered Mary, and he climbed onto the driver's perch.

It was the first time in Mary's life that she had ridden in a proper carriage. The experience, on the whole, left her unimpressed. Her father's farm wagon was far sturdier and absorbed the bumps in the road better than the hansom. The cab moved too quickly through the streets for her to get a good picture of the layout of the town. At one point, she smelled freshly mowed grass and tucked her head out the window. The cab rolled past a park where several people were gathered around a man who stood on a box and shouting at the top of his lungs. She kept her head outside the hansom to take in the landmarks. The cab skirted the edge of a lane lined on both sides with trees. Behind the trees stood houses large enough to hold her whole parish. The cab did not linger long in this end of town. It sped through the gentry's neighbourhood before she could get a good glimpse of the surroundings and realize what she had been deprived of since birth.

Mary closed her eyes. The jostling of the cab over the broken cobblestones lulled her to sleep. A good half-hour passed before she awoke, lapsing into a coughing fit. After regaining her composure, she scrunched up her nose at the fetid stench that had awakened her. She wheezed and tried to hold her breath as she thrust her head out the window of the cab. It was true what she heard on the boat. You could smell Whitechapel before you could see it. Rows of dingy red brick buildings blackened by a great cloud of soot above the rooftops greeted her.

A rock sailed through the window, missing Mary by an eyelash. She craned her neck and saw a young boy race down the street. The driver cursed and shouted after him, "If I catch you, I'll flail you alive."

A young woman exiting a tavern with a sign of a cluster of bells strung together like grapes painted above its doorway stumbled off the curb. The driver pulled up his reins and lashed out at her. "Out of my way, you slut." The woman blew him a kiss. She turned around and bent over to lift her skirt to show him her naked ass. The crack of the driver's whip sent her scurrying back into the tavern.

The cab leaned to one side as it rounded a corner and stopped in front of a set of open wooden gates. "No sooner asked than delivered, miss," the driver said. Mary climbed out of the cab and looked through the open gates at the squalid courtyard lying behind them. "Driver, I told you to drop me off at Mother Cantons boarding house."

The cabby pointed at the clapboard buildings surrounding the courtyard. "That's what I did, no more, no less." The driver reached between his legs and tossed Mary's bags at her feet. "If the accommodations ain't to your liking, look me up. I'm sure I can put you in touch with some gents who know how to use your talent."

Mary picked up her bag, held it to her ear, and shook it. Nothing had broken as far as she could tell. "Is this how you treat all your passengers?"

"Ah, come on, there's nothing in there that you couldn't replace with a little effort on your part. I'd mark that a strapping lass like you could go all night without taking a breather."

Mary's face grew hot. She picked up her other bag and glared at the driver. "I know where you're going with all this, but I'll just mark it off as a case of bad breeding."

The driver wrapped the leather lead of his rein around his gloved hand twice. He said before giving the rein a quick snap, "Don't play coy with me. I have been around these parts long enough to know that sooner or later, your type ends up between the sheets. Sooner is better than later while men are still willing to ante up for a choice piece of thigh."

"If you'd come down from that perch of yours, be sure I'd teach you some manners." Mary's anger burst forth in such force that it startled the horses.

The driver deliberately snapped his whip and steered the hansom through a puddle. The front of Mary's dress was splattered with its green stinking liquid. "Can't smell any worse than the piss you're already drenched in," he cackled.

Mary fought back the urge to cry. The shrill laughter of the driver taunted her. She started after the cab, but it rapidly gained distance on her, rounded the corner, and disappeared. She inhaled deeply and marched down the wooden sidewalk through the open gates.

The courtyard was enclosed by three rickety structures, the tallest of which faced the street. From the stench and squealing of pigs, Mary immediately recognized the structure on the left side of the yard as a barn. The building on the right served as a livery. It was left open to the elements. It had four stalls, only one of which was occupied by a sway-back cow whose udder hung past her knees. Mary turned toward the barn and saw a man shovelling manure out of a wheelbarrow and tossing it on a dung heap. She tapped him on his shoulder. He whirled around, holding the shovel in front of him like a pike. Mary controlled her urge to run. His face looked as though it had been doused with boiling water. Layers of scar tissue rose and fell like the swells of an angry red sea. A black hole existed in the place where his nose should be. It sprayed a mist of wet air as he breathed. The man dropped the shovel and yanked a dirty tan scarf over his face, leaving only his eyes exposed.

Mary swallowed her revulsion. "I'm sorry if I frightened you."

The man rubbed the corner of one eye with his thumb, taking away a yellow gob forming in the corner. "As well you should be for scaring what's left of a man's wits out of him." The voice which seeped through the moist cloth was as tortured as his face. It travelled erratically up and down the musical scale like a defective pitch pipe.

"I'm truly sorry, sir," Mary repeated.

"Never mind., my fault, really. I should know better than to work out here without covering up." He chuckled and rapped himself on top of his head with his knuckles. "But it gets so bleeding hot with this thing pulled over my mouth that I can scarcely breathe. Now, what can I do for you, miss?"

"I was told this is where Mother Cantons boarding house is located."

"True. That building straight ahead with the balcony is Mother Cantons. For my part, though, I'd rather sleep in the barn; better class of animals there, you know."

Mary took a step forward. Her foot sunk into a pile of muck

covered by sawdust. The noxious fumes of pig manure concealed under the sawdust enveloped her.

"Sorry bout that, miss." The man ran over to the stable and returned with two planks, which he laid end to end as a boardwalk for her. "Meant to clean up that mess when I got around to it. Not enough hours in the day though to do what needs to be done." He turned his back to Mary and pulled down his bandana. He reached into his hip pocket, removed a bottle, and took a long swig before pulling up his kerchief and facing Mary again. "Straight ahead it is, miss." He continued to place the boards in front of Mary as she walked toward the building. "Mind the sow if you come out on your own. She'll do you for sure if she sees you near her piglets."

Mary stepped off of the plank and onto a raised platform that functioned as the building's porch. "Thank you for your help." She lifted the latch holding the doorway closed.

"Name's, Farrow, miss, though everyone around here calls me the Major cause I...." He failed to complete his sentence and coughed. "It is unimportant. I'm here now, and that's a sight better than being in some of the places I've been in."

"My name is Mary Kelly, Mr. Farrow." She reached out and touched the man's hand.

He cleared his throat and stepped to the side. "Since we're going to be neighbours, call on me if there's anything you need." He lifted his eyes to a room above the stable. Out of place with the surroundings was a stained glass mosaic window.

“I will,” she lied and leaned against the door. It sprung open without warning. Mary fell across the threshold and landed face down in the hallway. “For the love of Jesus,” she cursed and blushed as she crossed herself and stood up. “That’s one for confession,” she remarked and limped toward a set of stairs leading to the upper floors.

“No need to lay waste to the place. If the door’s broken, it’ll be you who pays for it.” She heard a whiny voice say. She walked around to the side of the stairs and saw a small man under the staircase. He was seated behind a door laid on top of two crates. Tacked to the back wall was a hand-lettered sign.

MOTHER Cantons BOARDING HOUSE
NO JEWS, WOGS OR WHORES NEED REGISTER!
ALCOHOL AND OPIUM FORBIDDEN !!
PAYMENT IN ADVANCE !!!

The man spat into a bucket in front of the makeshift desk. He looked Mary up and down, scrunching his nose when his eyes came to rest on the dried muck on her dress. “Aye, Gawd, no telling what the cat will drag in.” He reached inside his sweat-stained shirt and scratched his chest. When he removed his hand, he studied a louse trapped between the pads of his thumb and finger a moment before crushing it and wiping it off on his pants. “Well, out with it. How long will you be staying?”

Mary tucked her hand inside her bag and withdrew a letter. “Mother Cantons sent this to my Da to confirm that she’d received three months rent in advance for my board and keep.” She handed him the letter.

The man ripped the end of the envelope open with his teeth. He scanned its contents before tossing it on top of his desk. “You owe me another 6 shillings.”

“I owe nothing of the kind. My Da made the arrangements with Mother Canton and paid in advance. I have a receipt to prove it.”

“That was then and now is now.”

Mary turned away from the little man, gaining control of her emotions. When she faced him again, her eyes were fixed on his throat. “I want to speak with Mother Cantons.”

He propped his elbows on the plank top and leaned forward. “Can’t do that. She ain’t here, immigrated to America.”

“And how long ago did she do that?”

The man flicked off a roach crawling across a plate. He picked up a biscuit and sniffed it before popping it into his mouth. He grinned at her and swallowed. “Let’s see, she sold me this place nearly two Christmases ago.”

“But the sign, the advertisement my father wrote to,” Mary protested.

The man burst out laughing. “Course, I kept the name of the place. Do you have any idea what it costs to change a sign? I didn’t want to destroy the goodwill the old gal cultivated by word of mouth from your sort travelling back and forth to Ireland. Merely good business to capitalize on her reputation. Besides, who'd want to stay in a place called Lucky Snodgrass Doss House?"

"I don't give a tinker's damn what you call this establishment." Mary slammed her palms down on the desk. "It does not alter the fact that my father paid three months' lodging in advance."

The little man hunched his shoulders and dropped his head to one side. "There are a great many unscrupulous bastards in the world who would deny that any sort of transaction took place. Not me. It is true your father sent me what at that time would cover your stay. I'm an honest man. My word is my bond. But, times being like they are, I have to meet my expenses. So, like it or not, I have to ask for my lodgers to help me keep the doors open by chipping in a bit more."

"Return me my money, and I'll find another place to stay," Mary demanded.

"As much as I'd like to, I can't give you what's been spent." The man smiled and pushed the plate of biscuits to Mary. "Go ahead, take one." He stared at the ceiling as he scratched his neck in what passed as a moment of deep reflection. "My heart goes out to you, lass. What has happened is inexcusable. I tell you what I'll do to make amends. Give me the extra to cover your three months, and I'll throw in a change of linen once a month at no additional cost."

"A change of linen, what kind of arrangement is that?" Mary clasped her hands together to keep them off the pimple-faced dwarf's throat.

"I can see how you'd be surprised by my offer considering how most places around here require you to supply your own bedding. Since I am truly consumed by guilt, I'll, against my better judgment and to my financial ruin, toss in a hot bath once a week. There I've said it, and in saying it, I feel a great weight has been lifted off my conscience."

Exhausted by her journey, Mary nodded. Turning around, she dipped her hand into her bodice and pulled out a note. Reluctantly, she allowed the man to take it from her. She knew surrendering her money made it imperative she secure a job at Hollens within the week as she only had enough left to last her a month. "I'd like that hot bath you promised," she said.

The man shook his head sadly. "That'll cost you four pence."

"Nonsense," Mary screamed and reached out for her money lying on the desktop. The man was faster than her and snatched it up before she could get to it.

"You'll get your free hot bath. Let it not be said Lucky Snodgrass is a dishonest man. But you see, we only heat the water on Fridays."

"Listen to me, little man. I'm tired. I'm dirty, and I'm fast on my way to saying and doing things that will make you lose what hair you have left."

The man put his arms behind his head and smiled benignly. "A cold bath will cost you nothing, provided you draw it yourself. The tub's inside the livery stable. Don't get much call for it. Each room has a washbasin and chamber pot. Them articles meet the hygiene needs of the majority of my guests." He leaned over and picked up a cigar box off the floor. Inside the box were several keys attached to wooden sticks. "Here you go, miss, room 12. That'll be one floor up on your left."

Mary trudged up the unfinished pine treads to the next story. Her shoes stirred layers of dust carpeting the naked floor of the corridor. She passed an overstuffed armchair and sofa spilling its stuffing out of its sides. A sign on the wall with an arrow pointing down to a bucket read "SPIT HERE NOT ON THE FLOOR !!"

She located her room. A padlock secured the door. She inserted the key into the lock and jiggled it several times before she heard a click and forced the lock open. She entered the room and closed the door behind her. The door could not be locked from the inside. The room was bare except for a cane bottom chair and rough-hewn bed slightly larger than a coffin. The canvas tick on top of the bed was blotted with yellow stains and smelled of mouldy straw. Mary cursed herself for not remembering to take the sheets and blanket the toad of a hostler had promised her. She was too weary to make the trip downstairs. She stripped off her soiled clothing and fell into the bed. The sour smell of the mattress was worse than the stench of her dress. "Tomorrow, I'll wash my clothes and put everything in order," she mumbled and closed her eyes. Hardly had she fallen asleep when a loud banging on her door awoke her. "What now," she protested and made it halfway to the door before she remembered she was dressed only in a cotton shift. She picked up her dress from the floor, held it up to her neck, and opened the door a crack. The stablekeeper stood outside the door with his hat in his hand. His scarf was pulled up to the bottom of his eyes. He kept his chin pressed in the folds of his neck, avoiding eye contact with Mary.

"Sorry to disturb you, but I thought you might like to know I heard about your problem with Gus."

"Gus?"

"Gus, who for some reason known only to himself prefers to be called Lucky, the keeper of this palace-" Farrow's eyebrows lifted as he smiled under the cloth. "-agreed that if I'd heated the water, he'll allow you a hot bath at cock's crow."

"Cock's crow, hot bath? I thought that bloke wanted blood for that luxury."

"It's been taken care of." Farrow waited until Mary shut the door before leaving. She stood a few minutes with her ear to the door, listening for any sound in the hallway. She crossed herself and peeked outside. The corridor was empty. She shut the door and jammed the chair under the doorknob. It was, she recognized, a laughable attempt at barring intruders from her room.

Chapter 5

The steamship arriving from New York passed under a smog bank, the accumulation of three centuries' worth of foundries and tanneries belching their waste into the atmosphere and water. Bryson flicked the end of his cigarette over the ship's rail when London came into view. He felt a peculiar ambivalence toward England. At the same time he acknowledged she was the bad bitch mother of his country.

Thanks to the hype that Morris had telegraphed to England, Bryson's impending arrival had been covered briefly in the local Fleet Street rags, "WILD WEST JOURNALIST TAKES ON LONDON!" Granted, his arrival was not in the same league as Mark Twain, but still, he was mildly offended by the reception awaiting him. Five derelicts barely able to stand on their feet waved American Flags and held up a banner welcoming "Bryson Wort Last Man to Ride with the Daltons".

"Bob, Grat, and Emmet may have been hot items in New York for a couple of weeks but over here they mean nothing," Bryson thought. The British press was more concerned with covering the exploits of Sir Henry Morton Stanley than reporting on the nickel-and-dime exploits of a clan of misanthropes from Oklahoma.

On disembarking, Bryson picked up his luggage before one of the hundreds of porters working for pigeon feed could load it on a trolley. He carried his bags listening to the musical lilt of the porters cursing him for cheating them out of a coin. "Beautiful language the way these boys speak it," he thought.

A thin man dressed in a blue pinstripe suit and bowler hat with a catch loop attached to his coat's collar shoved aside the derelicts holding the banner. Bryson walked across the dock to meet him. When he was within arm's length, he dropped his bags and reached out to shake. The man ignored Bryson's hand. He cradled his umbrella in the crook of his arm like a carbine. "Mr. Ward, Mr. Bryson Ward of the New York Tribune?" He asked in a voice so formal that Bryson swore he smelt mothballs on the man's breath. The last time Bryson had been addressed so stiffly was in Baltimore when a couple of bulls from the morality squad put the brakes on him for filing a story on how lily-white southern belles were taking up with gentlemen of considerably darker complexions to ply the world's oldest profession. The bit was just a filler, not to be taken seriously. The unamused policemen took him to their precinct and beat the hell out of him before putting him on a northbound train.

"You are Mr. Ward, I presume?"

"Right-O Gov, I'm your man. That's how you boys say it, isn't it?" Bryson joked.

"Not with anyone with whom I am acquainted," the man replied. "Are those your bags?"

Bryson glanced at the portmanteaus at his feet. "I believe in travelling light. It's easy to do when you can cram everything you own into two bags."

The man pointed at the luggage with the tip of his umbrella. Two derelicts waving the American flags rushed forward to take them. “Mr. Ward, please come with me. I have arranged lodgings for you.”

Bryson crossed his arms over his chest. “Whoa buddy; before I head off with you don’t you think introductions are in order?”

“Perkins,” the man fired off too quickly for Bryson to hear.

“Come again.”

“Perkins, Ezra Perkins, your office wired us to expect your arrival.”

“Who is us?”

“Mr. Ward, I would prefer if we carry on this line of questioning on route to your hotel.”

“Lead on Ezra.” Bryson followed Perkins up a steep set of stairs to a cobblestone street. Perkins raised his umbrella and hailed a black hansom. He opened the cab’s door and motioned Bryson to enter ahead of him. After he had settled himself on the red leather cushion covering the bench, the derelicts placed Bryson’s bags at his feet. “Whew,” Bryson whistled and leaned back. The padded backrest took on the contour of his body. “This is what I call travelling top drawer, if you know what I mean.”

Perkins sat next to Bryson. He stood his umbrella upright between his legs and folded his hands over the curve of its ebony handle. “Your editor asked that I escort you around London until which time, as you Americans say, you get the lay of the land.”

Bryson turned his head to study the passing street scenes. "I don't know anybody who says that."

"I beg your pardon."

"I don't know a single guy who talks like that. Get my drift, Gov?"

"Quite," Perkins said. "I deserve that. I was rather abrupt with you."

"Forget it. I appreciate the red carpet treatment you're giving me, but I don't see why Morris thought I needed a nursemaid."

Perkins banged the tip of his umbrella against the cab's floor. "I am not a nursemaid. I am the representative of your paper in the United Kingdom."

"I don't get it. All our European copy is straight off the wire. We just reprint it word for word back home."

"You are quite correct. Perhaps I failed to define my position with your paper clearly enough. I am a telegrapher. I edit and transmit the latest news from the continent to your employer on a weekly basis."

The hansom stopped. An old man in a donkey cart trundled in front of the carriage. He sang at the top of his lungs, "Knifes sharpened, pots and kettles mended good as new, buttons and threads and needles for sale."

Bryson cringed as the cab driver heaped the foulest sort of abuse on the old man. "Get your Yid arse out of my way."

The old man wore a long black coat and a broad flat hat. He

nodded politely and smiled. “And good morning to you too,” he said and combed his fingers through his white beard. “It’s not my arse that’s slow but is my ass’s arse. He’s too old to move faster than he wants and is too young to stop moving altogether.”

“Listen, you black-hearted devil. I don’t have all day.” The driver raised his whip and laid it across the back of the donkey.

Bryson stuck his head out the cab’s window. “Let it go. No one in here in that much of a hurry.”

The driver raised his whip again. Perkin’s face went taut, and his eyes became blacker. He slammed the crook of his umbrella into the roof of the cab. His posh voice turned into something guttural, threatening. “Lay off the whip, or I’ll be laying into you.”

The old man managed to coax his donkey out of the hansom’s path. Bryson started to pull his head back into the cab when three emaciated children whose faces were as dirty as the soot-covered buildings ran up to the cab. The eldest of the children pulled her shapeless dress over her head, exposing her plum-sized breasts. “What the hell,” he exclaimed when the smallest of the gang snatched Bryson’s skimmer from his head. The boy tore down the street and disappeared into a narrow alley. The other two children stuck out their tongues and raced after their friend. Bryson pushed open the door. Perkins yanked him back into the cab as it lunged forward. The door swung shut, catching Bryson on his funny bone. He turned his face to the window to hide his pain. It travelled from his elbow to his fingertips.

"If I had allowed you to pursue those urchins, I fear I would be transmitting the news of your demise to your home office tomorrow morning." Perkins allowed what passed for a smile to creep across his face.

Bryson wondered what was so important about a factory on the corner ahead of them. A line of over a hundred people composed of women and children crawled along the street like an immense centipede. A hand painted sign hung outside the building, HOLLENS TEXTILES established 1798.

Perkins stretched his arm across Bryson and pulled down the blind. "Excuse me, Mr. Ward. As first impressions are generally the ones that linger, I do not want Whitechapel to be the lasting memory of London that you carry home."

"It looks pretty rough out there."

"It is the equivalent of what you Americans call a slum. Pimps, prostitutes, trade unionists are free to exercise their business in this quarter."

"You should send over some dirt on the goings on here. My readers would eat it up."

"An unhealthy diet at best."

"Maybe, but it sells papers."

"Two weeks ago, I telegraphed your office with the details concerning the discovery of the body of one of the leaders of the labour movement. He, or rather what was left of him, was found hanging from a lamppost. His assailants had disembowelled him and wrapped his entrails around his neck. Out of good taste, I took the liberty of sparing your readers the gruesome details."

Bryson tugged at the bottom of the blind. It snapped open. "That corks it," he whispered.

Perkins leaned to the side. He pointed at the Tower of London when it came into view. "Corks what, Mr. Ward?"

Bryson chewed on his thoughts in silence. "The son-of-a-bitch has ears like a bat."

"Please go on. I detect a note of criticism."

"If you want to sell a copy in Manhattan about London, then it is best to take off your white gloves and tell it like it is. There's nothing you can write that would put my readers off their feed."

Perkins placed the handle of his umbrella under his chin. His eyelids narrowed to slits. "My task is to report the facts, not embellish them for the sordid entertainment of your readers."

Bryson met Perkin's steady gaze. The Brits had mastered the art of the self-righteous stare centuries before he was born. He was convinced that it was this ability of their's to look you directly in the eyes while saying they had killed three thousand of your people to preserve civilization that enabled them to build an Empire. Bryson broke off the contest. He removed a tobacco pouch from his coat pocket and rolled a cigarette. It was a habit he picked up in Oklahoma. He remembered watching Grat Dalton roll one last smoke before riding into Coffeyville. The vision of the back of Grat's head reduced to oatmeal haunted Bryson. He couldn't bring himself to buy machine-rolled cigarettes after that. It was his tribute to the death of the Wild West. He closed his eyes and dozed off. When he awoke, Bryson saw green patches of lawn barely larger than a sandbox in front of immaculately kept row houses. The cab turned down a side street, travelling through the residential area until it reached a section of town where small travellers' hotels dominated the surrounding area.

Perkins knocked on the roof of the cab. The hansom stopped in front of a white brick five-story building. Its double doors were flanked on either side by Grecian-style columns supporting an overhang. "I searched all over London for a room suitable to your means. It is one of the newer establishments. There are several reasonable restaurants near here. As for the type of entertainment you seemed so enamoured with back in Whitechapel, well, in so far as that goes, you're on your own."

"You sure know how to make a fellow seem at home, Perks." Bryson pushed open the door with his boot and stepped out of the hansom.

Perkins closed the door. "If you do choose to return to Whitechapel, walk under the gaslights for your own well-being."

"Shoot, Ezra, and I was beginning to think we didn't hit it off. I'm really touched by your concern for my safety."

"I would prefer to remain as a transmitter of news instead of an exporter of dead American journalists. Mr. Breck informed me you have an uncanny ability of finding yourself in situations in which divine intervention is required." Perkins signalled the driver to move on. He stuck his head out the window. "I will be by in the morning at 7:00. Be so good as to meet me at the curb."

Bryson dropped his bags and chased after the cab for a short distance. "Hang on there!" he shouted. The scowl on the driver's face betrayed his annoyance. Perkins stuck his head outside the cab.

"Hey Ezra, why don't you come inside the hotel for a quick drink?"

"I regret, Mr. Ward, that I am unable to join you. I must return to the office to transmit my file of stories to your paper."

"Don't be more Catholic than the Pope. A day one way or the other isn't going to make a difference to Morris."

Perkins raised his arms and spread them out from his sides, palms up. "Mr. Ward, I am a creature of habit. As such, I am condemned to adhere to my set regime without deviation."

Bryson shrugged and stepped back. "Yeah, it's been a long day. Maybe we can knock back a few some other time."

Perkins' lips stretched into a forced smile. "One day, we may have an occasion to share a pint together. In the meantime, I'm at your service for as long as you're in London."

The driver sneered, "He's a bleedin' gentleman, now he is. But I knew him when he'd sooner bash your brains in than give you the time of day. I saw him beat the prayer out of..."

"Shut your gob and get moving," Perkins ordered.

*

Bryson approached the hotel and set down his valises to lift the heavy door knocker. It fell against a green metal plate cast in the image of a griffin. The door opened before Bryson could lift the knocker again. A tall man wearing a saffron-coloured turban bowed slightly. He stepped to the side to allow Bryson to enter. The man's skin was the colour of chestnuts. Bryson scrutinized the man. He had never seen the likes of the man's uniform, even at P.T. Barnum's Circus Emporium. Around the man's chin was a gauze-like sling that kept his flowing beard off his crimson waistcoat. The military cut of the coat was accented by two rows of brass buttons fastened up to the man's neck as large as twenty-dollar gold pieces. Instead of straight-legged trousers, the doorman wore pants that ballooned at the thighs and fit tightly from the knees to his ankles.

"Looks like you're expecting trouble there, buddy." Bryson pointed at the curved dagger tucked into a wide band of cloth encircling the man's waist.

"It is ornamental."

"Until it isn't," Bryson said.

"Hopefully not, and most regretfully so." The doorman's English was so formal and precise that he made Perkins sound like an inbred yokel. "Sir, if you are concerned about the rumours of the growing threat to one's safety in London, put your mind at ease. The Parthenon is known throughout Britain as a quiet and dignified establishment. It permits neither actors nor politicians to take up residence." He snapped his fingers. A young boy, just on the slant of thirteen, if that, rushed over and picked up Bryson's bags. The boy was dressed in the identical uniform of the doorman. He carried the bags over to a counter at the far end of the marble-tiled lobby and put them down.

Bryson leaned his back against the countertop and studied the lobby. A huge mural depicting the seven labours of Hercules covered every wall. He looked above him, whistled and blurted out, "Damn that will get you tossed in the clink in Boston." A fresco of plump nude women dancing around a young Dionysus, naked except for the wine goblet hiding his private parts, occupied the entire ceiling.

"May I help you?" Bryson turned around. He had seen undertakers with more colour than the desk clerk wearing a sombre charcoal evening coat over an equally drab vest and white shirt.

"I'm here to check in."

"Are you registered with us?"

"I reckon so. Look for the name of Bryson Ward."

The desk clerk lifted the pince-nez attached to his lapel to his eyes. He bent over to study the hotel ledger. He licked his fingertip, flipped the pages, and ran his finger down each line. "I am quite sorry. I have no room registered under that name."

"That's not possible. The guy who dropped me off said he took a room for me."

"Perhaps this, guy," the clerk spit out the word guy like a piece of bad meat, "was mistaken."

"Forget it. Just sign me in."

"Regretfully, I am unable to register you. The Parthenon, like other respectable establishments, accepts guests only on a referral basis. We have a strict policy of discouraging street trade."

"Wait a minute. Are you trying to tell me that I can't snag a bed because you have to have someone clear me first?"

"Correct, sir." The clerk walked away but stopped and returned to the counter. Perhaps he felt that his British sense of fair play dictated that he explain the rules of the game more fully to the uninitiated. "I regret if this has caused you any inconvenience. It is necessary if we are to maintain our reputation as a respectable traveller's establishment. Many of the better hotels, such as the Parthenon, prefer to have their clients, especially ones from abroad, registered under their firm's name. By doing so, we are able to ensure our guests will associate with people of the highest character."

Bryson realized it was futile to argue. "Mister, before you scoot, do me a favour. Do you have anything reserved in that book for The Manhattan Tribune?"

The clerk's finger stopped midway down the ledger. He slipped his pince-nez into his breast pocket. "I do have a room reserved under that firm's name." He raised his arm over his head. The bellhop rushed back to the counter to pick up Bryson's bags. "Take this gentleman to his room. Make certain he is comfortable." The clerk handed a key to the boy.

The boy struggled to carry the valises to the elevator. A similarly uniformed boy sitting on a high stool inside the lift's cage slid the wire grid open.

“Fifth floor,” the bellhop announced. He dangled his arms at his side. He opened and closed his fists several times to regain the sensation in his fingers from toting Bryson’s bags.

“If you boys don’t mind, I think I’ll take the stairs.” Bryson remained outside the elevator. “I’m not real comfortable riding in one of these things.”

“Nonsense,” the lift operator said. “It is safer to ride in a lift designed by James Otis of Chicago than it is to cross Piccadilly Circus.”

Bryson refused to be swayed. “That may be the case, but I’m still not getting in there. Now, if you’d just point me to the stairs, I’ll meet you guys on the fifth floor.”

“That will not be possible,” the lift operator said. “The stairs are reserved for the servants of the hotel. With the exception of the bellboys, employees are restricted from riding in the lift to prevent them from fraternizing with the guests.”

Bryson caught the smirk on the bellboy’s face in the mirrors inlaid in the rich teak panelling of the lift’s cabinet. “Damn-it-all,” Bryson said. “It’s just a machine, right? Besides, five stories aren’t that great of a height to fall from, are they?" He swung one leg forward like a blind man searching for solid footing. He stood in the elevator with his eyes closed. The constriction in his throat did not lessen until the whine of the pulleys hauling the cage up the narrow shaft ceased.

“Please follow me,” the bellhop said when the doors opened. Bryson bent over and picked up one of the bags.

“Guests are not allowed to carry their own luggage, sir.”

“Don’t worry about it, kid.” Bryson nudged the kid out of the lift. The bellhop led him down a corridor illuminated by flickering newly installed electric bulbs spaced twenty feet apart. The halls smelled of fresh paint and cigars. They passed an alcove where three men dressed in black suits and wearing starched high-collared shirts sat in armchairs reading newspapers. “Over there is the smoking alcove. It is the policy of the hotel to request that its guests refrain from smoking in their rooms.”

Two doors down from the lounge, the bellhop stopped outside a room. He inserted a key in the lock. He pushed the door open and picked up the bags. Bryson followed him. A room twice the size of the jail cell he’d occupied in Coffeyville. In one corner was an iron-framed bed with a mattress, the thickness of an overcoat folded in half. The mattress was covered in a bedspread made out of the same seaweed green material as the drapes drawn closed over the window. Bryson bumped into the mirrored shaving stand as he maneuvered his way between it and the end bed and a wardrobe. The bellhop placed the suitcases on the floor. He kneeled at the foot of the bed. He pulled out from beneath the bed a porcelain chamber pot sitting inside it a washbasin. “The conveniences are located at each end of the corridor. Please ensure you hang the occupied sign on the hook provided outside the W.C. when you are engaged.”

Bryson nodded and opened the drapes. "What the hell!" He stared at the windowless plaster wall concealed behind the curtains. He retreated to the bed and sat down.

"If you require anything, I will be at your service," the bellhop said.

"Hang on there." Bryson bounced off the bed and ran after the boy. He dropped his hand onto the boy's shoulder, dipped into his pants pocket, and took out four copper-coloured coins.

"What is this?" The boy looked puzzled when Bryson forced the coins into his hand.

"A tip? You know, a little something for your troubles." Bryson wondered if his unfamiliarity with the local currency made him appear to be a cheapskate.

"Are you a Canadian?"

"Nope, American."

"Without meaning to offend you, may I tell you something?" The boy handed the coins back to Bryson.

"Sure, every bit of info I can get to help me learn the ropes around this burg would be appreciated," Bryson replied and closed his fingers around the coins.

"It is considered bad to offer gratuities to help. If I were to accept your money, I could lose the position my uncle has secured for me working with him here."

"Thanks for the advice." Bryson stuck out his hand. "By the way, kid, don't call me sir. Just call me Bryson."

The boy looked at Bryson's hand as though someone had offered him a dead eel. He overcame his aversion and grasped Bryson by the ends of his fingertips. "I am called Kit Singh."

"What do your friends and family call you?" Bryson asked. He leaned against the wall and took out his pouch of tobacco.

"Kit Singh." The bellhop watched with fascination as Bryson rolled a cigarette with one hand.

"Well, Kit Singh, I'll be seeing you around. Who knows, I might even ask you to give me a tour of the city."

The boy smiled when Bryson handed him the cigarette. "Can you show me how to do that?"

"Drop by for a lesson anytime," Bryson entered his room and closed the door. He tossed a valise on the bed and opened it. He dug under the stack of neatly folded socks, underwear and shirts and removed an object wrapped in newspaper. He spread the newspaper and untied a string that secured an oiled sheepskin cloth around the object. His good hand, his whole hand, clutched the smooth deer bone grip of a single-action Colt 45 peacemaker. The voice of Emmett Dalton haunted him. "Always keep your pistol cleaner than your prick. You never know when you might have to use it." Bryson held the gun up to the light and spun the cylinder. Bryson had never fired the pistol and probably never would. He carried it with him as a memento of a bad man who loved rock candy more than whiskey. He looked around the room for a place to hide the weapon. Finally, he lifted the mattress. He weighed the advantages of hitting the bricks and knocking back a couple of brews versus hitting the sack. Exhaustion and common sense won out. Bryson kicked off his boots and collapsed into bed fully clothed.

Chapter 6

At sunrise, a single powerful knock sprung open the door open and toppled the chair to the floor. Mary Kelly leapt from her bed. In her state of half-consciousness, she grabbed the chamber pot and swung it at the silhouette of the man standing outside her room. The shadowy figure jumped to the side, narrowly levelled by the piss pot.

"Good gawd, go easy there," the stableman rasped.

Mary Kelly jerked the itchy wool blanket she had brought from home off the flea-infested mattress and wrapped it around her. She knelt by the single chair and lit the stub of a candle standing in an empty sardine can and carried it to the open door.

"Mr. Farrow, I took you for a gentleman."

"I am, miss. I didn't mean to startle you."

"Startle me! You frightened me to death."

The stableman stepped into the dim light of the candle. A clean purple scarf wrapped his face from nose to chin. "Miss, for you." He raised his arms. Two buckets of water dangled from his hands. His hands and fingers were suited for more delicate, precise work than shovelling manure. In the chill of the early morning, steam rose off their rapidly cooling contents.

"As promised, hot water for your toilet."

"My what, Mr. Farrow?"

"Your toilet, your bath, that's what they say across the channel."

"That's all well and good, Mr. Farrow, but you don't think I'd be taking a bath without a tub to stand in or curtain to keep your eyes off me."

The exposed part of Farrow's face turned crimson. He set the buckets down. "My flesh may be scarred, but that doesn't mean I'm corrupted on the inside as well, nor is my brain addled. I came to escort you to the washroom. My intention is to stand guard while you bathe." He pointed at a shed protruding off the far wall of Mother Cantons in the yard below. That is the washing room, miss. I'll place the buckets inside it for you." He lifted the pails and trudged down the stairs of the balcony to the yard below.

"Wait, Mr. Farrow," Mary called out. "I didn't mean to offend you. I would be very grateful if you would stand vigil outside for me."

"With this face, I learned not to take offence. I'll pour your bath and bring you more hot water as this lot has cooled."

Mary Kelly dragged her carpet bag from under the bed. She removed a bar of green soap, a dark long-sleeved dress with a neck-high collar and a petticoat dingy with age that had once belonged to her mother. She slipped her bare feet into a pair of tattered mules and gathered up the clothes she had worn on the trip. Mr. Farrow was waiting for her in the courtyard. He pushed open the door of the little building that jutted out of the rooming house. A kerosene lamp hanging from a hook illuminated an oval tub in the middle of the slat wood floor. Mary stepped cautiously inside the room. She dipped her foot into the milky water. It was tepid. As she turned to close the door, Mr. Farrow walked into the bath shed. She moved to the side. His eyebrows rose as though he was smiling under the scarf.

"This will take the frost off." He emptied two boiling pails of water into the tub. "I'll station myself outside to make sure no one disturbs you." He walked out of the washroom.

Mary closed the door behind Farrow. There was not so much as a drop-latch to prevent someone from barging in while she bathed. Though the soap burned her skin, she rubbed it briskly over her breasts and between her legs. Its astringent smell of ashes, fat and lye brought back memories of home. Water sloshed over the edge of the tub when she stepped out of it and ran between the wide gaps in the floorboards. She towelled herself dry. A free bath was not something that should go to waste. She tossed her dirty travelling garments into the grey water. She attacked her clothes with the bar of lye soap. When she was done, she called out, "Mr. Farrow, would you be so kind as to bring me a bucket of cold water."

"Yes, Miss," the stableman said.

She slipped her chemise over her head as she waited for Farrow. A scraping sound and heavy guttural exhalation came from behind her. She glanced around the room. Light shone through a plank on the back section of the wall abutting the main building. Mary shuddered and quickly got dressed. She dashed into the yard barefoot and saw Farrow returning from the public water pump out in the street with a bucket of water.

Farrow placed the buckets without spilling a drop. "Good lord girl where are your shoes?"

Her words tumbled out as a mélange of curses and frightened sobs.

"Slow down. You say someone was spying on you inside the shed?"

Mary nodded. He picked up the buckets and marched into the washroom; Mary kept close at his heels. He lifted the wet bundle of clothes from the wash tub and set them on top of the buckets. Farrow took a running start and crashed through the back of the shed. A cry of panic came from the other side of the wall. The legs of a man stuck out from under the collapsed wall. Farrow cleared away the wooden debris in armloads then pulled Lucky Snodgrass to his feet. He wrapped his hands around the neck of the man and lifted him off the floor. The eyes of the landlord bulged as Farrow slowly strangled him.

"Put him down," Mary shouted.

Farrow sighed and heaved the man to the side. The landlord gasped for air. Despite nearly being strangled, he stared at Mary's full bosom straining to escape the thin fabric of her chemise. She snatched her clean dress off the door peg and quickly put it on.

A flash of light danced across the ceiling as Farrow drew a curved knife with a gutting hook from inside his jacket. He held the knife in front of the landlord's eyes. "You know what this is, don't you, my little peeking Tom?"

The landlord's whole body trembled. The front of his trousers went wet and stank of urine.

"You know why they call me the surgeon, don't you?"

The answer came as a shudder.

"You're lucky she's present."

The landlord started to speak but stopped when Farrow placed the flat of the blade under his neck and pushed his head back. "All I want to hear from you is silence. All I want at this moment is for you to wash this young woman's clothes. Do I need to say more?"

The landlord shook his head.

"I don't believe you." Farrow dragged the man to the washtub and dunked his head in the dirty water. Mary tugged at Farrow's arm, afraid that the pathetic little man was drowning. Farrow released him. His head popped out of the water like a cork. He spit water across the room. Lucky Snodgrass started scrubbing Mary's clothes as though his life depended on it because it did.

Farrow pulled the scarf off his face. His mouth stretched in a hideous smile, revealing his blackened gums and broken teeth. A fetid mist sprayed through the cavity where he once had a nose. "Now I believe you. In the future, I expect you to protect her privacy and respect her person." He twisted the landlord's wet hair and jerked his head back. "There's one more thing I expect of you, Lucky. Return her money and give her three months free lodging."

"The hell I will."

"You will," Farrow said and walked out of the shed. Mary watched the landlord rinse her clothes in the buckets of clean water.

He spoke from the side of his mouth, keeping his attention focused on the task at hand. “Think you have a friend there, do you?”

“Yes, I do.”

“Be warned. Even the bloody devil himself knows well enough not to look cross-eyed at that one.”

Mary went into the yard. The stableman was sitting on an overturned bucket. His back was toward her. He lifted a dark bottle to his mouth and swallowed. “Mr. Farrow,” Mary said to warn him of her presence. Farrow slipped the bottle into the bib pocket of his leather apron and pulled the scarf up to the bridge of what was left of his nose.

“I thank you for what you did, but I’m afraid that your action may have cost you your job.”

The stableman stood up, threw back his head, and laughed. “What job would that be, Miss?”

“Your livery and yard duties.”

“I own this yard and all the properties on it,” Farrow said. “That cretin is my tenant. He rents this doss house from me.” A low growl escaped Farrow’s throat. “Don’t you have something better to do than stare at me, Miss?”

“Thank you again, Mr. Farrow,” she said and dashed across the yard and up the stairs to her room. Mary kicked off her boots and pulled on a pair of woollen stockings, then slipped her feet back into her boots and tied them, ready to apply for a position at Hollens Textile Factory.

Chapter 7

Bryson rubbed the sand from his eyes. It was a rough night. He'd dreamed of Grat Dalton being flung forward in his saddle. Grat's exploding head haunted him, but not so much as the image of the Bluetick hound drooling and gulping down his thumb without chewing. Grat and the dog dream merged at times. At one point, Grat stroked the dog's head. "Bryson, it ain't so bad on the other side. You get to relive the best and worst moments of your life. It ain't so bad, just repetitive. But hell, it's a lot less terrifying than waking up from a nightmare and discovering the world is in the same fucking mess as when you closed your eyes."

He looked around his digs. A silent valet stood unused in the corner next to a wash table topped by a flowery porcelain wash basin and pitcher. Clothes were scattered throughout the room. The high-crowned cowboy hat he'd carefully packed in his valise as a memento of his time playing a desperado hung from the corner of a picture frame holding the portrait of Queen Victoria.

Bryson dropped his legs over the side of his bed and made his way barefoot to the table. The cold from the floor worked its chill up his thighs and settled in his crotch, shrinking his penis and balls. "Jesus," he said. He had forgotten to light the gas fire when he arrived at the hotel. It was too late to bother with it, but he would pay Kit Singh on his way out to get it going before he returned that evening. He picked up his coat from the floor and sought out his tobacco pouch from its side pockets. He didn't know what the custom was in England for starting the day, nor did he give a rat's ass about it. Riding with the Dalton's had taught him that your first cigarette of the day may well be your last one, so get on with it. He didn't really like the taste of the smouldering cigarette so much as he enjoyed the minute it took to roll it. Bryson lit up the cigarette and inhaled weakly. A faint whiff of smoke passed his lips. He lifted his arm and buried his nose in its pit. He smelled like sour milk but not so bad that he couldn't wait another day to bathe. He crushed out his cigarette in the porcelain basin when he noticed a bottle of lavender toilet water, most likely left by a previous guest. He splashed the liquid into his palms and doused his chest and armpits. Pouring water from the pitcher into a glass, he dribbled a couple of drops of the lavender water into the glass and proceeded to gargle. With unerring accuracy, Bryson spit a seamless stream into the chamber pot next to the table.

He heard the tinkling of a bell from the hallway, followed by a gentle rapping on his door. The doorman who had greeted him on his arrival stood in the corridor holding a ladle. Next to him was Kit Singh. The young boy was carrying a steaming pail of water. The doorman walked over to the washstand. He dipped the ladle in the pail and was about to spill it into the basin but stopped. His eyes narrowed to slits while he studied the remains of Bryson's stubbed-out cigarette. He picked it up and deposited it in his pocket.

"Please refrain, Mr. Ward, from using this basin as cendrier."

"Sorry 'bout that, but I didn't expect company."

"A complimentary measure of hot water is provided every morning to our patrons."

"What about a bath?"

"The management provides this convenience gratis as well. It is necessary, however, that you schedule it with the concierge."

"You boys thought of everything," Bryson winked at Kit Singh, whose face remained as impassive as a bronze statute. "Well, pour me some of that hot water and hand me a bar of soap."

"Regretfully, guests are expected to supply their own toiletries. I would suggest you complete your ablutions fairly quickly, sir. Breakfast is being served in the great room."

"Where'd you learn that big word?"

"Breakfast?"

"Ablutions."

"In school, sir."

"Guess I should have stuck with it." Bryson dipped his fingers in the hot water and dabbed it behind his ears. "I'm ready to go."

The doorman shook his head and mumbled. Bryson only caught the tail end, something that sounded like, "White monkey."

When Bryson exited the elevator, a tall man wearing a black frock coat, dandy ruffled shirt and white-on-blue pinstriped trousers crossed the lobby to meet him. The man kept his head down. His features were hidden under a wide brim frontiersman hat, the sort that that James Butler Hickok favoured.

The stranger croaked, “Bryson Ward?” and raised his head. The luxurious black handlebar moustache and sunken opal-coloured eyes made his yellow pallor even more pronounced. If the man wasn’t sure who Bryson Ward was, Bryson was dead certain who he was. Bryson had read most of Bret Harte’s stories and admired his work as much as Mark Twain despised both it and the man in the ruffled shirt.

“Mr. Harte, it’s an honour to meet you.” Bryson wiped his palm on his trousers and stuck out his right hand sans thumb to shake, then pulled it back and stuffed it into his pocket.

Harte either had not seen Bryson’s attempt to conceal his mangled hand or was gracious enough to pretend he had not. “Mr. Ward, I ran into Ezra Perkins this morning at my club. He asked if I’d show you around.”

“You know that tight-ass Limey?”

“He’s a friend.” The glint in Bret Harte’s eyes and the crispness of his voice was sufficient warning for Bryson to curb his tongue. “Ezra gives his apologies for not being here to meet you this morning. He had to go to the morgue and check out a story on some other fellow they found swinging from a light post.”

“Suicide?”

“Not unless he was able to disembowel himself and use his own intestines to string himself up.”

“What’s on the tour, Mr. Harte?”

Harte inspected Bryson from his scuffed shoes to open his

collar. "Mr. Ward, you look like you and two other men slept in that suit. I suggest you go upstairs and get cleaned up because I'm going to see if I can get you admitted to the Royal Geographical Society today. If we're lucky, you'll be able to interview some of its members and get their perspective on Stanley's latest scheme to Christianize and create unrest in Africa. The only person to do more damage to Africans than that Scottish bible thumper is King Leopold."

"Yeah, Mark Twain wrote a piece last year on the slaughter going on in the Congo."

Harte reached into his breast pocket, pulled out a handkerchief and started coughing. When he regained his composure, he stuffed the blood-spotted cloth back into his pocket. "Twain and I might disagree on a lot of things, but we both agree that what that Belgian cocksucker is doing will come back to haunt the entire so-called civilized world for centuries."

He pointed his black walking stick, the head of which resembled a lion, at the elevator. He didn't have to say a word. Bryson dashed for the lift and rode it to his floor to get changed. It didn't take him long to put on a clean but wrinkled white shirt and attach a stiff winged collar. He had wisely chosen to bring four suits over in case he was called on to entertain or be entertained. One was a lemon-coloured number he had made after he saw Buffalo Bill strolling down Park Avenue dressed in the same outfit. Bryson chose a long black coat and matching pants to be in line with Bret Harte's costume. When he tried to put on his tie, Bryson cursed a blue streak.

It was impossible to do up any kind of knot minus a thumb. Back in New York, a friend of Ward's prepared one for him when the need arose. Bryson would just slip it over his head and pull it taut. Unfortunately, he had lacked the forethought to see his friend before he left and had no ready-made ties on hand in London. Bryson stuffed the damn thing in his coat pocket. Maybe the fancy doorman could give him a hand doing it up.

Bryson became alarmed when he did not see Bret Harte in the hotel lobby. He opened the double doors of a room above which a sign read Gentlemen's Lounge. Bryson entered and was nearly asphyxiated by the pungent aroma of Turkish cigarettes and cigar smoke. Harte sat in an armchair, taking long draws off a dog leg cigar. He tossed a newspaper he had been reading onto a side table. The end of Ward's tie dangled out of his pocket. Without asking, Harte pulled the tie out, pushed Bryson down into the armchair, and draped the tie around his neck. Within a few seconds, he'd created a perfect Windsor knot.

"Now you look fit to see the cream of the Royal Geographical Society." Harte offered Bryson one of his black cigars. Ward declined, pulled out his pouch of shag tobacco and rolled a cigarette. His eyes drifted to the front page of the paper. He had time to scan it while Bret Harte smoked his cigar down to his knuckles.

The main headline screamed in bold type, "Progress of Stanley's expedition to rescue the Emin Pasha." Further down was an article on negotiations between England and France on ownership of the

Suez Canal. Bryson flipped through the rest of the paper, barely reading the storylines until he stopped at a small news item tucked beneath an advertisement for Latham's Unguent, The Kingdom by the Sea's Relief from the Distress of Piles. The piece was about a suicide in Whitechapel. The item was short, to the point. A man had hung himself from a street lamp in this seedy part of London. His common-law wife, Emma Elizabeth Smith, claimed it was not a suicide but a case of murder designed to silence the emerging worker's unions. No credence had been given to her assertion as the woman was a woman of notorious reputation, a known prostitute.

Bret Harte tapped Bryson on the shoulder and pointed at the article with his cane. "Guess I was wrong," he said.

"About what?"

"Seems it is possible to gut yourself then use your own innards as a rope."

*

When the hansom rolled up in front of a two-story red brick building adorned by fake peaked roofs and a shabby white-washed upper balcony, Bryson Ward wasn't sure if he'd arrived at the Royal Geographical Society or the Women's Suffrage and Temperance meeting house. Harte waved at Perkins. He pushed away from a pillar he was leaning against and walked over to greet them. The words Royal Geographical Society engraved on a brass tablet secured to the pillar became visible.

"Didn't think you'd be here," Harte said.

"I saw what I needed to see," Perkins replied.

"Is it what you thought?"

Perkins shifted uneasily on his feet. "We'll talk about it over tea or something with more character."

"I gather the Royal Geographical arseholes won't give us entry?" Bret said.

Perkins shrugged, "They'll see you, but not an unwashed Yankee tabloidist. As for me, you know how the caste system works here."

"Indeed I do. Want me to open the doors for us? I was the Consul General, after all."

"Leave it alone for now. I'll find a way in on my own. If they think I'm using privilege to storm their bastion, they'll fasten the doors tighter than the Royal Mint."

Bryson started to walk off. "Fellas, I appreciate your concern, but you can use my name or talk directly to me."

Perkins called out, "Stop where you are. You are to go nowhere without my permission."

Bryson spun on his heels. Harte tried to block his path, but Ward sidestepped him and backed Perkins up to a wall. Ezra stuffed his hands into his pockets and lowered his eyes.

"Listen here you prissy Limey cocksucker. No one tells me where I can or where I can't go."

"If you have a problem, I suggest you wire your editor. He told me I was to assist you."

"Calm down, Bryson," Harte said.

Ward shoved Perkins hard and pinned him against the bricks. “Does assist imply that you have the right to dog my heels?”

Perkins’ clenched fists appeared from his coats sleeves. “Remove your hands.” His black eyes disappeared as he shuttered his eyelids.

“I would recommend you listen to him,” Bret Harte said.

Bryson laughed and pointed at Perkins’ balled-up fists. “Or what, Little Lord Fauntleroy here isn’t going to invite me for high tea?”

As the insult left his mouth, Ward found himself flipping ass over elbows when Perkins executed a grappling move and caught Bryson before he landed face down on the pavement. He helped Ward to sit up.

“Please remain seated. In a few minutes, the vertigo you are no doubt experiencing will dissipate,” Perkins said.

Ward nodded. The Englishman’s martial skills had convinced him that he did not want a rematch.

"You should have listened to me and calmed down.” Harte handed Bryson a Turkish cigarette. “You’re lucky he flipped you instead of using his fists. Prior to being an employee of your paper, Mr. Perkins boxed under another name, compared at one point to Daniel Mendoza. Like that legendary Jewish boxer he went toe-to-toe with brutes three stones heavier and set them on their backs watching their souls escape from their bodies after he pummelled them.”

Perkins held up his hand to stop Harte. “As I was saying, your editor instructed me to assist you in whatever way I am able to help you complete your article on Stanley's latest African fiasco."

Bryson blew out a cloud of tobacco smoke. "Perkins, did that tub of lard editor of mine give you any more instructions concerning me?"

"I'd prefer not to discuss it." Perkins slipped back into his prim and proper gentlemen's helper persona.

Bryson took another hit off his cigarette and exhaled his words along with the smoke. "Out with it, man. It can't be any more demeaning than being tossed in the air like a rag doll.

"I was ordered to keep three eyes on you. You have a reputation of meandering off and getting into situations ranging from embarrassing to bloody well life ending."

Bryson kept his temper in check. "That's what I thought you were told. Let me set the record straight. I don't need a nursemaid. I need a newshound. Someone who smells a story and goes after it."

Perkins ignored Ward's comment. "Since we are unable to gain entrance into the RGS today, we might as well visit some of the sights of London. Have you ever been to Westminster Abbey?"

Bret Harte pulled two cigars from his vest pocket. He held them out to Bryson and Perkins. "I think he'd like that."

"Besides the official nursemaid cornstarch you were fed Perkins, what else were you told?"

"I'll refrain from embarrassing you further in front of your fellow, albeit more intelligent and accomplished fellow citizen."

Bryson flushed as he entertained the idea of going a second round with Perkins. Common sense intervened. He sighed, and his chin sank into his neck.

Harte slapped his newspaper against his thigh. "Westminster Abbey is worth a trip to London alone."

"I don't care to see where all the cream of Britain's tyrants and poets are deep-sixed. I want to squeeze some juice from the guy on the streets. See if they give a tinker's damn about some religious fanatic in search of another Bible thumper." Bryson grabbed the paper from Harte and pointed to the piece on the so-called suicide in Whitechapel. "I want to go here."

Perkins looked toward Bret Harte for support. Harte took the paper from Bryson. "Whitechapel is no place to seek opinions. Most of the people there barely know what's on the other side of the city, much less what's happening on another continent."

"Maybe, but there's another story I'd like to check out. Something that would appeal to my readers more than one about Stanley and his cronies at the RGS expounding on their duty to bring civilization to folks who aren't interested. Say like a story about some poor woman's hubby dangled on a lamppost with his own entrails."

Bret Harte jabbed his finger into Bryson's chest. "Spare yourself a trip and possible thrashing. Whitechapel is no place for tourists unless accompanied by a flock of badges."

"I've been in rougher waters and managed to swim to shore."

Perkins exploded, dropping his veneer of polite British civility.

"Listen, this ain't the so-called Wild West. This ain't Manhattan. This is Whitechapel. This is where people applaud the mutilation of not only whores but of national heroes like General Gordon in Khartoum. This is where people collapse from drink or starvation in the fucking river of shit that flows down the gutters. More men and women are stabbed, shot, strangled or beaten into an unrecognizable facsimile of a human than you can imagine."

Harte agreed. "The Outcasts of Poker Flats is a romance. Whitechapel is the true untamed frontier."

"That may be the case, but I want to see for myself. Gives me something to do while waiting for the Grand Poobahs of the Royal Geographical Society to grant me entrance."

Perkins regained his composure and slipped back into his best King's English. "Mr. Harte, we can agree that our companion is beyond reasoning. He prefers to ignore his assignment and prefers to cater to the tastes of the basest elements of society."

Bryson snatched Perkins' hand and shook it. "You're catching on. Those bottom feeders you maligned are the folks who buy the sheet I write for."

Chapter 8

Bret Harte declined the invitation to join Perkins and Bryson for an evening tour of Whitechapel, declaring that if he wanted to contract cholera or syphilis, he'd book a steamer for New Orleans. Perkins leaned his head out of the hansom and told the driver to proceed to Dorset Street. The driver leered and said, "See you gentlemen are in mind for a little entertainment of the more robust nature."

Perkins sat back and folded his arms over his chest. "Cretin."

"You seem to have a good word for everyone," Bryson said.

The cab bounced its passengers as high as its roof over the cobblestone street. Bryson looked at the line of trees planted precisely four feet apart in the middle of the boulevard. Each trimmed tree a mirror image of its neighbour. Nannies outfitted in black skirts and jackets and white shirts topped off with equally black bonnets pushed prams across the road to green splashes of parks facing rows of brick three-story houses.

"You Brits sure like to wallow in the glory of sameness," Bryson muttered. He closed his eyes and listened to the sounds of children laughing, dogs barking and the plinking of spinets coming from inside the houses.

"Excuse me," Perkins said. "Did you have something of note to share?"

"Nope, just thinking aloud."

"Must be a tremendous strain to think and talk to yourself at the same time."

Bryson cracked one eye open to take in a Gothic church, a grim reminder of sectarian human bonfires that served as public entertainment two centuries prior. His head lolled back against the banquette. He did not awake till the cab had passed through London's emerging quartier of well-bred merchants, bankers and aspiring parliament members. The transition from sunlight, manicured lawns and patches of flowers to a rutted street of mud and broken bricks, squeezed between a collection of dwellings that leaned into one another, waiting for a spark to set them ablaze, was immediate. Even Dickens' most lurid descriptions of the city's underbelly seemed like utopian musings compared to what Bryson observed.

Perkins knocked on the roof of the cab. It stopped in front of a building on a corner. A sign above its lintel read The Ten Bells. Two women were going through a man's pockets who had passed out. Perkins hopped out of the cab. He pointed his umbrella at the driver. "Meet us here at eight sharp."

"The gaslights ain't even lit before seven. The birds don't start preening until it gets dark. Better for them and lot better for the blokes who don't have see them in the daylight."

"Eight sharp," Perkins repeated.

Still drowsy from the ride, Bryson stepped out of the cab. The sound of his boots being sucked into a black puddle woke him. The stench that rose from the puddle nearly made him vomit. He tried to pinch his nose with the index finger and thumb of his left hand. "Shit," he growled recalling his thumb had been digested by a hound in Coffeyville.

"I'd venture a mixture of that and other revolting ingredients as well." Perkins smiled. It was the first time Bryson had seen Perkins stretch his lips in something approximating mirth.

"It was remiss not to instruct you to leap from the cab onto the footway. The streets are Stygian in nature. A vile river of excrement, dead animals and the occasional aborted fetus. It has been said that even Noah's deluge would fail to wash away the corruption of Whitechapel."

The women had ceased exploring the drunk's clothing. One of them spread her legs apart and raised her skirt. "Take a good look. It'll be waiting for you when you has the need." The other woman told her companion to stop messing about. They stripped the drunk's clothing and rolled him into the gutter. Bryson could tell from the slack jaw of the naked man and open milky eyes he was dead.

Perkins walked into the Ten Bells ahead of Bryson. The journalist's confidence dissolved in the grey mist of Dorset Street. He thought he had dealt with every form of low life in his reporting days in New York's version of Hell, the Five Points.

When Bryson entered the pub, the clink of glasses and profound silence of its patrons, interrupted by the occasional moan or garbled curse, greeted him. The clientele of The Ten Bells were scattered around the dingy, piss and vomit-stained interior like mouse droppings. The men showed no sign of animation except when reaching for another pint placed squarely in front of them or when swatting away some chippy trying to steal their beaker of forgetfulness before staggering off to beat their wives and children.

Bryson followed Perkins to a vacant table at the rear of the pub. He bumped into a woman who veered off her path into him. "Eh there, don't be touching less your intentions are pure." Her blouse hung off her shoulders, sliding down to reveal the pink areola of her tiny breasts. "Find yourselves a chair worthy of your station," she said and walked over to a slab of wood that functioned as a bar. The man behind the counter pushed three mugs of beer and six full measures of clear gin to her. She loaded them on a tray and circulated through the pub, depositing the drinks. When she returned to Perkins and Bryson, she chirped, "Thought I forgot you, did you? What's your pleasure, gin, beer or both? I'd offer you sherry, but we're fresh out. The Duke of Arsehole came in earlier and quaffed the whole barrel. So I ask again. What's your pleasure? For a small fee, I can direct you where your expectations might be met."

Perkins stood up and pushed his chair back so hard it toppled to the floor. He started to walk away. Bryson followed him. They threaded their way through the tangle of bodies roaming the pub. The barman came out from behind his counter and blocked their path to the door. He wiped his hands on his apron, then reached inside and pulled out a leather-covered cosh. He smacked it against his open palm. “You gentlemen thinking of leaving without paying, are you?”

“We didn’t order anything,” Bryson said.

“You must have ordered something, seeing how long Nell lingered near you two.”

“No, we didn’t order so much as a glass of water.”

“You know, lads, round here, nothing comes at a dear price. The time you warmed our chairs staring at my customers like they was Bedlam inmates is worth at least a few bob.”

Perkins snatched the cosh from the barman and threw it across the room, narrowly missing Nell as she passed by. “Oi, you gibfaced dullard, we’re going for a stroll. Should we reenter your establishment, you’ll be wise to greet us with genuine hospitality. Perhaps a pint on the house.”

The tough veneer of the man turned as soft as overheated butter. “Sorry Perez, I didn’t recognize you. Just a lark, no offence intended.”

“None taken,” Perkins hooked his arm through Bryson’s elbow and steered him out of The Ten Bells. On the street, he spun him around. “This is the first stop of the tour of London’s black heart you so desperately want to experience.”

They walked past a woman sprawled in a doorway and a man retching in the gutter. Row after row of flophouses and gin mills, some of which were no more than a canvas-covered lean-to, stretched from one end of Dorset Street to the other end. Perkins stopped at a pub with the royal name of The Princess Alice. "One of the finest establishments amongst the worst. Best curb your tongue. Leave me to open the talk. The denizens infesting this fine old grog shop will scatter like fleas on a dead cat if you press them."

Once inside, a squat man wearing a nightshirt over a pair of hemp trousers stumbled into them. Perkins dragged the man back by his shirt collar. "Hubie Cross, you know better." He held out his palm. The man gummed an apology and handed Perkins a wallet.

"Give over the other one as well." A second wallet Bryson recognized as his own materialized. Perkins opened his purse. "You're getting clumsy, old friend." Perkins handed him a few coins. The man pulled a pocket watch from his sleeve and dangled it in front of Bryson. "Not so clumsy that this one noticed." He tipped his hat, handed Bryson the timepiece and dashed out the door.

They sat at a long table occupied on either side by men in varying degrees of lost sobriety. Bryson felt something brush his leg. He peeked under the table and saw a man trying to unlace his boots. He kicked the thief but he persisted tugging at the boot. A bald man who had to duck to clear the ceiling beam put down a tray of drinks and signalled Bryson to move his chair back. He dragged the boot thief out by his hair. He gave the thief a swat with a varnished cudgel. He slung the thief over his shoulder and dashed to the open doorway. The publican threw the unconscious boot lover outside. He turned and bowed to acknowledge his appreciative clientele's applause. "Beat my last toss by at least three feet," he announced.

Perkins ordered two ales apiece. Bryson leaned over the table and asked a guy who looked somewhat alert what he thought of Stanley's search for the Emin Pasha. The fellow shrugged and pointed at one of the mugs of ale. He drained the mug without stopping to breath then pointed at Bryson's other ale.

Perkins pushed the mug toward him and slipped into a voice far from the plummy accent Bryson had become accustomed to. "Well, mate, what do you have to say to this Yank? He's a scribbler, works for a shite sheet in America."

The man finished his ale. "Don't fuckin' care, don't fuckin' wants to know. Got enough blood and guts tales on this patch of hell to care 'bout what's going on with Mr. Stanley and his I presume. This strip of misery is far darker than anything in Africa."

The pub filled up rapidly with customers coming in batches of six. All the tables were soon occupied. The latecomers leaned against the wall or stood shoulder-to-shoulder at the makeshift bar. The majority of people were employed by the local textile factories. They were released from their shifts a half-dozen at a time thirty minutes apart. Perkins explained it minimized the chance of disgruntled workers coming in contact with others and staging a protest. The 1871 Paris Commune rebellion was still fresh in the minds of industrialists and governments throughout Europe.

Two women with kerchiefs covering their hair and wearing identical long grey dresses stood just outside the doorway, scanning the room for somewhere to sit. The younger woman put one foot inside tentatively, like someone dipping her toe into the ocean to test its temperature. She was softer-looking than her companion, an innocent introduced into a world that was not yet understood nor feared. The other woman pushed her into The Princess Alice. The woman's face was etched with wrinkles around her eyes, and her brow furrowed from constantly squinting to detect a flaw in anything or anyone that fell under her scrutiny.

"Mary Kelly, step lively," the woman said. "Lest some peeler takes you for one of them lot and shackles you." She pointed at a woman leaning on a man against a wall with her hand tucked down the man's trousers. "For Gawd's sake, Emma, take it outside. The floor is slippery enough as it is," she yelled at her.

The woman withdrew her hand from the man's pants and wiped it on his shirt. "Miss High and Mighty Catherine Eddowes, don't be shunning me. I wager it won't be long before I sees you fiddling with some bloke's tool once your man has been butchered for attacking the hand that feeds him."

"I have no man and intend to keep it so."

*

Perkins and Bryson exited the pub in time to see a lamp lighter leaning a ladder against a gas pole. Perkins walked ahead of Bryson and then stopped. "Three hundred years ago, a king slept there." He lifted his umbrella and jabbed it at a dwelling on the other side of the street. Under the layers of coal soot, a spot of white appeared. Bryson jumped back when a slate roof tile broke off and clattered to the cobblestones. Perkins moved it to the side with his shoe." It's rumoured a saint from the Middle Ages lies beneath its foundation. A saint who no doubt liked to burn us alive." Perkins remarked more to himself than Bryson. "Cromwell may have quartered his troops there."

"Yup, you sure have a heap of history piled layer upon layer."

Perkins ignored Bryson's remark.

"Looks like it has seen better days. What is it now, a warehouse or something?"

Perkins turned away from the building. "Or something. Once the resting place of a king and the bones of a saint, it's now an abattoir, sometimes a morgue to store an overflow of cholera victims. Upstairs, whores who have no place to go take their clients. Either to ply their trade or lead them to their pimps' knives. With luck, they'll only lift their purse instead of slitting their throat."

"Sounds like you know this area pretty well."

"I was born here, in a rooming house behind a sorting station. Perhaps when we are on a trusted first-name basis, I'll tell you about my amazing rise from the gutter to the footpath of middling society."

"Bryson."

"I beg your pardon?"

"Bryson, call me Bryson."

He stared at Bryson's outstretched hand and clasped it. "Ezra, as you already know." He turned his attention away to watch an old man pulling a trundle cart.

The man's white beard hung past his throat, fanning out on his shirt and long black coat. The man paused every few feet to remove his wide black-brimmed hat, underneath which was a skull cap, to wipe his brow. The cart was piled with rags, bottles, and scraps of metal. A gang of children dogged his heels, taunting him and throwing stones, then running up to snatch things from the cart. Perkins approached the cart and faced the old man's tormentors. He bent over, picked up some of the items on the ground, and put them back in the cart.

The most vocal of the gang spat. "We knows what you are, don't we?"

Perkins pulled a thin blade from his umbrella's hollow shaft. "Then you know well enough to leave, don't you?" The leader of the group turned his back and hurried away, followed by his flock.

Bryson helped Perkins gather the items the kids had taken from the cart.

"My grandfather was a totter," Perkins said out of nowhere.

"A what?"

"A rag and bone man. He knew what was scrap and what was worth picking from a hundred feet away. He succeeded well enough to get us out of this cesspool and opened up a small shop far enough from where the gentry lived but close enough to attract their servants. Became known for the occasional loan if one of the brick house's help needed an Uncle." Perkins put the last of the things on the street back in the cart and got behind the cart. He gave it a shove so the old man could be on his way. "I still remember my Zadie praying every morning, laying on the Tefillin. My father told him to dress like the others, not to draw attention to himself or us now that we'd escaped Whitechapel."

"Perkins doesn't sound very chosen, well you know to me."

"Mr. Ward, my father found it more advantageous to change our name from Perez to Perkins."

"Don't see why he had to switch from Perez to Perkins. Last name like that could be Spanish."

"Have you ever heard of the Armada? Despite having passed the Catholic Act some sixty years ago, the majority of Church of England parishioners still harbour ill will toward both Spain and the Pope with just a touch less enmity toward my people. Mr. Ward, let us keep this between us, off the record."

"I told you, call me Bryson. You know the only way to keep things on the hush-hush is to maintain silence at the git-go."

"We have one more haven to visit of those who cling to life despite the world outside Whitechapel's blindness to their misery." Perkins veered into a narrow alley a few yards before the Ten Bells. Standing two abreast, they could touch the dank walls of the passage on either side. The odour of rancid fat, smouldering coal and feces filled the alley, impossible to disperse by even the most ferocious North Sea gale.

Inside a doorway, a woman teetering on the threshold called out, "I'm not engaged at the moment. Two for one is a gift you'll not see again." She stepped out off a stoop and fell into Bryson's arms. She pushed herself away and smoothed her smock. Her pupils were the colour of dishwater. "Come on, gentlemen, you didn't come all the way to Paradise Row for the fresh air."

A small girl wearing a flour sack tugged at the woman's sleeve. She was as wilted as a dying peony. The woman struck the child's face with the back of her hand. "Off with you, can't you see I'm busy chatting with these fine men?" She shoved the girl to the ground. "Can't go cockering the young ones, or God knows where they'll end up."

Ward trotted after Perkins to the end of the alley. Once outside, he took in a deep breath of the marginally fresher air. Perkins pointed out a file of women circling a squat church with a square steeple across the street. The women kept looking over their shoulders. "They're shankers of a higher order than the skank we just met. The police leave them alone as long as they keep moving,"

"Is all of this area a shit pit?"

"The economic foundation here is based on prostitution, gin and the exploitation of honest labourers who live on wages too thin to feed a louse."

"That last part could get you beaten to a pulp by the Pinkertons back home."

"Delighted to see the severed colonies still maintain a connection with the mother country." Perkins crossed the street. Their hansom driver leaned against the cab, talking to a young woman.

"Christ, not again!" Bryson's feet sank into a soft horse patty. The soft excrement crept over his laces and seeped into his boots.

"I have to agree with Mr. Breck. You seem to have a talent for stepping into it wherever you go."

Bryson scrapped the bottom of his shoes against the curb. "I hated horses in Kansas, hated them in New York and sure the hell don't like them any better here."

Chapter 9

Mary Kelly descended the rickety stairs to the courtyard of Mother Cantons. The sun was just rising above the rooftops of Whitechapel. It shone as a faint orange light through the haze of smoke cloaking the city. She felt a breeze disturb her hair. It was then she remembered she had left her bonnet on the bed. She took the stairs two steps at a time to retrieve it from her room. She had debated about the necessity of wearing a bonnet but decided she wanted to be perceived as a respectable and serious woman. Underneath the bonnet, she discovered the letter of introduction to Hollens Textile.

At Hollens, a windowless building save for a narrow strip of transom windows where the roof met the pitted bricks, Mary realized she could have worn a bucket on her head or dyed her hair green for all it mattered. A line of women in various degrees of dishevelment snaked around the corner of the mill. In the hands of the twenty women ahead of her, Mary recognized the same paper as the letter of introduction she had been given back home. Behind her, another hundred women held the identical letter.

For over an hour, the women shuffled from foot to foot in the cold, waiting for someone to open the iron gates of the factory. Two identical pasty-faced men dressed in long frock coats and top hats appeared. They directed the first twenty-five women in line to follow them into the building.

"Brother Julian, seems as though father's letter has proven effective," one of the twins said as he herded the women into a room, unfurnished except for a short bench.

"Indeed, Brother Archibald, I think once he sees how many applicants have come, he'll not regret engaging an agent in Ireland."

The brothers kept one arm behind their backs as they passed down the line of women. They crooked a finger at whatever woman they selected to step out of formation. Two young girls, no more than ten years old, jumped forward. Their cheeks were sunken, revealing the outline of their skulls trying to break through the flesh of their emaciated faces.

"How tall are you?" Julian asked.

"Don't know," the shorter of the two girls replied.

"How old are you?" Archibald followed up.

"Been told by Ma I came a few months after my sister," the other girl answered.

Julian pulled the bench away from the wall. "I want to see how nimble you are. Crawl under this bench and return as fast you can." He started to count.

The two girls flattened themselves on the floor, slithered under the bench, and came back before Julian reached four.

"Show me see your hands," Archibald inspected their palms and moved their fingers up and down. "This one will do as a scavenger, faster than the other by a margin and appears very flexible."

"And the other?" Julian asked.

"Hands are smaller, well suited as a piecer."

"Stand by the wall," Julian told the girls. The brothers continued down the line and passed by Mary. They selected ten other women.

"What about this one?" Julian pointed at Mary. "She looks a sight more healthy and sturdy than the rest of this lot."

"Never, remember thirteen were present at our saviour's last supper and see where that ended."

"Sir, sir," one of the chosen women spoke up. "If it's not too much to enquire, how much will we be earning?"

"One shilling for the children, three shillings a week for the loomers and stitchers."

"That can't be," the woman objected. "Your advert stated 5 shillings."

Spittle flew from Julian's mouth. "Want to know how much you'll take to the ale house even before you start, do you? Leave now with others. Leave now before I summon someone to evict you forcibly."

"With that one gone, we're one shy," Archibald said.

"This one will do." Julian pushed Mary to the woman's vacant slot. "Thank God we're not hiring twelve virgins, or we'd be scouring this Gomorrah for years to find one."

Julian reached into his pocket and pulled out a silver bosun whistle. On the first shrill note, a man who had been standing in a darkened corner of the room wormed his way forward. He removed his cap. His eyes settled briefly on his employer's feet but quickly shifted to an inspection of the women. His study took in all aspects of the women, roaming over their bodies from the floor to their breasts, seeming to strip away their layers of clothing.

"Mr. Fitch, send the others away, then take this lot to Mrs. Stride."

Fitch threw open the door leading outside. "Off with you, come back bright and early tomorrow to see if we needs anybody."

The women outside refused to budge. One woman spat at Fitch. "Dirty bastard, you promised me you'd have me on."

"I did have you on. Don't you remember, darling? You were on top." Fitch laughed at his cleverness and slapped his cap against the wall. "Now get outta of here, or I'll call my boys to drag you into the street."

*

The Hollens twins left through a side door. Fitch circled around the women. Out of the corner of her eye, Mary saw him rubbing his hand over his privates as he paused to whisper something to a woman. The other women stood stone-faced as he crept down the line. Fitch spent an inordinate amount of time with the two young girls. Mary shuddered when he stroked their bare arms and patted them on their bums. He caught sight of her reaction and smiled broadly. He leaned into her. "You looks like a peach ripe for the plucking." He smelled of kippers and pickled eggs. Mary pretended to lose her balance and brought her heel down on Fitch's big toe.

"You clumsy cow," he cried.

“I’m so sorry, sir.” Again, Mary lost her balance. She brought the full weight of her other heel down on the same toe. Fitch hopped away. He pointed a tobacco-stained finger at Mary. “I’ll see you pay for this.” He raised his arm to strike her but dropped it when a voice so deep and unwavering it sounded like it came from a bassoon said, “That’ll be enough of that, Mr. Fitch. You should have brought these women to me ages ago.”

A woman at least six feet tall and three feet wide stood at an open door at the back of the room. “Ladies, don’t take note of Mr. Fitch. He’s nasty but harmless, been cursed with a perpetual lobcock rather than gifted with a stiff staff.”

Fitch slunk back to his corner. “No call for that, Mrs. Stride, no call at all. I was just establishing a report with them.”

“It’s pronounced rappor not report. The T is silent.”

“Fuckin French should says it as it’s spelt.”

“That would require you to know how to read and write. Would it not, Mr. Fitch?”

Mrs. Stride clapped her hands. “What are you waiting for, girls, the Lord Chamberlain to serve you tea and biscuits?” Like ducklings, the women marched in step behind Mrs. Stride. They passed down a long corridor with wainscotting aged a chestnut brown and pictures of four generations of Hollens men suspended on the walls. An immense sliding door closed off the end of the hall. On either side of the door were two identical paintings of a pastoral scene replete with cows, sheep and a herdsman. Stencilled above the door, the admonition “BUSY MINDS AND IDLE HANDS ARE THE DEVIL’S WORKSHOP” set the Hollens’ expectations of their workers. “Burn those words into your souls,” Mrs. Stride said. “For those of you who don’t heed it, it’s a quick trip to the streets. This is the last time you will ever walk down this hallway. In the future you are to enter at the rear of the factory gates where your presence will be recorded. Failure to do so will result in your immediate dismissal.” Mrs. Stride pounded on the iron door and waited as it slowly rolled open. Seven women lined up like a row of plaster saints stood on the other side of the door. They held out grey dresses and head scarves.

“These are your work clothes,’ Mrs. Stride said. “They identify you as proper employees of Hollens Textile. They’ll be deducted from your salary on a weekly basis for three months. Show up dressed in anything else, and you’ll find yourself on the street.”

The ceaseless whirl and groan of metal against metal and clack of wood frames against wood frames drowned out whatever thoughts or dreams the women working at the shuttles and looms entertained. A young girl crawled under the looms and shuttles, cleaning the grime and tufts of cotton deposited on the spindles and gears. Another child leaned over the moving shuttles to repair broken threads and pluck out bits beyond saving.

Mrs. Stride pushed the two young sisters toward one of the seven saints. “Catherine Eddowes, have these two watch what those girls are doing for an hour. The one with the smaller hands is to be a piecer. The other one’s quicker, fit to scavenge under the machines.”

Mrs. Stride came nose-to-nose with Mary and peered deeply into her eyes. She used one dirty finger to draw down the bottom of Mary's eye. Her cloud-free whites and cat's green irises were examined by Mrs. Stride. "Go with Catherine, you're perfect for a stitcher."

Catherine did not bother to look at Mary. She nudged the sisters toward the machine and told them, "Watch what the two colleens there are doing carefully. Don't take your eyes off of them as if your life depends on it because, my sweet darlings, it does."

The sisters observed the girl under the machine and the one bending over it perform their duties. The smaller girl slithered out from under the machine, and the other girl backed off from the top of the machine. "Eh, youse two give it try," the girl from under the loom chirped. "Not hard, just needs be nimble."

The other girl added, "And be quick." They both joined in and sang "Like ol' Jack jumping over the candle stick."

The thinner, quicker of the sisters went belly down on the floor and did as she had studied, snatching balls of dust and shreds of cloth and gobs of dripping oil from under the workings of the machine. Her sister bent over the rods moving up and down and from side to side and tried to pick out broken tails of thread.

Catherine Eddowes looked over and screamed, "Back away," when the girl leaned too far forward. Her tangled hair fed in the moving shuttles of the loom. The girl's face entered the maws of the monster. Her sister, hearing her shrieks, tried to slide out from under the crushing down strokes of the apparatus. Her dress got snagged in its gears. She was pulled into its pistons while her sister's face was stripped of all human features. The sound of wet flesh and crushed bone barely made a peep over the incessant rumble of machines in the factory. Only when both sister's bodies had been drawn sufficiently into the monster's belly did it squeal and ceased to work, satiated with its latest sacrifice.

"Didn't expect that, did ya?" The girl who challenged the sisters to give it a try asked.

"Not me, leastwise not on the first day," the other answered.

Cat tore off her kerchief and dropped to her knees. Mary moved toward the two lifeless bodies. She struggled to pull the child from under the machine. It was futile as the quicker of the two was thoroughly trapped in its teeth. The other sister's arms waved spasmodically as the last pulses of energy flowed through them.

Mrs. Stride approached the two bodies with as much concern as one observing her own shadow. She sighed and said, "Better now than later when we're in a full run. Catherine, tell Mr. Fitch to send over a machinist to get this mess clear and the monster humming again."

A young man wheeled a basket laden with pry bars, spanners and other tools to the machine. Mary recognized him from the train. He tipped his cap as though greeting a neighbour on a quiet Sunday morning. "Welcome to the working class," he said and went about prying open the wood and metal of the monster to free the two sisters.

Mary buried her face in her hands and wept. She sucked in her tears when Catherine dropped a hand on her back. "They can't hear you, and there's no work left to be done today or even tomorrow until they clean them wains from the machine and starts it up again."

"It's horrible," Mary said.

"Horrible it is, but it's just part of marvels of the new age. Do you partake?"

"Huh?"

"Imbibe, drink."

"No."

"Darling, it's never too early nor too late to start. The day's done, and The Princess Alice is calling."

*

"Heave ho!" A man carrying what at first looked like a sack of potatoes over his shoulder yelled as he threw a body past Mary and Catherine. He said something that met with a raucous cheer of approval, then went over to a counter and lifted the flap gate to take his position behind the bar. Mary kept close behind Cat as they made their way toward a wooden table with benches on either side. Catherine stopped to exchange words with a woman trying to crawl into the body of a man propped against a wall. Two men who looked definitely out of place in the pub stood up when Catherine and Mary glanced around the room for a place to sit. The taller of the two motioned them to take their place. He was an odd-looking duck, wearing a yellow jacket over a gold vest. He reached up to tip his hat but failed miserably as his left hand was unable to gain a hold of the brim.

Mary ordered a ginger beer to the obvious disapproval of her friend, the server and the half-conscious patrons on both sides of the table. "Come on, gal," Catherine said. "Surely, after what you saw within the first hour of your first day at glorious Hollens should put you in state for more than a sip of watery sugar and spice."

"You're right at that. Puts me in mind to go to mass and light a dozen candles for those poor children."

A woman came up behind them. "Cat, it's time we rose up to put a harness on those who see us as no more than fodder to feed their machines."

Catherine placed her finger against her lips. "You should know better Polly Nichols than to go talking like that in public."

"No to worry, dear. The lot here is so lost in the din of their own troubles they're deaf to the world's misery around them."

"Scoot over Mary. Give Polly here some board. She barely takes up enough room to warrant half a cheek of plank."

The woman's face had an unnatural tint. She covered her mouth as she spoke. "There's to be a meeting. It would be splendid if you chose to give a presence for the women mill workers. A few of the lads from the SDF and Machinist Guild, as well as the Irish Brigade, will be there."

"What'll you have, Polly, a beer or a soon-to-sin gin?"

Polly placed her lips against Catherine's ear and whispered. Catherine elbowed Polly away. "Come on, gal, don't you know enough to keep silent in public? This ain't 1871 Paris and surely isn't Bloody Sunday 1887 London. Neither date could rouse our people to action considering how things turned out."

"If we don't take a stand now, we'll never be able to rise off our knees," Polly said loud enough to attract the attention of a bluebottle, one of Sir Robert Peel's finest, entering the pub with a three-foot rod in hand. His long blue coat, stovepipe hat and lantern hanging on his wide belt inspired one patron too drunk to measure his words to jeer, "Oi there, please light your lamp so I can see if it's your head or arse under that topper."

The policeman whacked the jokester across his mouth with his finely polished baton. "Hard to laugh while spitting out your teeth, isn't it, boy?" The policeman made a direct line to Polly. "Is this the one?" He asked. A plump hairless man save for his mutton chops in a suit of wool so rough that he scratched himself every time he moved came out from behind the constable. "Yes, she's the one who's been causing a stir at Bryant and Mays."

The policeman inserted himself between Polly and Mary. "Hello darling, should I nip you for whoring or for being an offence to our eyes?" He clamped his hand on Polly's jaw and pulled it down. In the dim light of the pub, her ulcerated gums glowed a phosphorus greenish white. "Don't think your employer has much to worry about this one. Her phossy jaw will do her in before she can mount a revolution." The policeman released his grip. "Be a good girl, shut your gob and go back to making matches so you can pay for your funeral." The policeman turned his attention to Mary. "Haven't seen you around before." He picked up her glass and took a sip. "Good girl, stick to ginger beer and avoid the likes of these two labour rousers, and you'll do fine."

"You know I'm no troublemaker, Milton," Catherine said.

"Not yet, but it's etched in your face that you're on the path. One more thing, just because we may one day be friendly doesn't give you the right to call me by first name. Not in the pubs, not in the street and not between the sheets."

"You can count on that constable. You'll never hear me address you under your bedding."

The policeman got up. His path was blocked by Darcy and another man. He tried to step around them. Every time the policeman went left or right, they moved with him until he finally made it to the door. He brandished his rod. "I know you, Darcy Darnell. I know what you're about. Keep it up, and I'll introduce you to the proper etiquette to show a peace officer whose sworn duty it is to maintain order and decency."

Darcy draped his arm over the mutton chop little man who had tried to remain inconspicuous behind the policeman. "Milton, take this one back to his master. He reeks of obsequiousness. As do you."

Milton slid his baton out of its sheath and took direct aim at Darcy's head. Even before Mary yelled, "Look out!" Darcy sensed the intention of the peeler. He moved gracefully, almost like a dancer. He leaned to the side as the baton passed by his head and pivoted on one heel catching the copper with a knee to his kidney and slamming his elbow into his nose. Milton dropped to the floor and was quickly swooped up by the bartender who launched him into the street past his other ejection. "Got a good two more feet on that one," he acclaimed to a solid round of hoorays and whistles.

Darcy walked back to Mary. "Why is it, Mr. Darnell, whenever we meet, blood and bile accompany you? That man, though rude, poised no threat to me."

"Until you open your eyes and see Whitechapel for what is, don't presume to know what is or isn't a threat. Cat, keep this lamb close to you." He said.

Catherine nodded and helped Polly to her feet. "Take her home, Darcy. With all the talk she's been doing about organizing the girls at Bryant and Mays, it's not safe for her to go wandering the dark alone."

Polly squeezed Darcy's hand. "Will you be coming to the meeting?"

"Of course, Polly, I'll bring my boys too. If nothing else, it'll make the powers think twice before breaking it up."

"And you Catherine?"

"Polly, the conditions at Hollens might be a disgrace and the pay a pittance, but it's still better than nothing. My showing up alone would mean one more opening on the line."

"Then get all the women to come," Darcy said.

"Easy for you to say, Darcy. You're a first-rate mechanic, harder to replace."

"Oy, thought you was going to add because I'm a man."

Catherine winked and slapped his ass as she led Mary past him. "Some things don't need saying."

Chapter 10

Mrs. Stride protected her girls to the best of her ability. As long as hands were busy and complaints kept to a whimper, she banished Fitch and the other drooling lobcocks to the periphery of the shop floor. Only the mechanics, notably Darcy, were permitted to cross the imaginary border to keep the monster running.

Mrs. Stride stood behind Mary as she inspected each yard of cloth coming off the beast with a beadle's scrutiny. At one point, the factory matron tapped Mary on the shoulder. "Didn't think you'd make it through the first day, girl, but I see you're here to stay. How do you feel?"

"Tired," Mary said, then realized she might be coming off as a whinger. "But good, good tired. I imagine I'll not even notice it after I get used to it."

"Wouldn't count on it, girl. The beast won't let you get used to it. Everyone's tired in Whitechapel, so know you're one of us."

A woman coughing up phlegm and twisted with obvious signs of cotton lung stumbled past them. Mrs. Stride barked, "Nancy, Nancy Marsh, go fetch the bin and start loading up the deadbolts and take them to the disposal dock."

It seemed a cruel thing to force Nancy to perform such a hard task. The bin, even empty, took a great deal of effort to push. Mary decided to confront Stride and tell her that Nancy could not stand the strain of rolling the bin back and forth across a factory floor as long and wide as a football pitch a hundred times a day.

Catherine said, “Leave it alone. Stride is a good sort. Taking Nancy off the line will give her time to recuperate.”

“Recuperate, and then what?”

“And then continue to feed her children and crippled man.”

Nancy rolled her cart by, and just as Catherine stopped talking, she toppled face forward into the bin of rejects. Before either one of them could pull Nancy out of the bin, Mrs. Stride rushed over. She used one arm to lift her out of the bin and propped her up with her wide body against the push bar as Fitch rushed over.

“What’s going on here?” he demanded. He tried to get around Mrs. Stride’s bulk to get a look at Nancy.

“Go back where you belong, Mr. Fitch, or I’ll tell the twins about your plunging anything that has a hole and your in-work-hours tippling. You know how damning proper the Calvinists are.” Mrs. Stride kept her body pressed to Nancy’s as she rolled the cart to the back of the factory. When she returned, she pulled Mary to the side. “Go to the disposal area and take over from Nancy. She’s on her last leg. Keep your head down so nobody knows it’s not her.”

“For how long?”

“By days end, we’ll send Darcy to spirit her away. Leastwise, this way, she gets a full shift’s wages.”

Mary kept her face covered and her head down as she pushed the cart back and forth the factory floor. Mrs. Stride had hidden

Nancy behind a stack of pallets. She gave Mary a cup of water, a chunk of bread and a bit of cheese for the woman. At the end of the day, Darcy rolled a wheelbarrow next to the pallets. Mrs. Stride lifted Nancy by her shoulders while Mary and Catherine picked her up by her legs. They placed her in the barrow and started for the front of the factory, where workers stood in line to be checked out and receive their day's wages.

Darcy pushed the wheelbarrow up to a far older version of the Hollens twins at a counting desk. "What's this?" The man adjusted his spectacles on his nose and looked at Nancy.

Mrs. Stride stepped in front. "It's Nancy Marsh. She put in a hard day and collapsed near three minutes ago on her way to be ticked off."

"Nancy Marsh?"

"Aye, Mr. Hollens, she's been here near long as me. You brought her on."

"Oh yes, Church of England as I recall."

"No sir, Scot Presbyterian. A regular pew warmer."

The old man pulled at the tip of his nose. "Hhm." He took out the quill from its ink pot and made a check next to her name, then placed a few coins in her open palm without noticing that her eyes had rolled into the back of her head and her flesh was cool to the touch. "Mr. Kelly, return that wheelbarrow to where it belongs. It's the property of the mill."

"Will do, your royal arseholeship," Darcy mumbled.

"Excuse me," the senior Mr. Hollens said.

"I said, right away, governor."

The women lifted Nancy out and propped her up between them. Once on the streets, they waited for Darcy to round the building with the wheelbarrow. Mrs. Stride took some coins from her apron pocket. "Give these to her man, likely the last bit of salvation they'll see now she's gone."

Darcy added a few coins, as did Mary and Catherine. "It won't keep them from a pauper's warren, but it will fortify them on the way there," he said and rolled the dead woman down the dark street until he passed out of sight down a blind alley.

Mrs. Stride placed her skillet-sized hands below her breasts. She lifted them and let them fall. "I was once perky like you girls. As was Nancy there. Save your wages and beat the devil to get out of here before the devil beats you," she said and walked away.

"I told you she's a good sort," Catherine said. "As long as you keep on her good side."

"And what side would that be?" Mary asked.

"Don't know, never got around to her other side."

Chapter 11

Despite her meagre wages, Mary managed to send her father money. Wages which Hollens and Sons, as well as other factory owners, denounced as scandalously high, leading to their workers' gin-soaked gutter wallowing and open fornication at the base of Lord Nelson's statue. She hid her money in her mattress tick, rarely taking any out except for necessities. Her father's words held permanence in her mind when the urge to spend a farthing more than called for tempted her. "There are those who sleep on the beds of gold stuffed with the tears of others," he would say before retiring to his corner of the shack to gasp himself asleep. Mary pressed her face against her pillow and sniffed the sour history of others who had occupied the same room. She was content with imagining two sets of fresh linen. Ignored the pricks of straw penetrating the mattress and dreamed of being wrapped in a clean sheet decorated with flower petals that smelled of roses.

Mary's fifth month's rent came due. Reluctant to do a face-to-face exchange of currency, much less have her fingertips graze the worm-like fingers of Lucky on the chance she contracts some unknown but soul-killing malady, she slid the money under his door.

Fortunately, her sentinel appeared every Thursday when Mary returned to the bathhouse. The licks Mr. Farrow had laid on the diminutive peeping tom had induced the doss housekeeper to seek grace, if not salvation, between the thighs of Emma Elizabeth Smith. She had been recently expelled from her rooming house for her persistent attempt to get the authorities to investigate the murder of her man. She had warned Polly Nichols about the danger of supporting the emerging labour unions. Though Polly's lower jaw was barely hinged to her upper, she continued to enthusiastically persuade her fellow workers to link hands and walk off the site of poisonous vapours of matches and watch faces for insomniacs.

The landlord's daily violation of Emma Elizabeth Smith, a truly virtuous woman who turned her head and recited the Rosary as he ploughed into her like a bent share in sterile ground, abruptly ended. Her partly naked body was discovered in the black dog-coloured effluence of a tannery. Emma Elizabeth Smith's throat had been severed so violently that her head bobbed up and down in the slow-moving stream, and her nearly detached breasts floated to her sides.

Mr. Farrow promised Mary not one but two hot baths a week. At first, she was disinclined to accept his generosity. She loathed being in anyone's protection. She equated it with seigneurial privilege. But she accepted when she realized that Mr. Farrow lacked the inclination to fulfill any carnal musings. She accompanied Mr. Farrow to the doubly secured walls of the bathhouse. He glanced at Mary's swollen face and the red balloons under her eyes. She sneezed and accepted the mandatory bless you, then clutched herself to fend off a non-existent breeze.

"Good lord, you sound like you're talking from the bottom of a well."

"Just the sniffles. It's Sunday. I'll rest and be right by tomorrow."

He put down the buckets of steaming water. "What you got won't be cured by slumber." He raised the clean bandana covering his disfigured face. "Come." He pointed at a set of stairs that led to a floor above the stable. She followed him. He opened the door and stood aside to let her enter. The scent of sandalwood wafted over her. Along the corridor leading into the main room, brass plates with engraved images of mythical creatures adorned the walls. A wall tapestry hanging at the back of the apartment depicted a turbaned warrior riding a black horse above a landscape of palaces out of the Arabian Nights. A low circular teak table surrounded by pillows dominated the centre of the parlour.

"Sit."

Mary inched her way toward the front door. "Think I should go back to the bathhouse before the water goes cold."

"Nonsense," Farrow growled. "The buckets can be reheated. What's ailing you will not be cured by a splash of water and a pad of soap."

She sat on a pillow. He made his way to a galley kitchen and lit a paraffin stove. Mary craned her neck and saw Mr. Farrow set a small brass pot on the open flame and spooned two full measures of a black powder into a small copper pot. He waited until it came to a boil and sprinkled sugar into it. He poured the thick liquid into two demitasses. He carried them on a tray that held tricornered biscuits and a small bottle of Arak to the table. Farrow poured a thimble of the anise liquor into his Turkish coffee.

Mary placed her hand over the mouth of her cup. "I never touch spirits."

He set aside the bottle. "Worried what Mrs. Stride might say, might give you the sack?"

"No, I've seen the damage it's done to others back home and to so many more here."

Mary nibbled a corner of a biscuit. It tasted of spices she'd never encountered and smelt of rose water. The portrait of a young officer in full dress uniform hung above a door leading to another room. "He cuts a very striking figure," she said to part the thick silence between them.

"Does he?" Mr. Farrow let out a short, nasty laugh. "Truth be told, he cut a far less romantic figure sometimes after. One of the last men standing at Khartoum. Major Joshua Cyrus, one of five less than fortunate survivors."

Mary held a vague recollection of the fall of a city in Africa which General Gordon vainly defended against wave after wave of the Mahdis' desert warriors. "Did you know him?"

"Well enough to hang the good army surgeon's portrait. Major Cyrus and a few others the Crown had sent to Sudan were imprisoned for several years. Went through the normal hell of the captured. Spat upon, mocked, beaten and tortured. As for Major

Joshua, he suffered no worse than our own not-so-distant monarchs dealt out to those who opposed them. The wheel, drawn and quartered and the like. He was among the last to be released, actually ransomed. His captors jeered that the Mother Sow was calling her litter home. Prime Minister Robert Gascoyne-Cecil honoured the returnees anointing them as the true JUWES, I mean jewels, of Britannia."

He paused and turned his face away from Mary and pulled down his covering to blow through the cavity of his missing nose. He pulled it up, and he returned to Mary. "All in all, I hear he did well. Even called upon by those in power and behind the power to do their bidding. Sure you won't have a dribble of Arak to cure the grippe? Mrs. Stride would approve. She's been known to down four pints or more in secret when the bruises of others become too much for her to bear."

Chapter 12

The telegraph from New York contained few words. Just enough for Bryson to envision Morris Breck chomping on a cigar and draining a beaker of whiskey mixed with dyspepsia relief powders.

ANY NEWS ON EMIN PASHA SEARCH? (stop). IF NOT WHY THE HECK DID WE SEND YOU $$$! (stop)

Bryson, accustomed to the Tribune's concern for the price of each letter, knew Morris expected an equally truncated but meaningful reply.

BIBLE THUMPER HAS NOT REPORTED BACK TO POWDER WIG GEOGRAPHICAL SOCIETY (Stop)

MULTIPLE MURDERS OF WOMEN IN WHITECHAPEL (Stop)

THIS MORE TO OUR READERS' TASTE (Stop)

Morris Breck's reply was delivered that evening by Perkins.

"WHORES OR WOMEN OF GOOD STANDING (Stop)

Bryson handed Ezra his response.

DOES IT MATTER-WHORES OR VIRGIN SAINTS YOU CHOOSE (Stop)

Chapter 13

Six weeks had passed since Bryson staggered down the gangplank of the tub that brought him across the Atlantic. His day consisted of meeting Perkins and standing until two o'clock in front of the British Geographical Society, waiting for an invitation to enter. He received no such invite. The gatekeepers of the society barred him from putting a toe over its threshold, much less engaging in conversation with its brandy-sipping members. After receiving the go-ahead from Morris Breck to pursue the murders in Whitechapel, Bryson sauntered into the smoking lounge where Perkins and Harte waited for him to begin yet another dreadful tour of the city.

"You look like someone whose least favourite aunt died and left him a million dollars," Harte said.

Perkins scowled. "Seriously, Mr. Ward, you believe the horrible events in Whitechapel are worth your time?"

"Ezra, is it not better to spend it where real news is happening? Standing outside that mausoleum is a true waste of time, capped off by dining on boiled beef and potatoes, washed down with warm beer every evening. Not to mention hearing about the next story Mr. Harte contemplates writing. No offence meant, Bret."

"The truth hurts but rarely offends," Harte said.

"So where do we begin to learn why and who filleted this latest chippy?" Bryson asked.

Perkins raised his voice, “Emma Smith, her name was Emma Elizabeth Smith. She was no more a whore than I am the Bishop of Canterbury.”

Bret Harte patted Perkins on his shoulder. “I heard you speak of her husband a few times after synagogue. Sorry about her passing.”

Perkins swept Harte’s hand off. “I’d hardly call being butchered like a hog a passing. Her only failing was that she married a labour agitator and tried to convince the authorities he was murdered.”

“Sounds like you boys know a lot more about these doings.”

Perkins swivelled on his heel. “My task is to get you into the RGS to interview the leather chair mummies about the exploits of Mr. Stanley and their opinion on how to bring the fire of Christianity to the wilds of Africa. It is doubtful they will open their mouths to condemn the savagery of what is going on in the mills and workhouses of Britannia.”

“Where do we start?”

“In a place that never changes, Whitechapel,” Perkins said.

Bryson nodded and returned to his room to retrieve his pistol from under the mattress. He strapped the holster across his torso like a bandolier and concealed it under his long overcoat. He briefly gave a glimpse of it to Perkins on his return.

*

“Murder, Another Murder in Whitechapel,” a kid hawking papers announced outside the hotel. Splashed across the front page was the rendering of a woman lying on her back with her arms to her sides and a ribbon of black blood representing the deep slash across her neck.. Bryson tossed the kid a coin. He unfolded the paper and read aloud, "The body of Martha Tombram, a well-known prostitute frequenting..."

Perkins tore the tabloid in half. "Now they've stooped to labelling an angel a slut. Martha's only fault was sheltering the dispossessed and feeding the starving. Her crime, she belonged to a movement that cared for workers withering away in the factories of Whitechapel and beyond."

*

Bryson had become so accustomed to the squalor of Whitechapel that he barely blinked when an old woman wearing barely enough rags to keep her decent threw herself in front of their hansom. The driver jerked the reigns, and the cab veered into the curb. He jumped off his perch and started to shake the woman. Bryson and Perkins left the cab to restrain him, but before they could intercede, a huge black-haired man dressed like he was going to an opera lifted the driver off his feet. He tossed him to the side as easily as he would a feather pillow. He helped the woman to her feet and opened the carriage door. He took out a blanket intended for passengers, wrapped it around the woman's shoulders and gave her a fistful of coins. "Next time you are determined to remove yourself from the pangs of the living, throw yourself in the path of a beer wagon. Much less nimble than this transport."

The driver picked himself off the street and confronted his

assailant. A deep pulsating scar travelled from the top of the man's ear to his cheek. The man's obsidian eyes, embedded in his sun-scorched features, warned the driver to retreat. The driver removed his cap, pressed it against his chest and backed away to his cab.

"Wait."

The driver froze. The man took his wallet out of his coat pocket and removed three bills. "One note is for your blanket; the other two are to remind you that the old woman could have just as well been your mother given where this nation is headed." He patted the driver like a faithful dog and entered The Princess Alice. Perkins followed the man. Bryson, on the scent of something worth investigating, tagged behind them. The toughest-looking thugs in the pub gave way to the man. Even Hubie kept his arms behind his back. The man barely acknowledged the thimble-twister, but stuffed four smiling kings into his pocket.

Only Milton, now accompanied by two of Robert Peel's finest, dared to intercept him. "And what is your purpose in this haven of the perverted and depraved, Sir Burton?"

Burton backed Milton against a table and brushed aside his mates like whips of grass. "Two purposes. One to teach manners to the person who bashed a good friend of mine, one Oscar Wilde. And two...," He paused to stare Milton into a chair at the table. "And two," he continued and cocked a finger at the constable "And two, to discover why Sir Robert Anderson and Charles Warren with all their runners and turd drops such as yourself are unwilling to acknowledge, much less pursue whoever is butchering women in Whitechapel."

"To the matter of that Irish bastard poet and sodomite, the Marquis I hear is well-tooled to deal with him without our help."

"I have heard the same, you mottled prick. Know this, should you or any of your maggots touch him again, even the Ganges will not accept your earthly remains."

"Is that a threat, Sir Burton?"

"Have some dolly read the accounts of my travels to you, and you'll gain I never make idle threats."

"Can't ya count beyond two, Sir Richard?" Milton crossed one leg over the other and propped his chin up on his elbow.

Sir Burton kicked the chair from under him. His ass bounced off the floor. He grasped at his underlings to pull him to his feet.

"Go back to your kennel," Burton said. "Your masters are calling."

Milton swept away the arms of his subordinates. "I know men of influence."

"I am a man of influence."

Perkins tapped the man on his shoulder. A teeth-bared smile indicating either a greeting or a bull mastiff's warning before it attacks appeared on Burton's face.

"Easy there, Sir Richard, there's no reward in anointing that one."

Burton relaxed, his sharp teeth retreated under the cover of his drooping moustache. He wrapped his arms around Perkins and lifted him off his feet. "By God, what brings the wandering Jew back into this valley of despair?"

Perkins slipped out of Burton's grasp and squared off in an unorthodox boxing stance. He let fly a flurry of jabs with his left hand that stopped short of the giant's scarred face before tapping him with a straight right on his chin. The man clapped his hands together so soundly that it could be heard above the din in the pub. "By God, what a waste Perez. If you had chosen to stick to your real calling instead of..."

"Instead of what, Sir Richard?" Ezra held up his open palm to stop him from continuing." Instead of joining Her Majesty's army as I did?"

Burton shook Perkins' hand. "You could have been the next champion of the British Isles."

"A Jew in uniform or a Jew in the squared circle is still a Jew in the eyes of the gentry. I found that out quick enough in the service of her Royal Highness."

"And so, my friend?"

"And so Richard, I have perfected the art of blending in. I go to mass, Church of England of course, buy a Christmas goose in honour of your, our, addition to the long list of supposed Messiahs and vote for whoever is in fashion at the moment and who hopefully prevents us from entering frivolous wars to inflate our Rule Britannia lungs."

Burton walked over to four toughs and tossed four coins on their table. "I presume you fine fellows are seeking establishments more to your liking." Each man pocketed a coin and left.

Bryson skimmed his newly acquired Bowler across the table. "Neat trick, huh? Saw Bat Masterson do it once in Queens at a boxing match he fronted." He extended his hand to Burton. The explorer put his arms behind his back. A thin smile crept across his face. "You're keeping odd company these days, Ezra."

Bryson pulled his hand back. "I'm Bryson Ward of The New York Tribune."

The man patted the concealed pistol inside Bryson's overcoat. "Sir Richard Francis Burton, discoverer of the source of the Nile, adventurer, the only infidel to enter Mecca, translator of the Kama Sutra. Need I go on?"

"No need, even across the big blue puddle we've heard about you."

"And what's your claim to fame, Mr. Ward? Rode down any desperados, rescued any lily white damsels from the clutches of bloodthirsty Indians or reported on the annual Tulip and Rose festival in New York City?"

Bryson pulled up a chair. He sat down with arms resting on its backrest. "Nothing that exciting, Dick. Sorry for my slip, I mean Sir Dick. Not so sure about the Nile bit, think that's still up for discussion."

Burton pulled out a chair and sat likewise, leaning so far over its backrest that Bryson could feel his hot breath. "Only when the odour of gunpowder has cleared will my findings be validated and Mr. Speakes' assertions proven to be as misguided as his hunting ability. The only debate left will be whether the poor fellow tripped and blew his head off or sat down and placed the shotgun between his knees and blew his head off rather than have the courage to face me on the location of the true mother of the Nile."

A waiter arrived with a bottle of rum and three tumblers. "The pistol so poorly concealed under your coat, I take it is a Colt single-action revolver? What your dime story authors refer to as a peacemaker."

Bryson drew his coat closer around him. He folded his arms over his chest to hide what he realized was the distinct shape of his pistol's holster. He leaned forward. "It's said God created men, but Samuel Colt made them all equal."

"Given a choice of weapons, I prefer something with less thunder and more accuracy to dissuade enemies intent on placing my head on a pike. Such as the Webley revolver. Mr. Colt may have contributed to the lore of the Wild West, but the Webley helped build and maintains our Empire." Burton held up his glass to the streak of light seeping through a grimy window. He pulled out a handkerchief, ran it inside the glass and around its rim, and passed it to Perkins, who repeated the ritual and gave it back to Sir Richard.

"Perez, I rather like this former colonial. Let's meet again. Perhaps I can ease him past the guards of the RGS inner sanctum."

Chapter 14

Catherine Eddowes ordered a tumbler of a clear liquor that smelt of pine and lamp oil at The Princess Alice. She slid it across the table to Mary. "Go on, gal, have a proper drink. It will calm your nerves. With luck, it will muffle the screams of young girls being fed to the machine and the sight of women older than their years being trundled out in wheelbarrows." Mary held up her ginger beer and passed the tumbler back to Cat.

"That won't do, Mary. Mustn't insult the owner of this fine establishment. He adds his own sweat to this brew of snake venom." Catherine gulped down the drink and two more of the same before Mary finished her ginger beer. "Now it's time for me to do some serious forgetting." Catherine inhaled three more tumblers. She became less and less coherent until every sentence was prefaced with a sob and punctuated with a long belch. Finally, Catherine rounded the bend and could no longer speak except to utter a desperate plea for help. "Mary, guide me home. Yours or mine will do."

Mary had experience leading her Da home when the weight of poverty and little hope existed for a brighter future. When the black dog of depression entered him, he drank himself numb, and Mary had to search for him outside the doors of the local pubs. He clasped her hand like a toddler fearing abandonment. Often pausing in front of the absent landowners' mansions, he cursed them and the Widow at Windsor for the sanctioned piracy of the common grazing fields. He reserved his most ferocious imprecations for the vermin inside the squat building of the Royal Irish Constabulary. The British soldiers were less odious. They neither volunteered nor wanted to be in Ireland. Not so with the RIC, more mendacious than Judas, they betrayed their own for a glint of silver and brass uniform buttons. Once, he spotted four Black-and-Tans staggering out of their private watering hole. He tried to bring up enough saliva to give a proper spit. Mary pulled him back before he could confront the men. In the morning, he thanked her for saving him a thrashing and possible disappearance in a bog. The night before, he had chastened her for interfering with his freedom to express his contempt.

Mary relied on Cat's grunts and arm gestures for directions to her rooming house. Grateful that Catherine's binge took place on Saturday evening, Mary prayed that the Sabbath would give her friend a full twenty-four hours to right herself. She lacked the mind to stand erect, let alone clock a full sixteen hours at the beast. Within a few hundred feet of her place, Cat doubled over and spewed a stream of yellow vomit into a gutter filled with garbage, dead rodents and human waste that flowed into the Thames after a heavy rain.

Catherine wiped the slime off her lips. Smiling crookedly, she stabbed her index finger at a row of two-story wooden shacks squeezed between an opium den on one end and a rendering shed on the other. "Home fecking sweet home, darling."

Mary led Catherine to the door. Her friend pointed a wavering finger at it. A large man flung the door open, barring their entry. He wore a pied-coloured jacket, tight-fitting trousers of the same design, and an orange pork pie hat. The cigar clenched between his teeth, he spat at Mary's feet. "Excuse me, my dove, I did not see you entering whilst I departed." He removed his hat and bowed. "Crude and unforgivable of me, I pray you have in your heart to forgive me."

He wouldn't have been a bad sort of looking fellow if he had only decided what side of the river he belonged on. Too perfect teeth and clean nails to hail from Whitechapel and too garishly attired and perfumed to roam Regent Street.

"Please, sir, stand aside. My friend is out of sorts."

The man placed his fist under Catherine's chin and lifted her head. "Aye, looks like old Cat has broken her pledge of sobriety. She looks two skips away from becoming a hedge creeper." He flicked his tongue against the back of his upper teeth, making a clicking noise. "Really, Cat, is this what being an honest woman is all about? Hell bitch, paying for your own gin seems daft when you could have a line of punters funding your cups for the pleasure of poking you."

Catherine shoved the man back, leaving a wet handprint on his fancy jacket. "Away with you, Charlie Barnett! I'm quit with you."

"Stand aside," Mary demanded.

He held the door open for Mary. "Not meaning to be rude, but Catherine is wasting her talents, as no doubt you are. She has as much of chance of making a decent living in the Whitechapel mills as I do of having tea with the Queen. If she dreams of such nonsense then she should at least be well lubricated when she realizes she's been shat into the gutter when she's too decrepit to stand at the looms or too old to open her thighs in an alley."

Mary tried to guide Catherine around the man, but he spread his arms between the door frame and blocked their path. Catherine glanced up at him, chuckled and heaved what remained in her stomach on his trousers. Without a hint of anger, he slapped Catherine so hard she fell back on the street. He reached down and tore off a sleeve from Catherine's smock and used it to dab the vomit off his pants. He tossed the rag aside and then wiped his hands over Mary's breasts, pausing to squeeze them. "Firm they are, ripe enough," he laughed. Mary's knee came up but stopped short of his groins when he danced away. "Really, lass, you have to be quicker than that to nail an experienced gentleman like me. I paid you a compliment. Your breasts are firm, just the way my clients like them."

Catherine crawled to Barnett and tugged at his cuffs. "Leave her alone. She's a good girl."

"You stupid cow. If I choose to add a worn-out cunt like you or a fresh peach like this one to my stable, I'll do so."

Catherine used the lapels of the man's jacket to pull herself up to his chin. "Get behind me, Mary," she hissed. "Charlie Barnett, if you touch her again, I'll have a piece of you."

Barnett raised his fist over his head, ready to bring it down on Catherine's face.

“Cat, you’ll have to stand in queue,” Darcy Darnell’s calm voice rose behind them. “So much as a twitch of your nose, Barnett, and you’re a meal for the wharf rats.” His voice was made all the more threatening by its friendly tone. Barnett did not have time to respond. Darcy grabbed him by his arm and threw him across the road. He planted his boot across the pimp’s throat.

“Let off. I was gaming; I was just having a bit of fun.” Barnett squeezed out a plea as Darcy’s boot pressed harder on his throat.

“Let him up,” Mary cried. “For sure, he’s a pig, but you’re liable to break his neck.”

Darcy lifted his foot slightly before he bore his weight down on his Adam’s apple again. “Charlie, you know me. You know I don’t like what you call gaming, having a bit of fun. If I ever see you bothering Catherine, Mary or for that matter any skirt in Whitechapel again, you will have to answer to me or...” Darcy removed his boot and waited for Barnett to complete the sentence.

“Or answer to no other.”

“That’s right, Charlie,” Darcy said with the same flat tone of voice, free of any hint of menace. “Now get out of here. And Charlie, get a new suit, you look like a fucking clown.”

Barnett dusted off his trousers, planted his hat a-skid, and searched the gutter for his cigar. He clenched it between his perfect teeth and strode down the street. He turned when he was certain he was too far away for Darcy to catch him or too far to bother for him to exert himself. “You and these mares have not heard the last from me or my protectors." Barnett timed his escape well. His body seemed to rise out of the air as he sped down the street without looking back to see if he was being pursued.

"Let me introduce myself, though I think we've been near a formal get-to-know-you more than once." Darcy helped Mary support Catherine and led her into her flat. He lowered his head to make it through the low doorway. Mary followed him into a windowless room scarcely larger than a utility closet.

"You know well we've met before," Mary said. "You near caused blood and bones on a train, scooped out the remains of two kittens devoured by the beast, barrelled out a poor soul who no longer could stand the rigour of the mill, assaulted a member of the constabulary and ..."

Darcy laid Cat on her straw tick mattress. He lit a candle near the bed and sat down on a three-legged stool, the only stick of furniture in the room. "And wish to make a better impression on you, Miss?"

Mary hesitated. Catherine's deep snoring nearly drowned out her response. "You know my name. Mary, Mary Jeanette Kelly."

"Pleased to meet you. Since we are into formalities, I'm Darcy Flynn Darnell."

"I know your name and cannot say it is a pleasure to know you."

"Do you dance Mary Jeanette Kelly?"

The question took Mary back to her days in Ireland, pretending in the company of only herself and the chickens in the yard that she was at a glorious ball, dancing on polished marble floors under shimmering crystal chandeliers in a palace.

Before Mary could respond, Catherine bolted up from her bed and swung her fists at an invisible intruder tormenting her. "Out with you," she screamed and fell back. Darcy covered her with a moth-eaten blanket. Catherine curled into a ball. Clutching the corner of the blanket, she drew it up to her cheek and sucked her thumb.

Darcy sighed and asked, "Do you live far from here?"

"Not far, not far in daylight."

"There is no daylight in Whitechapel." He hooked his arm through hers and guided Mary through the labyrinth of alleys to Mother Cantons.

The gas street lamps spaced so apart that they looked like flickering candles in a tomb cast a milk stain light on the footpath they trod. Her Da on a visit to Dublin had shivered when he recalled how the gas lamps seemed to suspend the disembodied heads of Irish rebels who perished at Gibbet Rath in their wavering light.

Darcy escorted Mary through the tangle of streets and briar-like arms of the drunk and destitute, reaching for a lifeline but never salvation. He held her close to him, would stop short of a darkened recesses and survey the shadows beyond them.

"Really Mister Darnell, I thought your intent was to walk me home not protect me from the Bodach," Mary said, tired by the constant stop and go of their walk.

"A Bodach is a myth. Barnett is the vermin I keep an eye for. As a rat is most likely to come out of the dark to bite you, come from the place it calls home."

Mary shook herself free of Darcy. "I don't understand and don't know if I want to understand."

Darcy braced himself against the damp wall of one of the countless hovels on their path. "Mary Jeanette Kelly, you best open your eyes and learn quickly. Learn the rules of this jungle to survive or end up dead or worse."

"Grateful for your wealth of knowledge, Mr. Darnell, but my Da gave me better advice on how to swim upstream despite the current. Know yourself, don't waver from the self you know, and stand up for yourself, and you'll never have to question why you lost yourself."

Darcy placed his palm latticed with scars on Mary's cheek. "You sound like my Ma. She cautioned my sister, two brothers and myself to mind our manners and know when to tip our hats to those who held the purse or wielded a truncheon. She held to that belief even when she and my brothers were packed off to a debtor's prison, not to be freed till I, who remained free, could work off their debt."

Mary removed Darcy's jagged palm from her cheek. "And you saw them out?"

They walked another fifteen minutes. Darcy chewed the bones of his thoughts to the marrow before lifting Mary over a puddle at the entrance of Mother Cantons. "You might say I saw them out. They died of typhoid. I had to purchase their remains from the creditors lest they be sold off for dissection. Until the people of Whitechapel raise their souls from the gutters, they're worth more dead than alive."

"And your sister?"

He wiped his sleeve across his eyes. "A different fate awaited her."

Unable to express the sadness and anger crushing her lungs, Mary leaned forward and rose on her toes to kiss Darcy on his cheek before dashing across the yard to her room. Darcy patted his cheek with his pumiced palm. "Either Mary Jeanette Kelly will rescue me from myself, or I'll rescue her from here."

Chapter 15

Sir Richard gained entrance for Bryson into the Royal Geographical Society, where he was treated with equal doses of curiosity, derision and malice. Perkins remained outside preferring the company of the sweeper walking behind a horse than the mummified turds inside the RGS.

Bryson glanced around the reading room of the RGS to see if any former Colonials heads were part of the menagerie of exotic animals hanging on the walls. One man wearing a uniform from the glory days of King George III offered him a brandy. Bryson thanked him and extended his hand to take the snifter. The man tossed the brandy in his face. "I've not forgotten what you bastards did to my ship on Lake Champlain, not now and by damn not ever!"

Burton slapped Bryson on his back. "Think that's bad. He recognized Ezra from his days boxing under his real surname. He hit Ezra with a cane for coming from the loins of our saviour's killers. Naturally, I rushed to my friend's defence. I informed him the Hebrews had nothing to do with it. It was the work of the bloody, soon to be Christians, Romans."

Whenever Bryson approached the members of the RGS to ask, "Any word on Mr. Stanley's search for the Emin Pasha? What are your thoughts?" The fossils disappeared behind the enormous pages of the London Gazette or the latest Royal Geographical Society

Journal. “No comment, huh? What about the women being butchered across town? Seems you should have an opinion on that, Whitechapel being within smelling distance.”

A member dropped his paper to his lap and warned Bryson without looking up, “Desist annoying the patrons of the RGS or risk being bodily ejected.”

Sir Richard stood behind a man studying a painting hanging above a cavernous fireplace of Saint George slaying a dragon. Bryson pointed at him. “I'm his guest.”

The man snorted and vanished between the pages of his paper. “The next thing you know, Burton will be inviting Hottentots to dine here.”

Burton leaned forward and whispered something to the appraiser of the murderer of the fire-breathing lizard. The man turned. A broad smile appeared on his face. His lips were deep red and fleshy. Despite being far taller and heavier than Sir Richard, the man glided over the floor like a dancer to Bryson. His purple frock coat hugged his tapered torso. A green carnation was inserted in the buttonhole of his lapel.

“Oscar, this is the Yank reporter I told you about,” Burton said.

“So you're the scribe roaming the dark alleys and fetid drinking establishments of Whitechapel, the Sodom and Gomorrah of London.” Oscar Wilde clasped Bryson's hand so firmly that he nearly crushed it. "You have sailed across the big blue to be informed of Stanley's atest crusade to Christianize the natives and rescue a fellow fanatic, have you?" He glanced over his shoulder at the painting above the fireplace. "If we're not lionizing the slayers of innocent dragons, we're engaged in torturing contented pagans with the questionable Holy Book."

"Yeah, but it doesn't seem I got a chance of scraping a bit of lint off these stuffed shirts least wise getting a complete sentence."

"There is nothing to be gained here," Wilde said. He draped a cape lined with ruby-coloured silk over his shoulders.

The men exited the RGS and met Perkins outside. Wilde embraced Burton in full view of the carriage crowd with a passion reserved for long-lost lovers. Burton shoved the writer away. "Come on, Ozzie, you and I have enough trouble as it is without giving more grist to the mill."

"Limit yourself to one scandal a month," Ezra said, keeping out of reach of the writer's arms.

"Quite right, my favourite wandering Jew," Wilde said. "But one really can't fault me for keeping the fire of salacious innuendo blazing. Can one? I, for one, am bored and would relish a less rarefied atmosphere." He hailed a cab, and the four men got inside. "There's nothing like the stench of Dorset Street to overcome the hypocrisy and lassitude of the drawing room crowd."

*

The cab passed The Princess Alice. Beyond the pub, a barricade of overturned carts, chairs, planks of wood and barrels spanned the width of Dorset Street. Wilde walked toward a group of men bearing clubs. He chatted with them briefly and returned to the cab. "This should be an interesting diversion. There is a meeting being held of women protesting working conditions in Bryant and May and other factories."

"I surmise those brutes are there to dissuade the authorities from disrupting the gathering," Burton said.

"Show me a man wielding a club and nursing a righteous grudge, and I'll show you either an Irishman or one of Friedrich and Karl's disciples," Wilde replied.

Perkins marched straight toward the barricade. He raised his clenched fist above his head. "Remember 1848. Remember the Springtime of the Peoples. Remember Trafalgar Square. Workers unite!"

A young man answered, "Not bloody likely we'll forget. Stand aside, give 'em passage."

Burton slapped Oscar Wilde on his back. "Show me a fellow who knows his way in the squared circle and who has put up with over three thousand years of scorn, and I'll show you a man who can part the Red Sea."

They walked toward a gathering outside the double barn doors of an abandoned warehouse. Females outnumbered males by 3 to one. A sandwich board announced Women's Trade Union League-Men Invited. Bryson glanced over at a man with his arm looped through the arm of a young woman. He vaguely remembered her from a visit to The Princess Alice. The man wore a peaked cap and green armband with half a sunburst in its centre. Another woman, far more worn and thin, looped her arm through the young woman's other arm. Behind them, a person of questionable gender, but wearing a dress, stood with her arms crossed over her chest. She stood six feet tall and half as wide. She leaned over and said something to the man in the peaked cap. He removed his armband and put it in his trouser pocket.

Several people waiting for the doors to open, eyed Bryson and his friends with suspicion. A hunchbacked man armed with a wooden mallet stumbled toward them. He was accompanied by three men in overalls with patches on their bibs, indicating they were members of the International Workers. "Oi there, did they run out of chained brothers and sisters in Bedlam for you to gawk at or did you wander this way to take the names of honest workers to pass on to those who cripple our bodies and souls?"

Wilde removed his green carnation and offered it to the man. "My good fellow, this garish boutonnière indicates I too am a member of a persecuted yet necessary member of society. Just as you, through your labour, ensure our society is provided with not only silly luxuries for the idle rich and staples for the balance of citizens lacking title or wealth, I and my guild ensure..."

The man waved his mallet above Oscar's head. "Shut your yap. Ain't it enough your sort deprives us of a living wage without mocking us?"

Burton brushed the man aside. His path was blocked by the

protectors of the hunched radical. It was clear that the confrontation would not end well. Bryson touched the butt of the pistol under his long slicker. Wilde removed a derringer from his jacket pocket and concealed it behind his back.

"Back off, gents," Perkins said. He assumed the stance of a seasoned pugilist. "Solly, surely ya remember me?"

The elder man eyed Perkins from the top of his Bowler to his polished lace-up boots. "Sure, I know you, Perez, the reincarnation of Daniel Mendoza. The pride of our tribe until you changed your name and became a batman to some perfumed officer."

"One and the same. I may have left the covenant but never the tribe."

The hunched man tilted his head. His protectors parted to allow Perez and his companions to enter the warehouse.

The interior was packed its length and breadth with women and men standing shoulder to shoulder. At the front of the warehouse was a stage constructed of stacked pallets covered with sheets of plywood. Seven chairs with two men and five women, one of whom was dressed in the severe uniform of a Sally Anne, sat. Bryson heard the young woman who followed them in exclaim, "There's Polly, there's Sarah."

He watched the massive older woman shake her head. "They are far braver than wise, Mary."

The young woman addressed her friend, "Cat, what do you think?"

"When all you got left is the grave, courage is a diversion, not a blessing. Wouldn't you agree, Mrs. Stride?"

"Put a lock on it, Catherine. It's best to seal our lips. Show neither approval nor disapproval. The other camp has their jugs and ears. No telling who has infiltrated this gathering."

Bryson noticed the young man previously with Mary had taken his leave. He circulated the assembly, taking the measure of anyone who seemed out of place. He paused in front of a man wearing an ankle-length black Macintosh. A broad slouched hat obscured his face, a scarf was pulled over his nose.

The man stood rigid as a corpse propped up in an open casket. He pointed a long finger at the makeshift stage and, with his other hand, motioned Darcy to be gone. Neither man budged until a voice from the primitive dais shouted above the din. "Hush, be still. We have rented this space for only three hours and then best be gone 'fore Mr. Robert Anderson introduces his lesser demons into our gathering."

A man in the furthest regions of the audience held aloft a bottle of crystal clear gin. "Him and his flaccid lackeys can suck my full member before I let them break up our right of assembly."

"Mr. Ward, the poor chap mistakes the Magna Carta for what you Yanks call the Bill of Rights. You know, freedom of assembly, freedom of press and speech, all men are created equal sort of thing," Oscar Wilde remarked.

"It took a war between our enlightened States to resolve that issue."

"And has it been put to rest?"

"Hardly, especially the part that all men are created equal."

"Really, and when will that happen?"

"When all people are."

A woman on the stage wearing a shapeless brown dress stood up. She lifted a veil attached to her bonnet. One side of her face was raw, and a long brown welt squirmed on her cheek like a worm emerging from the earth after a heavy rain.

Bryson elbowed Burton. "Who's she?"

The explorer shrugged. "Haven't had the pleasure of meeting her. But I must admit I am impressed with how proudly she wears her scar."

The crowd grew silent as she approached the edge of the stage. "I have come from a distance far away from Whitechapel," she sang out. "Yet not so far that I neither hear the cries of starving infants wanting mother's milk when there is none nor the gasps of those drawing their last breath begging for one more day of health to put bread on their families' tables."

"This melange of destitutes grasp her every word," Wilde remarked.

"The cries in Whitechapel are echoed throughout our island, across the channel and the ocean."

"Annie Besant, she organized mill workers in Liverpool," Ezra said.

"Take heart. The international worker's movement has heard your pleas for Justice, Understanding, Equality, Welfare and Salvation. We are here to force the factory owners of Whitechapel and beyond to listen and address your needs."

Bryson faced Perez. "And how do you know that?"

"Because I was there when a bastard threw acid in her face. I know because I chased the coward."

Bryson took out his notepad. "You caught the guy?"

"No, he was too fast. Put the pad away. When I want you to record something, I'll let you know."

"Why were you there?"

"I was paid to prevent what happened from happening and failed."

Burton let out a coarse laugh. "Our invisible Hebrew has many secrets that he keeps hidden in his Perkins' trousers."

The huge woman clapped her hands so loudly behind Sir Richard's ears that he felt unbalanced. "Keep your yaps shut or get the hell back to your tea party."

Annie Besant threw her head back and roared to the rafters. "I am privileged. I have neither gone without meat nor bread. While you have fasted from dawn to dawn, I have feasted, shamefully nourished on the tears of your tribulations. Does this mean I have no right to stand here and implore you to listen?" She walked slowly to where Polly Nichols sat and extended her hand. Polly embraced Annie Besant as tenderly as a sister. She led Polly to the front of the platform and lifted her arm. "Do not listen to me. Listen to one of your own."

Burton stroked the scar running from his ear to his chin. "Besant, of course, she's the one pushing for women's suffrage. What's her clarion call?"

"As we breed leaders, we should choose who leads us," Wilde answered.

"I told you to clamp your lips, or I'll clamp them for you," Mrs. Stride threatened.

Polly Nichols's jaw was secured in place by a strip of cloth tied in a bow at the top of her head. She untied the bow. Her jaw dropped like a hinged door. She lifted it with two fingers and struggled to speak. "For sixteen hours a day, my sisters and I lick and dip sticks into pots of white phosphorus and then lick and dip again, maybe a million times a shift, so people can light their candles, fire their stoves, and the like. We don't ask for much, just fair wages and red dipping pots so we don't have to swallow the hellish powder that makes your matches. Yet our masters ask for more. More hours at lesser pay with no concern for our health. I know other factories have equal problems. Children fed into the maws of machines that never cease. Men and women with lungs so infested with dust and wool that to take a breath unhindered is a rare blessing. I cannot tell you what to do, but I can tell you what we Matchgirls are going to do." She pointed at a young woman on the dais. The girl picked up what looked like a rolled-up window blind. She stood beside Polly.

“The time left me is measured in eyedrops,” Polly said. “This girl’s in spoonfuls lest we take action.”

The young woman unfurled the blind. In bold black letters, JOIN UNITED WOMEN EMPLOYEES SYNDICATE stood out on the pure white canvas. “My name is Sarah Annie Chapman. Polly has given all she has to the cause for all who seek suffrage and the end to suffering. As of now, we are on strike at Bryant and Mays. We urge all the women and men slaving in the factories of England to put aside their differences and walk beside us for change.”

“She’s a brave one,” Catherine said.

“She should be terrified,” Mrs. Stride replied. “Now, let’s make haste and leave before we are reported for being here.”

“Reported by whom?” Mary asked.

Darcy swept his arm over the crowd. “By those who do the bidding of Anderson who in turn kiss the arses of those who own the factories and government that own us.”

They threaded their way through the crowd. Bryson moved a few inches to the side to allow Mary to pass. Their eyes met and flickered with a brief spark of recognition. Darcy jabbed his fist into Bryson’s chest. “Keep your eyes to yourself and your mouth shut when you meet them that sent you to spy on us.”

“Easy lad, he’s not a stooge. He’s an American journalist. I would call him an author, but that would be casting a slur on genuine practitioners of the art of poetry and prose.”

“Do you find our company amusing, Mr. Wilde?”

"Not at all. I find this building imbued with more honesty and gravitas than the fragrant swamps of salons and drawing rooms bereft of intelligence and passion I frequent."

Darcy walked away muttering, "Don't understand a word he said, but got to admit that Irish fop speaks well."

Bryson pulled Perkins toward him. "Damn-it man, forget Stanley and the Emin Pisser."

"That's Pasha."

"Pasha, Pisser who gives a rat's fart, Perez!"

"I prefer to be called Perkins while in your company."

"Enough of that crap. I'm tired of calling you by your starched collar name."

"I insist you do not insist."

"Listen Ezra, we all have norm de plombs," Bryson said.

"I think you mean Nom de Plume or, more correctly, an alias," Wilde interjected.

"The real story is here in Whitechapel, not at the RGS."

"And what story would be that?" Perez asked.

"Take your choice, Women Butchered in Jolly Old London or Anarchists and Marxists Encourage Work Stoppage in the Engine of Europe."

"Why not both?" Wilde said.

Burton, who had remained uncharacteristically silent, asked. "What are you alluding to?"

"Sir Richard, look at the victims and layer atop their affiliation with other recent murders and viola, you have the making of a delightful tale by Rymer and Prest or more recently, that Stoker fellow who I believe you and I met at some forgotten literati gathering."

"Has he put nib to paper?"

"Not yet, but you know, as well, that mediocrity takes time to flourish."

"Another one of your aphorisms, Oscar?"

"Unintentional, but worth recalling in the future."

"For Christ's sake, quit horsing around. The real story is in Whitechapel. Let's go after it."

"I know a young doctor and writer who revels in uncovering mysteries. Arthur may provide insight into how these two disparate happenings are linked."

Chapter 16

It took little cajoling on the part of Darcy to persuade Mrs. Stride to accompany them to the meeting at the warehouse. “If things get unruly, I’ll likely need a striking figure like you to calm the waters. Besides Beth, you have been working clandestinely for the cause so long that you’ll recognize the weasels hired to take names by those who want to crush us.”

“I’ll come if only to protect you naifs from yourselves. I don’t want Cat leaping up when Sarah and Polly take to their feet.”

The gathering at the warehouse went off without incident. Mrs. Stride spotted a few informers in the crowd, but even they seemed to agree with the speakers. A stranger dressed from head to boot laces in a black Macintosh alarmed her. A slouched hat covered his forehead, and a scarf was drawn over his nose. The man batted Darcy away as easily as a pesky fly. He vanished when the meeting came to an end. “The Reaper seldom lingers after choosing his next dance partner,” Mrs. Stride thought.

True to form, Darcy managed to engage in a confrontation with three well-dressed gentlemen, but nothing came of it. Out on Dorset Street, the crowd went in different directions, some to their hovels, others to the pubs and gin mills that were almost as numerous as the rats scurrying in the gutters. Mrs. Stride and her naifs travelled together without speaking.

"Hold up there," Bryson yelled after them.

"Not you three again," Darcy said. "Not enough that you got to see the beasts of Whitechapel in the wild? Now you feel like watching us retreat to our dens and perhaps toss us a bone."

Sir Richard propelled Bryson ahead of him. "It's your idea, Yank; come out with it."

Oscar Wilde added, "This American journalist desires to spread your noble cause across the globe or at least to his limited readers in New York City, that thriving metropolis of sin and misery only rivalled if not surpassed by the ground on which we stand."

"Put it to rest, Ozzie."

"Good lord Mother Stride, I didn't recognize you dressed in your finery. Have you shed a few stone since last we met at the conclave of socialists and other utopians?"

Mrs. Stride took a step forward and laid her hand on Bryson's shoulder. "What is it that you want?"

"What's going on here needs to be exposed. The working conditions, the poverty, the way people are treated like chattel and the murders of women who have no other option than to sell their bodies."

Mrs. Stride dug her fingers into Bryson's bicep. "Listen you sanctimonious dolt. Those women were no more whores than Sir Richard there is the Pope."

"You ain't the first and won't be the last hobby crusader to spread news of our misery," Darcy spoke up. "London is overrun with do-gooders who adopt us for a week then move on to complain about the rising cost of theatre tickets."

"Playwrights and actors need to eat as well," Wilder rejoined.

Mrs. Stride challenged Bryson. "If you truly want to understand what is going on here, then meet us next Saturday evening at the Princess Alice."

Darcy waited until Bryson and his friends had hailed a cab and rolled out of sight before taking Mary by the hand. Catherine and Mrs. Stride split off into alleyways. Darcy accompanied Mary to her lodgings. Every few yards, he paused and looked behind him. When they reached Mother Cantons, he watched Mary ascend the stairs to her room. "I can't promise you luxury, Mary Kelly, but I can promise you is..."

"Promise her what?" A voice from inside the stable interrupted. "Poverty and the lack of will to live."

"Is that you, Mr. Farrow?"

"Mary, don't allow this one to drag you to a place of no return."

Chapter 17

Bret Harte waited for Bryson in the hotel smoking lounge. Perez had told him that they were embarking on an investigation of the powder keg of worker discontent in Whitechapel and the recent murders of women.

"Keep out of it, Bryson. Allow the proper authorities to do their job."

"To do their what, Bret? Ignore what is going on right under their noses?"

"What would Morris have to say about you abandoning your assignment to delve into the cesspool of Whitechapel?"

Kit Singh entered the lounge and held out a hand-rolled cigarette to Bryson. "It looks proper, sir?"

Bryson rolled it between his thumb and forefinger. "A little loose, but that can be resolved with practice."

"Will you show me how to do it with one hand?".

"Sure, but don't let your uncle catch you smoking it or we'll both be out on our ass." Kit Singh quickly left before he was discovered by his uncle.

"Now, where were we, Bret? Something about what would Morris have to say about my wasting my time on a story in Whitechapel instead of wasting my time at the RGS." Bryson closed his eyes and clasped his hand behind his head. He conjured up the image of Morris bolting or at least making a prolonged effort to simulate a bolt from his rolling chair. He envisioned him with a wad of chew bulging inside one cheek and his cigar smouldering in an empty sardine tin on his desk next to a beaker of illegal Five Points barley whiskey.

Kit Singh stood outside the lounge. He glanced around to ensure no one saw him hand Bryson a freshly rolled cigarette when he entered the lobby. Bryson pocketed it and patted Kit on the back. "You're getting the hang of it. In no time you'll be able to roll shag blindfolded."

"Sir Richard and another fellow are waiting for you outside."

Bret Harte followed Bryson out of the hotel. "Richard, Perez, I thought you would have more sense than to go on a snipe hunt with Bryson. Nothing is going to come of this except angering the authorities. You will either be in the middle of a riot or will be mudding the investigation of those tarts' deaths."

Perez held his rage in check. "Whatever trouble takes place in Whitechapel will happen with or without us. As for the women who were butchered. They were honest factory workers."

"Whores or Vestal Virgins, Sir Charles Warren looks dimly on civilians intruding on his turf."

"Is snipe hunting a sport in America?" Burton asked.

"Only for those on a fool's errand, such as Mr. Ward."

"Bret, I know you're appealing to our common sense, but if common sense is so common, why do so few people, us included, possess it? As for tracking mud over Sir Charles' enquiry, he would actually require one to muddy in the first place."

"At least Oscar seems to possess a grain of it."

"You think so, Mr. Harte?" Burton interjected. "Our darling daisy has gone to get that Sherlock Holmes writer's opinion of these doings."

Chapter 18

In The Princess Alice, Perez selected a table hidden in the shadows for himself and Burton and Bryson. He ordered a round. Their drinks remained untouched for thirty minutes while they waited for Mrs. Stride. On her way to their table, she scanned the pub for possible snouts. Darcy walked behind her. He paused next to a man leaning against the bar counter and whispered something to him. The man nodded and went outside The Princess Alice where he stood sentry. His knuckle dusters were visible when he crossed his arms over his chest.

Burton offered a chair to Mrs. Stride. "I see you brought British Bulldogs as protection."

"Irish Wolfhounds," Mrs. Stride corrected him. "Darcy and Liam would retch to hear you compare them to a drooling pet of the aristocracy."

Bryson held up five fingers to signal for another round. Mrs. Stride folded one of his fingers back into his palm. "I am not here on a social visit."

Bryson reached into his coat pocket and took out his notepad and pencil. "What's with all the women at the meeting?"

"You were there, right? You heard what they had to say, didn't you?"

"Sure, but I want to know what set them off."

"Then you obviously weren't there if you don't know."

"Yeah, yeah, I know the chorus, better wages, less hours, more say so. I've seen enough worker theatrics back in the States to get an idea of their gripes. I don't find anything novel about this one, except women are leading the charge."

Mrs. Stride reached for Bryson's ale. "Idiot," she snarled. "Thought I'd practice temperance tonight, but I see I need to stoke the fire in my gut."

"You must admit it's a bit out of the ordinary to see women commanding the attack on the factory owners."

Mrs. Stride gripped Bryson's left hand. He pulled it away. His glove came off, revealing the stub of his missing thumb. He dropped his hand to his lap and scooted his chair forward. Perez picked up the glove and laid it on Bryson's lap.

"You have nothing to whine about, boy. I've seen children with their faces ripped off." Mrs. Stride drank the balance of Bryson's pint. "You want to know why those Matchstick girls are taking the lead, do you?"

Bryson struggled to replace the glove. "I got it, they have a tough life."

"If you mean they are going to die slowly but not before they turn into hideous creatures at their workbenches, then aye, they have a tough life. But not only that, the owners there as elsewhere and no doubt on your own soil, demand more products plus more hours while reducing wages."

"That doesn't explain how these women came to the front."

Perez helped Bryson put back on the glove. "The reason you see women leading the charge is because most of the men involved in the movement have either ended up in Newgate, shipped off to Australia or Canada or most recently were discovered dangling from lampposts. Tethered there by their own innards."

Mrs. Stride added, "The majority of factory labour is done by women and children. If we take a stand, then the higher-ups have to take heed, or the machines will stop humming. I fear when all the remaining men are gone, we will be shunted off as well."

The conversation ended when Hubie Cross staggered into The Princess Alice and collapsed. "For the love of God, give me a drink. Horrible, too horrible, give me a bloody drink!" Darcy helped Hubie to his feet. Burton and Perez left Bryson at the table to join him. Burton grabbed a bottle of gin from the bar and poured a four-knuckle measure into a dirty glass.

"Enough there!" The barman slammed his fist on the counter. "Sir Dickie, I don't give a hag's teat if you are the Lord Chancellor himself. This is my establishment, and I'm the one who decides what and how much to pour."

Hubie sank to his knees and held his empty glass above his head. "I can't rid myself of it. I pray I should go blind before I see the likes of it again."

Burton motioned the barman to fill up the glass. "My purse is covering each drop of your vile gin."

Perez took the empty glass from Hubie's hand and, without saying a word to the barman, waited for it to be filled to the lip. Hubie threw his head back and emptied the glass without coming up for air.

Bryson and Mrs. Stride joined the others at the bar. Hubie tugged at Bryson's coat sleeve. "I'd put out my own eyes to erase the sight." Ward backed off, patting himself for his wallet and watch.

"Enough of this, come to your senses." Mrs. Stride knocked the glass from Hubie's hand.

Darcy pulled the filcher to his feet. "You heard her." He trapped Hubie's head between his hands. "Out with it, man. What's so awful that it turned you greyer than cold porridge?"

The thief freed himself from Darcy's grasp. "Buck Row in front of the stable. Go see for yourselves."

"What are you on about?" Mrs. Stride demanded.

"Thought it was my charmed day, easy pickings. Lying all covered up with a tarpaulin. A drunk I thinks, dead to the world, so I reaches down to filch what I can. Only it ain't a drunk. It's a woman, truly dead to the world. Cut up so bad, even her own mother wouldn't know her."

Perez flew out of the pub and down the street. His companions chased after him. A throng of people, three bluebottles, and a man dressed like he'd just come from dinner at Hampton Court surrounded a body scarcely covered by a beige tarp. A charity hospital was only a hundred yards away. A few of the gawkers poked at the corpse with sticks or nudged it with their boots. Perez struck the nearest person and knocked him to the ground. Sir Richard held Perez back. Darcy knelt beside the body. Milton stood by idly with two other peelers, smiling as if sharing a childish joke.

Milton pointed his baton at Sir Richard. "Leave her lie there till we've gathered evidence."

Darcy brushed away the sodden hair obscuring a tortured face. Even in the dim light, the woman's deformed jaw cast a green glow. A gash so deep that the head could be detached by the slightest breeze ran across the woman's throat.

"Polly, Polly Nichols," Darcy said.

"The same Polly Nichols at the women workers meeting?" Bryson asked. Without forethought, he drew his pistol and took aim at a mangey dog dragging away what looked like a bloody sausage from between the splayed thighs of the corpse.

Perez forced the pistol under Bryson's coat before the peelers noticed it. "Displaying that much less firing it can land you six years in Newgate."

Burton covered Polly Nichols' face with his jacket. Milton placed a hand on his shoulder. "Pretty Polly if she ever was pretty ain't so pretty now; is she?" Burton raised his cane over his head. He stopped short of striking Milton when a clean-shaven man in evening dress stepped from behind the policeman. "Sir Richard, please exercise restraint. Constable Milton is a baboon, a baboon, mind you, who belongs to the Metropolitan Constabulary."

“What’s that mean?’ Milton protested.

“It means you are one of my monkeys. Go back with your fellow baboons and occupy yourselves picking each other’s nits until I summon you.”

“Fancy seeing you here, Sir Charles. It must be a special crime to bring you out on such a dreadful night.”

Chapter 19

Darcy waited on the curb six mornings a week outside Mother Cantons for Mary. When she appeared, they acknowledged each other with a smile. A queer feeling of being watched plagued Mary. The few words that passed between them were limited to the never-changing weather conditions of soot-ladened fog and rain or what they had brought for lunch. Until one day passing through Hollens Textile Mill's gate, Darcy asked. "Do you dance, Mary Kelly?"

"If I recall, I told you I do." She slipped through the narrow opening slot of the gate to be marked present by one of the twins.

"Three Saturdays from now, would you accompany me to a dance at the meeting house. "

"The what, where?"

"A remembrance of our Éire, a celli, where we heard the women from Bryant and Mays speak. Not to worry about staining your reputation by being seen with me. Mrs. Stride and Cat will chaperone. Should my hands reach further than seemly, rest assured Mrs. Stride will snap them off at my wrists, and Cat will escort me to the earth bed."

"I believe that to be true."

"That puts a bow on it. I'll pick you up at Mother Cantons."

"It means I will meet you there with Mrs. Stride and Cat. I can't promise you more than two reels or one quadrille, if at all."

"I'll take my chances."

Chapter 20

Oscar Wilde, having been absent for days, arrived at Bryson's room unannounced at five in the morning. His persistent knocking awakened Bryson from a fitful sleep. The dreams, rather the snatches of knives catching the reflection of terrified women and their O shaped vowels of agony flickered through his mind like magic lantern images projected on a soiled sheet.

Bryson flung open his door. "Jesus, Oscar, what are you doing here at this ungodly hour?"

Wilde held a single finger up to his pursed lips. "Discretion is my forte. I came early so none would be alarmed."

"Alarmed, you gotta be kidding. You probably woke everyone from here to Kensal Green."

"I doubt if the denizens of that neighbourhood would mind a turn in their bed of earth and worms."

Bryson poured a pitcher of water into the porcelain basin on the washstand. He scrubbed his face with a bar of eucalyptus soap and dabbed a bit of the foam under his armpits. "I'm as awake as I'm ever going to be. What's so damn important that you nearly broke my door down?"

"Don't blame me; it was Perez who sent me. Burton and him told me to fetch you."

"Fetch?"

"An expression that I thought you Yanks used commonly, like bring, retrieve, deliver post-haste."

"What's the message?"

"They want you to meet them at the English Eight Club. I have a cab waiting."

"Let me get this straight: they want us to meet them at some club to play golf?"

Oscar pointed at Bryson's bed. "You best take that barely hidden persuader with you."

Bryson lifted the corner of the mattress and retrieved his Colt.

*

Bryson dozed through the ride in the countryside. What he had expected to be a quick trip took over two hours. There were only so many cows and sheep grazing in pastures that merited his attention. Bryson felt a cool gust of wind when the cab's door swung open. Perez extended a hand to help him alight, but he refused the offer. He followed Perez to a white shingled board building with a red peaked roof. Sir Richard stood on the porch. He wore a holstered Webley revolver.

"Looks like it's going to be one hell of a round of golf," Bryson said.

Wilde popped his head out of the cab. "I will catch you fellows later. I have another rendezvous with Arthur Conan Doyle. I'm curious what he deduces is going on in Whitechapel."

Bryson followed Burton and Perez through the building. The

walls were lined with testimonials to members who had scored the highest points in various shooting competitions ranging from skeet to rifle and pistol accuracy. On one wall, a picture of a young woman dressed in a tartan jacket and kilt, feathered tam and shouldering a rifle stopped every passer-by. Bryson ran his finger over the brass nameplate at the bottom of the famed image, Annie Oakley.

"That girl outshot the best of the realm blindfolded," Burton said.

Perez patted Bryson's coat. He felt the hard butt of the Colt against his palm. The three men exited the building and stopped at a raised mound where a man holding paper targets awaited them. He walked down the range and hung each one of the targets on a bullet-ridden post about 50 yards away. Burton withdrew his Webley. He fired five shots in quick succession. Four of his bullets entered the human silhouette's torso while the last one went wide.

"Your go," Burton said.

Bryson shook his head. "I'm no pistolero. I'm a scribbler." He held up his thumbless left hand.

Burton slipped his hand inside Bryson's coat. "I've seen you write with your right one." He pulled out the Colt and handed it to him. Bryson raised the pistol and stood sideways as he aimed the revolver. He cocked the hammer and fired one shot hitting the target dead centre in the chest. His other bullets missed the mark, disappearing somewhere in the neatly manicured lawn.

"Mr. Ward, have you ever been involved in a frontier gunfight?

The kind I've read about in American versions of our penny dreadfuls." Burton reloaded and handed his pistol to Perez.

"I'm still standing. Does that answer your question? I've learned the only one who walks away unscathed from a gunfight is the one who refuses to be in one. From my experience, as an observer mind you, it's not who's faster but who's better at distracting the other guy. Deception and accuracy trump a hasty hand anytime. That and..."

"And what?" Burton asked.

"And hiding in the shadows and shooting someone in the back trumps deception and a steady hand always."

Burton looked disappointed. "No tales of men standing in a dusty street and waiting for one another to draw."

"Only one is worth recalling. A kid in Wichita Falls taunted the wrong man. The boy, maybe eighteen at the outside, wore a double rig low on his waist with butt ends facing out. The man he prodded was Emmet Dalton. Seemed playful at first, leastwise Emmet tried to take it that way. He tousled the kid's hair and told him no doubt the boy could skin his pistol before he could wink. Thought it would end there."

Perez raised Burton's Webley. "But it didn't." Without seeming to aim, he placed four shots in the head of the target and one in its Valentine-shaped heart.

"No, it didn't. How'd you know?"

"Because he shamed the lad in front of others."

"Some jackasses primed the kid with liquid courage. Told him

Emmet was making a fool of him."

"How did it end?"

The range man raced across the field to retrieve their targets. Perez held his target up to the sun. Light poured through the destroyed target's head. Bryson poked his finger through his own target's hole.

"Emmett met him on the street. He stood about thirty feet away from him. He told the boy to reconsider. The kid chuckled, probably thinking he was backing down."

Burton lit a cigar. "How did it end?"

"Two shots opened a hole the size of a watermelon in the boy's gut. The third took off the side of his face. Emmett had not even unholstered his sidearm. He shot the boy with a pistol concealed behind his back, loaded with notched unholy cross bullets."

"Not very sporting."

"Emmett told me not to varnish the story. Patted me on the head like a stray puppy. He told me cheating only matters if you're on the lead end of the cheat."

"Sounds like he could be in the House of Lords," Perez said.

Burton took his pistol away from Perez. "A doctor once asked me how you feel when you kill a man. I told him quite jolly. How about you?"

Perez kicked at a clod of dirt at his feet. "As a Jew, if I even dared to joke about such a thing, I'd be dangling from a hook like a Christmas goose."

"In my position, Ezra, I can proudly admit to committing every sin in the Decalogue and suffer no ill consequences other than being uninvited to social gatherings for a week or two."

Bryson balled up his target and threw it at Sir Richard. "I don't appreciate being awakened at five AM. Carted off to only God knows where for target practice and not even served bread and butter for breakfast. I don't see how it relates to anything going on that we're investigating."

"Next Sunday there is a dance in Whitechapel. Many of the players we saw at the meeting will be there, along with people who aren't there to waltz. We should be there," Perez said.

"I thought you wanted no part of this."

"I never said I didn't. I said it's best to be discreet about it."

Sir Richard removed the spent cartridges from his pistol. "Our association with Mrs. Stride and our presence at Polly Nichol's corpse has dashed any pretence of our merely being dandies searching for a bit of East London excitement."

"Why this target practice?" Bryson asked.

"In the event we hunters become the hunted, I thought it best to see if we have the necessary skill to make a show of it. I know Ezra possesses it along with other expertise. But I was not sure of you."

"And do I?"

Ezra smiled and said, "If the target is immobile, you pass muster. However, I think you would be better off just throwing your revolver at whatever villain confronts you."

Chapter 21

Mary carefully unwrapped her one good dress from its winding sheet of crepe paper. The scent of dried lilac sprigs wafted from it. Mary had only worn it once since arriving in London at what turned out to be the culling of women applying for work at Hollens Mill. Since that day she went and returned from the Hollens in their ghost grey uniform for which a substantial amount was deducted from each week's wages. She brushed her workday footwear to remove the accumulated misery of Dorset Street, then blackened them with soot from the remains of her coal fire. She had long since decided that coal was a luxury ill-afforded if she were to send a small remittance to her Da to help him afford the ever-escalating fee to graze his flock of skeletal sheep. She combed her hair as best she could, lacking a mirror to inspect herself. When she descended, each creaking tread to the courtyard, she questioned why she should step out with such a malcontent, an outright seditionist, to what he promised was to be a lively evening.

Darcy stood outside the gates of Mother Cantons. He handed Mary a touch of her homeland, a bouquet of desiccated flowers, heather and clover. He no doubt had purchased them at a discount at some florist shop evading Sabbath laws. She did not ruminate over his intention.

It was her free day. Mrs. Stride and Cat would be one on each of her arms to maintain a proper image in the eyes of her Calvinist employers, Church of England high thumb-suckers, and more importantly anti-unionist oligarchs who held the realm together.

In her dreams, Mary imagined herself at the ball in a crystal palace. Her actual dances took place inside the stable of her father when the single cow, a disinterested bull and the dim-witted sheep who could not distinguish a predator from a friend were turned out to pasture. Mary had the barn floor all to herself. Quadrilles, waltzes, even tip-toe twists of ballerinas she had caught a glimpse of on posters infused her with hope that something better awaited her besides the malaise that defined the landscape.

"Where are you off to?" Mr. Farrow's raspy voice called after her.

Darcy entered the courtyard. "To Buckingham Palace. The Famine Queen has a rat problem."

Mr. Farrow blocked Darcy's entry. "Treat the young lady with care. Avoid gatherings that will compromise her good standings and safety."

"Nothing to fret about, my friend. She'll come back as pure and rosy as when she left."

"Mary, pay heed. Watch that you and this fellow keep well away from the cauldron of trouble on the boil in Whitechapel."

"I think I've seen that bloke before," Darcy said when they were clear of Farrow.

"I surely doubt it. He rarely ventures more than a hundred paces from his yard."

Just past the communal water pipe, Mary spotted Mrs. Stride and Cat Eddowes waiting for them. Mrs. Stride slapped a man trying to sneak his hand up her skirt.

"No disrespect intended," he apologized as he righted himself. "Just trying to ascertain if a bull or cow is hidden under all that fabric." Without turning, Mrs. Stride swung her arm. She clipped the fool under his chin, sending him into dreamland.

A pitiful blockade of sorts spanned the street leading to the vacant warehouse where the Matchgirls had announced their action. Mary saw the same well-tossed gentlemen she had noted at the previous outing. Bryson tipped his hat to her.

"Look at them, come to see us beasts at play," Darcy snarled. Before he could cross the road to confront Bryson and his friends, Mrs. Stride yelled, "Leave off. They are not the ones to worry about. Use your eyes. Anderson's peelers are out of uniform, and are looking for an excuse to put this evening to a stop before it has started."

Several toughs stood beside the police, who were dressed in civvies. Their clubs propped against a building. Charlie Barnett, still wearing his hat askew and pied coloured suit caught a glimpse of Catherine Eddowes. He thumped Milton on his back. "That one will come around when she has no other choice." He slapped his palm with a weighted sap.

Mrs. Stride took hold of Catherine and Mary's arms when she saw a short, hairless man wearing a tweed suit a size too small for him. He licked the tip of a pencil and wrote something in a notepad. More disconcerting was the sight of one of the Hollens twins standing just before the barricade. He likewise took out a pad and scrutinized each person filing past and jotted down something.

Mrs. Stride did an about-face and dragged Mary and Cat to an alley a few streets away. Darcy followed them. They arrived at the back of the warehouse and knocked on the door. It opened a crack.

"If you're here for the dance, go round front and enter through the big doors. If you ain't here for the dance, fuck off," a reed-thin voice instructed.

"Listen mate, there are spies out front taking names of all who enter," Darcy said.

Mrs. Stride threw her considerable weight against the door, sending the body on the other side tumbling across the dirt floor. She lifted a slight man to his feet. The young woman who had unfurled the banner with Polly Nichols pushed through a curtain separating the back room from the warehouse. "Really, Mrs. Stride, you have to be more gentle; Malachi is just doing his duty."

"Sarah Anne Chapman, after what happened to Polly, you should not be here."

"Because of what happened to Polly, I have to be here."

"Don't you think those taking names know this dance is merely a pretext to meet with other agitators on the sly?" Darcy asked.

"We came by the back way as not considered to be in your camp. We must be cautious." Mrs. Stride warned.

Despite her slight frame, Sarah Anne Chapman filled the space around her with a force and passion matching the fiercest Celtic women warriors of centuries past. "Caution is for the willingly oppressed. Malachi, go alert the committee that our dance may be interrupted. Make sure everyone holds their temper should the bluebottles and their pets burst in. Offer them a drink and cake. Treat them like lost relatives."

Mary tuned her ear to the sound of a fiddle, bodhrán and flute playing beyond the curtain. She tugged at Darcy's sleeve. "It sounds so lively. Are we not here to dance?"

Cat found a post to rub her back against to spell her temporally from the sensation of a colony of ants crawling down her spine. She whistled to get everyone's attention. "Mary's right. We're here to dance, so let's dance. You know, eat, drink, be merry, and pray to God you don't wake up in the morning hairy."

*

The warehouse had been transformed. Spanning the width of the building, local trade association ensigns, posters calling for workers to join together, and slogans of the emerging suffragette movement hung from the rafters. The dirt floor of the warehouse had been tamped down so firmly that the people milling about did not raise so much as a puff of dust. Burly men stood on either side of the barn-like doors inspecting each person who filed through, barring those they suspected of motives not in keeping with the evening. Bryson and his companions were denied entry at first, but Mrs. Stride signalled to let them in.

"I feel as out of place here as I did when entering Mecca. More so because then I was disguised as fellow Mohammedan on the Hajj," Burton said.

Oscar retorted, "Yes, we do resemble swine cast before pearls."

"This place is several steps above the cathouses that masquerade as dancehalls I've seen out west. What about you, Perez? Do you feel out of place?"

"I've never had the pleasure of feeling in place anywhere except a boxing ring. But like Sir Richard, I've managed to blend in when necessary for the most part."

Darcy weaved a path through the rapidly filling building. "Didn't you gents see enough of our menagerie last time? I'm thinking you must be employed by those seeking to harm us."

"Quite the contrary," Oscar said. "I am here to taste the delicious punch I see on the table over there. Sir Richard is here because he is here."

"I'm here, buddy, because I want to discover the who and why women are being murdered in Whitechapel," Bryson said.

"Name's Darcy Darnell, not your buddy. Why do you care what happens here?"

"Mr. Ward is not being totally candid," Perez said. "He is here to squeeze enough juice out of the bricks to tantalize his readers in America with the promise of more to come of the horrid events taking place on these streets."

“For the love of Jesus, talk like where you came from, not from where you pretend you belong.”

“I’m here to see this feckin eejit comes to no harm. I’m with him until he tires of our streets and plants his arse back home.”

Darcy returned to Mary. She closed her eyes and twirled around, imagining herself a Countess at a Viennese ball. Dancing on polished marble floors under candlelit chandeliers that reflected her image on mirrors covering every wall. “Are they your friends?” she asked.

Darcy held out his hand and led her to the dance. “Not sure what they are.”

Mary stood on one side of the warehouse with other women. Darcy joined a line of men on the other side. They crossed over and took hold of their partners. The music grew louder and faster. They danced to the middle of the floor, where they exchanged partners with the couples on their left. The formation seemed almost militaristic in the course of passing and returns.

Before another pass could take place, the dance stopped when Barnett and his hooligans breached the barn door and swarmed inside. The guards were thrown on the ground and beaten. The men rushed to the guard’s defence. They fought furiously while the women were directed to flee out the back of the warehouse. Just as it appeared Barnett and his toughs were losing, twelve plain-clothed bluebottles stormed in swinging their clubs and blowing whistles so loudly that the music was drowned out. Darcy shrieked when Milton struck him across his face. The flesh below his left eye socket split open, exposing his bloody cheekbone. He fell to the floor where Barnett and the peelers gave him the boot. Milton raised his club to split Darcy's head. Perez raced toward the peeler and knocked him out with one punch. Barnett and two of his men jumped Perez but were pulled off by Oscar Wilde. He tossed them aside like straw dolls. The melee ceased when two gunshots thundered in the warehouse. Burton fired another round into the rafters. Bryson cocked his Colt with his good hand and did likewise.

"I suggest you leave and take your rubbish with you." Burton levelled his pistol at Barnett.

"You ain't seen the last of us. I'm reporting you to the authorities."

"Splendid, Mr. Wilde and I will be glad to accompany you to ascertain who these authorities are."

The shadow man from the Matchstick meeting appeared outside the warehouse. His black hat was pulled down over his forehead, and his nose and lower face were concealed by a scarf. He pointed at Milton. "You heard him. Leave and drag that fool of a constable with you. As for informing the authorities, you best bite your tongue as I know you're not sanctioned to be here." Barnett and his men shrank as they hobbled past the man. The bluebottles carried Milton out of the building.

"Hang on there. I want to talk to you." Bryson approached the shadow man.

The man held up his hand to back him off. Burton and Wilde took it upon themselves to follow the dark fellow to see where he came from. The man's arms and legs moved in perfect unison as though he were on a parade field. He avoided the streetlights and vanished in the mist rising from a stream known to locals as the black ditch.

Darcy tried to rise from the floor. His nose was caved in. Bloody foam and shattered bone bubbled out of the gash below his eye, and bits of teeth out of his mouth. Bryson knelt down beside him to staunch the blood with his handkerchief. He and Perez draped Darcy's arms over their shoulders and supported him between them.

Mrs. Stride and her wards were waiting outside for them. Mary did not flinch when she saw Darcy's bloody face. She had seen just as bad if not worse beatings inflicted by the Black and Tans on men for no more reason than failing to give way when they met on the same footpath. "I know one who can help him." She motioned them to follow her to Mother Cantons.

"There is a hospital nearby by," Bryson said.

Perez shook his head, "Don't be daft. The only thing that comes out of that place are severed limbs and the dead."

"He's right about that. A charity hospital is merely a holding area for the soon-to-be dead, and a doctor is an apprentice to the grave digger," Cat said.

Mrs. Stride gave Bryson a push. "Get moving. Darcy is in no shape to join the conversation."

Like the three Marys at the crucifixion, the women walked behind the men. Their progress was halted by a peeler in uniform. The policeman aimed his baton at Darcy's slumped figure. "Where are you coming from?"

"From the wharves. Our friend caught a block and tackle in his face," Perez said.

The peeler directed his baton toward the women. "And you three?"

Cat fell backward and giggled, feigning drunkenness. "You're a handsome one. I'd love to gather you in my arms and kiss the life out of you. Oh gawd, best move back, love. I think my celebration is coming up."

Mary pressed her finger to her lips. "Please, sir, as you can see, we're escorting our friend home. She's in no condition to know left from right. In her state, she could easily be taken advantage of."

"Seems she'd have to go a long way to be compromised." The young peeler lowered his club. "Be on your way. I'm not here as Jesus monger preaching, it's better to seek salvation and not gin and sin."

His false piety reminded Mary of a priest who visited her turfed bothán uninvited while she scattered feed for the chickens. He announced he had arrived to persuade her to enter the sisterhood. To become an angel of mercy. She was destined, preordained to tend to the temporal needs of heathens in distant lands while the priests slaked the unbaptized spiritual thirst. "Your departed máthair will gain indulgences to reduce her time in purgatory," he whispered in her ear as he palmed her breasts with one hand and snaked the other down her thigh.

Mary's Da exploded out of their rough dwelling. He lifted the unholy father off his feet by his ears. "Listen, you black crow. There are enough sick and starving of our own in Ireland to care for. There is no need to travel the globe to find ones who are happy to be free of your filthy clutches. Should you ever pass this door again and bother my Mary, I'll give you a final introduction to the Father, Son and Holy Ghost."

"What's swimming behind that smile?" Cat asked Mary when they arrived at Mother Cantons.

"Just remembering my Da." Mary pushed the gate of the courtyard. It did not budge. "Mr. Farrow, please open the gate. It's urgent; we need help."

Her plea was met with silence. Beyond the gate was the figure of a man who stood like a statue. "Please let me in. Our friend is in dire need." The figure turned away and crossed the yard to the stairs leading above the stable.

"We'll take him to his room at Millers Court," Mrs. Stride said.

They covered the distance to Millers Court in more time than it would have normally taken. Bryson and Perez stopped every fifty yards for a breather and to ensure Darcy was still amongst the living. Once they laid Darcy on his narrow cot, Perez said he knew what to do. He had acquired the basics of stitching a wound from his days in the ring. Mrs. Stride and Cat wanted to stay but Mary told them to go home that she would sit with Darcy.

"I'll stay with her just in case the coppers get itchy and decide to see where we ended up."

"You're a real gentleman, Yank," Mrs. Stride said. "But I think Darcy had you pegged right. You're here to squeeze juice out of the bricks for a story."

"That's my job, but I'll put it aside tonight."

Mary lit the oil lamp and moved a three-legged stool next to the bed. Darcy's breathing sounded like bellows trying to raise a flame. Bryson searched the room for a pitcher of water. On an upturned barrel was a jug. Flies floated on its surface. He found a rag under the table, dipped it in the jug and placed the cloth over Darcy's forehead. The gesture served no healing purpose but made Bryson feel he was helping in some meaningless way. Mary laid her palm on Darcy's chest. She could feel his lungs pushing his breast up and down. "We went to dance."

Not knowing how to respond, Bryson quipped, "So you like to dance, so do I if the music is right and the partner is light."

Mary's eyes bore into him. "All this for what?"

Bryson leaned against the wall and rolled a cigarette. He had no answer as to why a seemingly harmless dance had become a battleground.

*

Daylight seeped under the bottom of the door Sunday morning. Mary stood. "I have to return to my room and pick up my Hollens uniform.

When Monday comes, I best be at the loom. Darcy is in no shape to work. God knows what little I bring in wages must sustain us both. I'll be back soon to spell you if you don't mind staying a bit longer."

Bryson was out of tobacco and had a low rumble in his stomach. He handed Mary a few coins. "Pick up something to eat while you're out. This place is as barren as a Paddies' pantry." He quickly regretted his jibe.

"No need to apologize for saying that which rings true."

*

The entry remained barred to Farrow's property. Mary pounded on the gate for several minutes. As she turned to leave, it opened slightly. An arm placed the carpet bag containing her few belongings outside before the gate closed again. Attached to the bag was an envelope. It contained a message written on fine stationery in exquisite penmanship and a five-pound bill.

Dear Mary, I fear you have gone down a path that will lead only to your ruin. Take this money and return to Ireland. Return now, or I fear you will be corrupted and never find your way out of Whitechapel save in a pauper's grave.

Mary beat on the gate with all her strength, begging Mr. Farrow to open it. "I am not a troublemaker. I am only a woman trying to make her way in a world which seems to have no use for me or anyone else who doesn't hold the purse."

Mary backed away when the gate flung open. A brown leather apron reached past Farrow's knees. It was the sort that battlefield surgeons wore. In one hand, he held a cleaver and in the other a long knife. Inside the courtyard, a pig hung by its rear legs from a tripod. It dripped blood from a neatly sliced gash across its neck into a pan. It made no noise, not even a wheeze, as it slowly bled out.

Mr. Farrow adjusted the mask covering his face. “Everyone bows before the purse. Some as the instruments of its bidding. Others as its sacrifices.”

“And which are you?” Mary asked.

He cut the rope securing the pig to the post. It dropped to the earth and was soon surrounded by rats that emerged from the recesses of the stable. “Both,” he said and kicked the gate closed behind him.

Chapter 22

Sarah Anne Chapman and her sisters at Bryant & Mays picketed in front of their factory daily carrying placards that simply demanded Safer Days for Better Pay. What had started as an action against one factory quickly spread to other factories beyond London. Sarah believed that every person since launching the strike was of her mind. She placed her faith in the assumption the innate goodness of people triumphed over avarice. Perhaps some few genuflected to Mammon but so few as not to be counted. This was her creed. A creed justified by Bryant & Mays agreeing to switch from white phosphorous to red.

After the storming of the dance, Bryant & Mays sought to disassociate themselves from the event. As Quakers, they resented being cast as heartless villains. The welfare of the body and soul and the belief the Kingdom of Heaven is open to all drove them to agree to the considerably watered-down demands of the strikers. Wages did not increase, but hours spent at the bench decreased from sixteen hours to twelve on weekdays, with Saturdays reduced to half day. As for the switch from white poison to red, it did not occur until 1905, far too late for Sarah Anne Chapman.

Sarah breathed easier now that things had been settled between the owner and the girls. She was on her way to meet the woman who had taken up the girls' cause. The Matchgirls' truest angel, Annie

Besant, an atheist angel at that, ferociously championed all causes that undermined the will of those who directed the life of the poor and disenfranchised from the pulpit, chambers of government and counting houses of industry. Annie Besant did not subscribe to Sarah's notion that people were at heart good, altruistic and sought to benefit humanity. Her views were far too lofty for Sarah to grasp. Annie Besants' mantra: Better remain silent. Better not even think if you are not prepared to act to rekindle the sparks of revolution not only in England but in places as far afield as Ireland and India.

Sarah was on her way to the other side of London on foot to thank Annie Besant for her aid, not as a sister in militancy. Best leave that struggle to those who never have to worry about having meat or how to slice a loaf of bread so thin for seven mouths that it lasts as many days.

Her mind sorted through a hundred ways to best express her gratitude to Annie Besant for her guidance and support. She stopped at a passageway on Hanbury Street that led to a windowless house. A tall man lurking in the darkness of the corridor coughed, startling her. He came forward a few feet but kept to the darkness. "I did not mean to alarm you, Miss Chapman."

"That's all right, my mind sailed elsewhere," she said without considering how the stranger knew her name.

"You and your girls are to be congratulated. To be held up as martyrs. Like Antigone standing resolutely against tyranny."

"Thank you, I guess. Truth is, I have no idea what you mean or who this Antigone is."

The man lifted his arms to his sides. His black Macintosh spread like the wings of an immense vulture. "No matter; she is no more."

"All the same, thank you. I think you mean well."

"Not tonight."

"Not tonight what, sir?"

The man stepped out of the passageway. Sarah tried to scream when he pulled her toward him. Her plea for help was muffled by a soaked cloth pressed over her mouth and nose. She inhaled a sickly sweet aroma. She fell into the man's arms. The slouched hat and scarf obscured his face.

"Why does the devil always keep to the shadows?" She closed her eyes and was dragged into the passageway.

The man gently placed her on the cold slab of pavement. "Because the light is offended by his presence." He drew a long, thin blade across her throat and waited for her to exsanguinate before donning a leather apron and performing his post-mortem mutilation. He cried dry tears as he started to work. There was no time for pity. He had a message to deliver.

*

A doss house tenant discovered the body when he went to the privy. He stumbled down the street and bumped into a policeman. His incoherent ramblings indicated to the constable the man had either ingested a bad batch of homemade gin or was a lunatic. The man dashed back to his tenement. When the peeler caught up with the man, he understood why the man seemed mad. It did not take long for other bluebottles to appear when they heard his frantic whistle.

When the police surgeon arrived, he declared without hesitation, “I know this carnage. It is the same killer as that of Polly Nichols and perhaps more.” He ordered two policemen to load her into a wagon and convey her to the morgue. When they lifted Sarah, one of the policeman’s hands sank into the cavity of her mutilated abdomen. When he bent over to vomit, his feet toppled a tub at his feet. A brown article rolled in a ball tumbled out. The police surgeon held it at arm’s length and shook it. It unfurled and was quickly recognized as a leather apron, the sort worn by butchers and more illustrious wielders of a knife and bone saw.

Chapter 23

It had been over two weeks since the bluebottles and bullyboys stormed the dance. Fourteen days of Darcy struggling to rise from his straw tick to rail against everyone from the Queen to a Jesus who seemed indifferent to the poor and meek he once championed. Mary would lower him back on the mattress and place a rag dampened with a mixture of water and rubbing alcohol on his forehead.

"The fever will break soon," she said. Bryson appeared every morning after Mary donned her work uniform and placed Darcy in his care before going to work.

When Darcy finally emerged from his stupor, he could barely see out of his crushed eye socket. He was alarmed to see a blurry figure sitting on the stool next to his pallet. Bryson easily evaded his poorly aimed blow. Darcy fingered the black bruise that dominated the side of his face. The threads of catgut Perez had used to suture the cut below his eye hung like dead worms on his cheek. A skill Perez had acquired from acting as his own and fellow boxers' cornerman.

At a rickety table, Mary pounded a boiled potato into mush suitable for a baby or man who could only slurp whatever food was presented to him. Mary handed Bryson the bowl of potato paste and a spoon and left for the mill. It pained Darcy to speak louder than a hoarse whisper through his swollen lips and chipped teeth. "Has she watched over me the whole time?"

*

Mary passed Perez and Sir Richard on the street on her way to Hollens. Perez called after her. "How does Darnell fare?"

"As well as can be expected after having the soul near beaten out of him."

They did not bother to knock when they arrived at Darcy's. Burton handed Bryson a newspaper. "More trouble in Whitechapel." A sketch of the young woman in a casket took up a quarter of the front page. Bryson recalled her face from the meeting and dance. He pushed open the door and read by the light entering from outside. The few details permitted to be printed in good taste were horrid enough.

Darcy forced himself to stand. He crossed the floor like a marionette. He squeezed a terse command over his chipped teeth and swollen lips. "Read it, read it to me."

Burton addressed Perez, "Illiteracy, a curse and frequently a blessing."

"Leave off. This is no time to be larking about." Perez took the paper from Bryson. He slowly read aloud.

When he finished, Darcy tore the paper from his hand and ripped it in half. "The bastards! Where do they get the bollocks to write such lies? They called her a whore. They didn't even get her name right. She was called Sarah, not Annie. She made matches, and all who knew her loved her."

Darcy gathered his clothing from the foot of his cot and dressed slowly. He took one tentative step after another before gaining his footing and marched out of his room. Bryson tried to hold him back. "Where are you going?"

"To Hollens. The same eyes that noted Polly and Sarah may have glimpsed Mary."

"You're hardly fit to work," Bryson said.

"I work with my hands, not my face." Darcy sneaked the sentence through his clenched teeth.

Bryson followed Darcy into the street."You have only one good eye."

"If you can't get the job of a mechanic done blindfolded, then you're not fit to do the job at all."

Sir Richard and Perez joined Bryson. "You know, he's right. They called her Annie, not Sarah." Perez said.

"Perhaps the fiend attacked the wrong woman by error."

Perez pounded his fist into his open palm. "The hell he did. He picked this Annie to notify Annie Besant to move on. If he'd gone after Besant, there would be a riot the likes of Black Monday."

Bryson reentered the room to await Darcy and Mary's return. Burton and Perez said they would be back in the evening. They chose to leave Whitechapel on foot to gather their thoughts.

A man waving a cleaver screamed obscenities at women passing his small stall where skinned rabbits and carcasses of pigs and hunks of beef hung on meat hooks. Perez took the cleaver from him and laid it on the butcher block of the makeshift meat market. The man's angry features softened. Perez dove into his pocket, and placed five coins on the table and returned to his companion.

"Who's that chap? Another member of your tribe?"

"I know him from my fields of mud and troughs of blood days in the service of the realm. He served as a cook. A cook who carved his way through a dozen enemies to save the lives of officers who barely allowed him to breathe the same air as them."

"From cook to an apronless butcher. A strange transition."

"Not so; the Empire is an ideal training ground for professions of savagery. He received a small pittance as a reward for his bravery and the pox from a camp chippy but no medal. Those shiny trinkets are reserved for men with gold epaulets and posh accents who watch the slaughter of the groundlings from horseback. Not tommies and most certainly not members of what you call my tribe."

"I meant no offence."

"You seldom do, Sir Richard."

Chapter 24

The man across from Oscar Wilde sat sideways on a chair. His desk was stacked with reams of paper held down by a stethoscope and a volume of Gray's Anatomy. On the floor, another tower of paper overflowed the waste bin. He had a habit of stroking his black moustache and then removing his watch from his vest pocket to check the time as if awaiting someone late for an appointment.

"Stop doing that."

"Doing what?" The man removed his watch again and dangled it in front of Oscar by its gold chain.

"Arthur, unless your goal is to mesmerize me, put the timepiece away."

"You want my opinion of who might be responsible for the untidy happenings taking place in the East end?"

"I asked for your opinion fifteen minutes ago."

Conan Doyle removed his watch again and glanced at its face. "Twenty-one minutes ago, to be precise."

Wilde listened as the mystery writer presented a hundred possible suspects, each one more bizarre than the previous. Given Conan Doyle's fascination with spiritualism and the paranormal, he briefly alluded to the possibility that the murders were the work of some malevolent entity expressing its rage from beyond the grave. Finally, he stood up. "Perhaps Oscar, you would be so good as to read my most recent story. I value your opinion."

"I agreed to read it twenty-one minutes ago."

Conan Doyle, having discovered a delightful way to annoy Wilde, said, "Twenty-seven minutes. Exactitude in all things from medicine to literature is required."

"Show some mercy. What is your take on the murderer?"

"The killer's motives are unclear to me. But, it is obvious the perpetrator is either a woman or a madman dressed as a woman. This accounts for his or her ability to slip away from the crime scene unnoticed."

"Seriously? I have been accused of creating unbelievable fantasies, but nothing so absurd as what you propose. How could any woman overpower one so completely and disembowel them in a matter of minutes without being discovered wandering the streets drenched in blood from her bosom to her ankles?"

"Perhaps it was the deed of two women or a man dressed as a woman and an actual woman. When you eliminate the impossible, whatever remains, however improbable, must be the truth."

"A quote from your latest story?"

"Sign of the Four. Brilliant, isn't it?"

"Your ego makes mine seem pitiful."

"I doubt that's possible. But I do not doubt the crimes were the act of a lunatic."

"Until evidence of the contrary surfaces, on this point, we agree."

Chapter 25

Charlie Barnett stood outside the gate of Hollens flanked on either side by two peelers. The older constable towered over his younger partner.

"Are you expected?" Barnett asked Darcy when he approached the gate. "If not, scamper off."

The taller policeman blasted Barnett. "I am the senior policeman here, the one authorized to ask questions and ask if a bloke is expected or not."

"Sorry, Mr. Hines, I got ahead of myself."

Hines unsheathed his police baton. He stepped closer to the man whose crushed face reminded him of someone he'd encountered before but provided him with only a hint of the circumstances. He rapped his baton against the post of the gate. "Are you expected? If not, scamper off."

"I just told him that," Barnett complained.

"As I informed you, it's my task to query whomsoever approaches the gate, not yours. I am an official representative of the Metropolitan Police Force. You are merely a door opener on hire by Hollens."

Darcy winced. The cold air penetrated the exposed pulp of his chipped teeth. "I'm the head millwright here."

"Constable Watkins, get someone inside to check this one out,"

Hines ordered.

The young policeman had not spoken a word since he was paired with Hines replied, “Do your own getting,” and remained fixed to his spot on the pavement. “I may have to listen to your bluster but I am not your lackey.”

Barnett leaned forward and studied Darcy. “No need, I know this one. He’s a troublemaker; he might even be IRB, an Irish radical, and might even have been at the dance over a fortnight ago during the troubles. Might have been with them that sent Milton and your fellow officers to the infirmary.”

Hines spat. “Nothing happened there. There was no trouble. Leastwise, that’s what we’ve been told to remember and remember what to forget.”

Darcy stood tall. “I am the single man who knows how to fix what is seemingly beyond repair in Hollens.”

A hand slipped through the bars of the gate and tapped Hines on his back. He turned to face one of the Hollens twins attired in a wardrobe so grim that even an undertaker would consider it overly sombre. “Constable, what goes on here? Do your job and send this vagrant away.”

Darcy stepped around Hines. “Mr. Hollens, it’s me, Darcy Darnell, come to work.”

“Good grief, man, do you think you can disappear then return to pick up where you left off? Hollens is a business, not a seaside resort.”

"I know, sir. I had a bad turn, an accident, and could not right myself to return before now."

"We are not a charity." The twin began to walk away but stopped when his brother hailed him. "Julian, what are you doing out here?"

"I came to inhale what passes for fresh air and ran into this impudent fellow. The scoundrel has been absent for more than two weeks and has the nerve to request his position back."

Archibald pressed his mouth against Julian's ear. Julian bolted upright. "Really, the fool can't repair it! How long has he been at it?"

"Too long."

Archibald pivoted on his heel and ordered Hines to open the gate. He smiled at Darcy like a benevolent protector. "Mr. Darnell," I spoke in haste. "There is a position awaiting you provided your injury will not prevent you from doing the tasks required."

"My teeth pains me, sir, but I work with my hands, not my mouth."

"All men should take pains to do so," Archibald said.

Julian Hollens added, "Of course, given your absence, we cannot reinstate you at the same wage. I trust you are in agreement."

Darcy swallowed his desired response. A response that would no doubt prevent him from working at Hollens where he could watch over Mary. A response that might well result in his being beaten senseless by the peeler so fond of his wooden phallic.

"Of course, sir, I could expect nothing other. Thank you for your generosity."

*

The tortured groans and metallic screeches of the machines penetrated Darcy's brain like molten spikes from a blazing forge. He searched the factory for his tool cart and discovered Fitch had taken it. He watched Fitch fruitlessly struggle to loosen a bolt as big as a full crown. Fitch held his breath. His face turned from white to red to blue. Sweat streamed down his forehead into his eyes. No matter how much muscle he applied to the wrench, the bolt did not move. "Mother Mary and her sisters be fucked!" He hurled the spanner behind him, coming within inches of Darcy's head.

"Good God Fitch, not only do I find you using my tools, you're using the wrong tool."

Fitch sat back on his haunches like a chimpanzee. "Ain't your things no more, Darnell, belongs to him that takes 'em."

"Wrong, the cart belongs to Hollens. The tools are bought and paid for by me." Darcy pulled the cart toward him and did a quick inventory of its contents. "If you were a master tradesman instead of Fitch the fetcher, you'd know that every mechanic owns his own kit and takes it wherever work is offered." He searched under the tools which, prior to his injury, were neatly arranged by function but were now mixed up like a bag of bones. "Where's my leather apron?" he asked.

"Don't know, don't use one myself. Not afraid of a little grease. Shows I'm a working man." Fitch's trousers were covered in grime where he wiped his hands, and his shirt was spotted with the same plus the remains of a month's worth of suppers.

"Saw Julian, or was it Archibald rooting through the cart for something."

"For what?"

"Not my place to ask if I aim to keep my place."

Darcy found the largest socket head in the cart and knelt down beside the machine Fetch had been playing with. He loosened the bolt with a downward thrust of the two-foot ratcheting handle and held it up to Fitch. "You stripped it. Go get me a new one and a tub of axel grease."

Fitch grumbled at being addressed like a flunkey but did as he was told. He lowered his head as the twins walked past him.

"Excellent, Darnell, to see you have not lost your touch," one of the twins said.

Darcy stood up. He did not bow his head. He had never seen the twins venture into the factory before unless they were accompanied by a peeler to escort a potential labour rouser or malcontent from Hollens.

"Keep up the good work, Mr. Darnell, and you'll be back to your former status and wages in no time."

The other twin came closer to Darcy. He stretched out his index finger and grazed Darcy's sutures. "Must have been a terrible fall to do that much damage," he said. "Lot of mishaps since the melee at that dance several days ago, actually a meeting of radicals and Irish Home Rule trash."

"Heard about it, sir, but wasn't present to see what happened or who started it."

"I imagine you weren't. We asked Mrs. Stride and those two women who are always at her side what happened."

"And what did they say?"

"Nothing, like you, they were elsewhere."

The other twin pointed at the jumble of tools in Darcy's cart. "Thought you would be more orderly than this."

"Not my doing. Mr. Fitch borrowed my kit and left it so."

"Fitch is an incompetent mechanic's helper, but he serves a purpose. Is that not so, brother Julian?"

"Very true, brother Archibald. As much as we value your hands at work, we rely on Fitch's tongue to keep us apprised of our workers' grievances."

Darcy finished repairing the damage Fitch had done to the machine. He rolled his cart to the other end of the plant where Mrs. Stride supervised the loom workers. He stopped at their workstation and knelt beside a metal plate covering the end of the machine as though inspecting it. Mrs. Stride came over to him. "Things are not right here or elsewhere since Sarah Anne Chapman's murder. Cat is canvassing every pub to gather support amongst the factory women for a general walkout. Feels like eyes are on us all the time."

"What about my Mary?"

"Your Mary, is she now?"

"You know what I mean. I owe her for sitting by me."

"I know what you mean, Darcy, but Mary has neither a clue to what you want nor who you are."

"Get your filthy paws off of her," Cat's voice rose above the dull thrum of the machine. Darcy saw Fitch standing behind Mary. Without pausing, she plucked strands of detached yarn from the loom. His hand rested on her bum. Mary moved to the side, but he kept behind her, his hand moving up her back. Cat shouted at him again, but he sneered and pressed his body closer against Mary. Darcy stood and grabbed a mallet from his tool cart. Before he could crush Fitch's skull, Mary whirled around and kneed Fitch in his groins. Fitch bit through his tongue. He crumpled to the factory floor. Mary shook her head when she saw the mallet in Darcy's hand. "No need for that, Mr. Darnell. I'm confident Mr. Fitch will think twice before pursuing his uninvited attention with me or others in the mill. Is that not so, Mr. Fitch?"

Cat bent over the writhing body of Fitch. "Two inches higher, and you would be brain-dead."

Mrs. Stride lifted Fitch with one arm to his feet. "This is what comes from wandering where you're not invited." She cupped a hand over her mouth, failing to stifle a laugh. Her roar lasted so long and was so loud that it overpowered the grumblings of the machine.

Fitch's cupped left hand protected his manhood when he stood. He swatted the air with the other. "Think you'll get away with this!"

"Away with what, darling?" Cat kissed her fingertip and then pressed it on Fitch's forehead.

"Go ahead and mock me. I have the ears of those who can and will make you pay." He glared at Cat with a look of hatred so alarming that even Mrs. Stride took a step back. "Let's see how much mocking you can do without a face to do so."

"Mr. Fitch, let us put this behind us," Mrs. Stride said. "To carry on this way will do little justice."

"Fuck justice! I want your dues paid in triple."

Mary placed a hand on his arm, "So much trouble, so much anger, for a trifling offence. It's my fault that this happened. Forgive me."

"Damn right bitch. This is your doing; You're on the same ledger as those two for payback."

Darcy rushed Fitch and dragged him away. "Leave off, man. You had this coming ages ago. Open your yap again, and I'll rip that nasty slab of pink out off your turnip head."

Fitch broke away. "Think I don't know what you and your brother IRBs and these whores are up to. I know, and soon, I'll let them know who owns the purse strings. They'll make you pay up, all of you. Just like the others." Fitch pressed his hand over his mouth, preventing whatever he was going to reveal from escaping.

Chapter 26

Bryson lay on his bed staring at the plaster scrollwork below the ceiling. He had to file a story soon, or Morris would have him sending dispatches from somewhere so remote that they had to be inserted in bottles. The doings in Whitechapel perplexed him. He thought back to the reports of all the murdered women since his arrival. Nothing seemed to mark them for such grisly deaths. Retribution came to mind. Retribution for what?

He had to send something to Morris that would allow him to drop the idiocy of watching inflated patrons of the RGS smoking their cigars and pipes while pretending to follow the going ons in the Empire.

Kit Singh knocked twice. "Mr. Ward, Mr. Ward, your friends are waiting for you in the lobby."

Bryson stepped into the hall. Kit Singh held up a perfectly rolled cigarette. "My uncle caught me making this. I told him you had only one good hand, and you are paying me to roll ten of them a day."

"Did he buy it."

"No sir, he neither smokes nor partakes of spirits."

"That's not what I mean. Did he believe you?"

"Of course. He knows I never lie. I am rolling ten of them a day for you, but I haven't decided how much each one is worth."

"You have promise, Kit."

Bryson joined his companions in the hotel lounge. Perez and Burton were engaged in a heated discussion - about what, he didn't know. Oscar Wilde threw his arms up in frustration. "It's not a tea party we've been invited to. Perez is right. We have to be discreet. We may not be in danger, but those we visit most certainly will be."

Perez looked at Bryson. "Annie Besant found out we've been frequenting Whitechapel and that you're digging for information on the murders. She wants to meet us."

"Where?" Bryson asked.

"Where unwanted ears and eyes are least likely to be," Wilde said.

*

The glass dome of the Royal Botanic Gardens Palm Exhibit leaked in places, contributing even more heat and humidity to the already stifling atmosphere. Perez scanned the greenhouse to locate the person or persons they were supposed to meet. A scholarly-looking older man fingered the various leaves and fronds in the artificial jungle and barked orders to young men, most likely students, trailing behind him. Some of them halted to sketch a particular plant that attracted their attention.

"Quit playing ghost in the graveyard. We're not invisible." A husky voice that defied gender came from behind a false waterfall near the end of the exotic tree exhibit. Around a towering palm tree, they encountered Mrs. Stride, Cat and Annie Besant sitting on two benches against the wall.

Annie Besant rose from her bench. "You're that American busybody."

"I'm a journalist for a New York paper."

"Is that what they call snoops nowadays? If your rag is anything like the ones here, it's hardly fit to wipe one's arse."

Mrs. Stride tugged at Besant's sleeve. "They were at the dance. Helped us make our way to safety. That one," she pointed to Perez, kept Darcy Darnell's head from being turned into gruel. The Yank and Sir Burton—

"I know what they did. By firing your weapons, you two idiots gave the authorities an excuse to bear down harder."

"Bear down harder," Perez said. "Mrs. Besant, how much harder can they come down? We saw the remains of Sarah Anne Chapman."

"Thank you for your well-intentioned if stupid actions at the dance. Darnell is a valuable member of the workers' association and Home Rule Committee, as is Mrs. Stride. Up until now, they managed to remain inconspicuous to those who would blot out any speck of what they deem as upsetting the natural balance of society. A balance which despite our numbers is weighted in their favour of money and the support of the government."

Sir Richard fixed his eyes on the scar on the side of Annie Besant's face. He licked the tip of his finger and traced his own scar. "Many in my circle of acquaintances consider you guilty of sedition. That you have aligned yourself with the radicals who desire to bring down the pillars of the temple and replace it with something else.

They believe you are aligned with genteel Fabians, anarchists and strident Marxists."

"If you mean I want to bury the old corrupt order and expose the horrors they inflict on those under their heels, then yes, I am aligned with them."

Annie Besant jumped when a man passing through the Palm House knocked over a spade. "Move on," she shouted. The man quickened his pace out of this wing into the next housing rare species of ferns and palm trees, including a fern so enormous that it dwarfed the giant palm trees in the chamber. She stood up and said without preface, "Tread lightly in Whitechapel. Sarah Chapman and the ones before her are meant as warnings to abandon the cause."

"What cause?" Bryson asked.

"Are you truly interested in exposing the truth, or just the number of papers you can sell back home by recounting the squalor and madness in East London?"

"I have to concentrate on the latter to bring forth the former."

Oscar Wilde removed a silver cigarette case from his jacket pocket and held it out to the women. Inside were machine rolled cinnamon scented cigarettes. "Why, Mrs. Besant, did you request we meet you?"

"To inform you that what you have heard of, seen so far, is just a smattering, I fear what is to come. Regrettably, I may have instigated the horrors by my giving a voice to the oppressed, notably the Matchgirls, that has resonated far beyond London."

"And what do you expect from us?" Bryson asked.

Perez rapped his walking stick against the bench. "It's obvious. She wants us to report what is happening to prevent other murders."

"Why us?"

"Because Mr. Ward," Besant said. "I am no longer welcome in England. My views have made me an anathema to the monied, the state and the church. So much so that I may have to leave Britain, perhaps to India, for my own safety and of others linked to me by mere passing."

"Again Mrs. Besant, what do you want us, me to do?"

"First of all, cease calling me Mrs. I belong to no one. My name is Annie Besant; no prefixes attached. And secondly, report honestly what is happening in Whitechapel and let the world beyond our shores know." Annie Besant held up the cigarette she had taken from Oscar. He struck a match. The aroma of cinnamon and tobacco lingered as she walked off without saying anything further.

Catherine Eddowes looped her arm through Bryson's. "Come, love, let's take a stroll through the gardens outside." She tilted her head in the direction of three men who had stopped a few feet away and seemed to be paying more attention to them than the tropical vegetation.

Burton took Mrs. Stride's hand. They walked behind Catherine and Bryson while Perez remained behind to see if the men followed them.

Chapter 27

Behind a pitted oak table that had occupied the chamber long before George III lost the American colonies to a mix of plantation slave owners and New England merchants, sat seven men in high back chairs dating to Cromwell, when punishments were dealt for such serious offences as whistling on Sabbath. In front of them, four men in scarlet waistcoats, their double row of brass buttons polished to a mirror finish, stood at ease. The fifth man concealed himself in the furthest corner of the chamber, his face turned to the wall. Sunlight scattered through a stained glass window depicting a medieval knight brandishing a sword. It cast a kaleidoscope of patterns on the pale marble floor.

"I think you officers know the gentlemen seated with me," a balding man said. Wings of white hair above his ears spread past his sideburns. Without waiting for an answer, he introduced each man, "James Fraser, Commissioner of the City Police; Sir Henry Smith, Assistant Commissioner of the City Police; Sir Robert Anderson, Head Detective Chief and expert on Irish insurrectionists."

"I not only know Sir Robert, I detest him," the man in the corner said. "He has maligned every murdered woman in Whitechapel by portraying them as harlots who ply their trade in the hope of securing the meagre wages of drunkards or men as degraded as themselves."

Sir Robert jumped to his feet and slammed his fist on the table.

Spittle flew from his mouth, wetting his beard. "I only pointed out the obvious nature of the women. Only cast them as such to comfort decent ladies elsewhere in London that they have nothing to fear."

"Sit down," the balding man ordered and proceeded to introduce the three remaining men. "Representing business interests are Julian and Archibald Hollens. And, of course, you know Mr. Purkess. His distasteful illustrations of Annie Chapman's visage in his paper has ratcheted up disquiet throughout the Kingdom."

Julian snorted at the mention of the tabloid. "Prime Minister, isn't it enough we have to worry about Whitechapel exploding in worker rebellion without fanning the flames in Purkess' filthy rag? His lack of decency is appalling."

"My thoughts as well," Prime Minister Robert Cecil agreed. "But even Caiaphas played a necessary role in the crucifixion, as does Mr. Purkess."

Purkess lifted his cheeks off his chair and broke wind. "Come now, Julie, my rag does a service for the likes of you. It pits the poor against one another; Irish against Italians, them against Poles and all of them against Jews."

"Your point being?" Prime Minister Cecil asked.

"The point being, as long as we nurture the hate they hold for one another, the realm is secure. They're too occupied to provide a meaningful threat to the natural order."

"What order would that be?"

"It should be obvious, us at the top and the others at the

bottom."

"And our role is what?" The voice from the corner broke through the discussion.

"Your role is as it has always been. You are commissioned to strike down those who oppose the natural order and to send a message to others who entertain thoughts of doing so."

The man in the corner spun around and hurled his parting words like venom. "Her name was Sarah Anne Chapman, not Annie." He made his way to the door, followed by his brothers-in-arms. Their scarlet jackets bled into the hall outside the chamber.

"Major, what is our task?" One of the scarlet coats asked.

He removed the mask and, through his mangled features, addressed each man. "We are the survivors. Uriah, you saw that religious general maniac's head paraded around on a pike in Khartoum. Wesley, you tried to save our soldiers and Mohammedans as well from the injuries that could not be healed and received no less punishment than a dog who spoiled a carpet. Edward, you managed to find sanctuary in a dung heap. And Silas, you held our colours aloft so high that the Mahdi pointed at you and said, let him stand as a reminder to the Queen that though our standard ripples in the wind, it is as meaningless as a cloud passing over the desert."

"And you, Joshua?" Uriah asked.

"I am the image of what lies ahead for the Empire. Despite this, it is my duty to serve that which cannot be protected on its own soil, much less in lands that it has no right to lay claim."

"All this to say?" Uriah asked.

Joshua replaced his featureless death mask and sighed. "All this to say, we have neither the permission to ask for nor will be granted absolution. Our initials will be scrawled on the wall of our deeds."

*

The chamber was empty except for Sir Robert Anderson. The Prime Minister and the other men had left after they were assured the scarlet coats had vacated the building. Anderson sifted through notes he had taken during the meeting. To trust a mere clerk to record what was said would have been disastrous should the information be revealed to the general public. A knock on the door preceded the entrance of his secretary. "What the blazes do you want, Stephen? I told you, I do not want to be disturbed."

"Sir Richard Francis Burton is in the hall. He seems very impatient. He is here for the appointment you requested."

Chapter 28

"Mary, Mary Kelly." Farrow's voice came from inside an alley as Mary returned from work. She had not come face to face with Mr. Farrow since he shut the gate on her. Though she thought she had spied him following her from Hollens to Darcy's place where, contrary to rumour, she slept on the floor while he occupied the cot. The closest they came to exhibiting anything other than friendship was once when she slipped on a wet cobblestone, and Darcy caught her around her waist.

She took a few furtive steps toward the voice hidden in the dark. "Stay where you are," Farrow ordered. He tossed a pouch. It landed at her feet. Crafted from soft leather, the serpent-entwined staff of Asclepius was embossed on it. Mary looked inside it and gasped when she saw it contained Bank of England notes three inches thick. "Take it, Mary, take it and flee this hell before it consumes you."

"This is not what I needed from you, Mr. Farrow. This is not what I wanted. I asked for you to open the gate to aid an injured man, a friend, and you closed it on me and whatever charity you had for the world outside."

Farrow moved closer to the alley's opening. He was dressed in a red military waistcoat and black pants with a gold stripe running down the sides. His face was concealed behind a Papier-mâché mask. A slit where the lips should be allowed him to breathe. "I do not have time to debate if the milk of human kindness flows as freely through my veins as vinegar and piss does through the arteries of the world at large. Take the purse and leave your friends to the fate they have brought upon themselves. The Crown and its puppet masters do not tolerate interference in their affairs."

Mary flung the pouch into the alley. "Mr. Farrow, it was your kindness I required, not your money." Darcy, who had lagged behind Mary to purchase a loaf of bread, came up beside her. Farrow receded into the back of the alley. The swelling on the side of Darcy's face had receded, but he still had not regained full sight from his damaged eye socket. "Thought I saw you talking to someone," he said.

"No one who matters."

*

Despite holding as much contempt for the church as he did for the government, Darcy accompanied Mary to Mass. On their return, Bryson and Perez were waiting for them on the street. "Perez, I like," Darcy said. "He's one of us, well not quite given his creed, but close enough. I can't say I like the Yank hanging around and mining us for dross."

Perez waved his arms frantically and yelled, "Get out of the way!"

Darcy saw a lorry racing toward them. The driver did not pull up the reins. He laid the whip harder on the horses. Darcy shoved Mary against a wall before the lorry ran them down. Darcy lost his footing.

He rolled to the curb, preventing the hooves of the draught horses and the iron-clad rims of the wheels from crushing his spine.

Perez and Bryson raced to where Darcy lay unmoving. They reached down to help him to his feet. He pushed them away. "Hands off. See to Mary."

They guided Darcy to his room. Perez noticed a fancy leather wallet on the table. He held it up. Mary clasped her hand over her mouth, recognizing Mr. Farrow's purse. Perez opened the pouch. Rather than the bills that Mary had seen earlier, a folded sheet of stationery fell from it.

Mary picked it up before anyone else could and read what was written. *The degree of punishment is proportional to the attempt to incite crime or disturbances of the social order by fomenting discontent or disaffection between different social classes of the crown's subjects. Dearest Mary, the bed you lie in is a nest of vipers. The bed you may find yourself in later is one of earth.*

Mary shredded the note and stuffed the pieces of paper between her shirt and undergarment.

Chapter 29

Catherine Eddowes and Mrs. Stride gave up any pretence of being docile servants of the machine and its lords. They led Mary to a secluded corner of Hollens and engaged in a futile attempt to get her to join their cause. The death, rather, slaughter, of members of the worker cooperative, as well as the judicial execution and banishment to the furthest shores of the Empire of men in the IRB and labour activists, had convinced them that covert action translated into no action. They canvased the mills and tankard houses for like-minded women and men who had had enough of the constant abuse they suffered with the blessing of the state. It was Mrs. Stride who reached out to Mary. Her case for joining the movement was simple. "We have no choice but to stop the cogs of the machine from turning, we are the grease that keeps it turning."

Mary hitched up her skirt. "I have seen enough of good intentions that lead to hell. I want to be left in peace. Peace to earn enough coins to send to my Da. Enough for him to buy his own patch of earth to graze his sheep and raise a few rows of vegetables."

"And what of Darcy, who has taken you in?" Catherine Eddowes asked.

"He did no more take me in than the innkeeper gave a room to the Virgin. I am not beholden to him nor him to me. No more beholden than I am to the American and his West End swells."

"On that, we agree," Mrs. Stride said. "We owe them nothing as they see us as nothing. Nothing but a cause of the moment to champion until another arises or until the Fox hunting season commences."

*

Bryson took Mary's sack of two-day-old stew meat, turnips, and potatoes on her return from shopping. He appeared every morning prior to Mary and Darcy leaving for Hollens to ensure they were not accosted and remained at their lodgings until evening. Darcy, though avoiding serious hurt from the lorry incident, concealed a slight limp to keep his position as head mechanic and to watch over Mary.

Perez held vigil at the top of their street and walked behind them. He knew that whatever danger Darcy faced would not be announced in advance by letter. He was wrong. On returning from Hollens, Darcy stepped on an envelope slipped under his door. In perfect penmanship, his name appeared on the envelope along with a more specific reference to Mary Jeanette Kelly, Cohabitant. Darcy handed the letter to Bryson. He read it aloud. Mary remained outside. She enjoyed the warmth of the rare rays of sun on her face.

Enclosed is enough money to allow you to take passage from England to Canada. Book travel soon or suffer the consequences. Your vaunted principles, though commendable, will lead to nowhere but the grave and that of our darling Mary. If you care nothing for your own well-being, then at least save her.

"Whoever penned those words cares a great deal for Mary so much that he appeals to me to spirit her away from here."

"Maybe you should consider it. Things are getting precarious around here."

"I am listed. Stamped as a seditionist, a member of the IRB here and a Fenian in your country. Neither permitted to leave these shores nor place a toe on your soil." Darcy bit the tip of his thumb and, after a moment of contemplation, said, "Mr. Ward, should anything befall me, I beg you take Mary as your charge and return her to Ireland or bring her to America. Her association with me has listed her as well, despite her reluctance to join."

"Darcy, I think Sir Richard's intervention and Mr. Wilde's connections to higher society will soon lead to more emphasis on protecting the women here. As for my part, I have let Bret Harte, who has the ear of your government, give considerable attention to improving the living conditions in Whitechapel. My own paper is running articles on the senseless brutality on your streets. Exposing the crimes perpetrated here will embarrass the authorities enough to deploy Scotland's Yards finest to capture whoever is the murderer."

Darcy patted Bryson's head. "Go ahead, hold to those beliefs. Maybe you'll run into a leprechaun who'll guide you to a pot of gold. Sir Burton is regarded by most of his class as a heathen and hedonist. His intervention is taken as a reason not to intervene. As for the playwright's connections, he has none. He is seen as a passing amusement, a purveyor of gossip and clever barbs, and above all a mandrake, a sodomite, who will be abandoned by all should he ever threaten their standing."

"If you're trying to get under my skin, it's not working. My paper is going to show the world the grimy underbelly of Whitechapel. I guarantee you things will change."

"Your readers do not give a tinker's damn about the happenings here. They don't care about the misery. They only relish the description of the filth of Whitechapel and the mutilated bodies of women whom they regard as dollymops."

Chapter 30

Ward you are onto something (Stop)
Our readers are licking the pages for a taste of the blood and sniffing the ink for a whiff of the blade (Stop)
Kill the social commentary. Our nitwit readers want to be entertained not educated (Stop)
Expect a full accounting of the money you were provided (Stop}
Whores throats being ripped out in Jolly Old England make the plight of own tarts seem humane (Stop}
Sin not Saints sell papers (Stop)

*

Bryson sat on the edge of his bed and read the telegraph from Morris twice. He folded it in half and in half again, then stuffed it inside his right boot to cover the hole that had started to form from hours of walking the uneven cobblestones of the East End.

Perez and a portly man wearing a Homburg waited for him downstairs. The man's jacket sleeves were so short that his frayed shirt cuffs protruded below them. Bryson brushed past the man. "Forget the living dead in the RGS. Morris has given his blessings, says to stick to the going-ons in Whitechapel." The lie he was about to say tasted as bitter as alum but slipped out of his mouth like honey. "He says to keep on the story and be honest. Write what is true and let the world know they are heroines, not gutter winches."

The man in the Homburg stepped in front of Perez. "I think introductions are in order."

Bryson took in the man's well-worn navy blue suit. A black tie with a perfect Windsor knot was tucked between his vest and white shirt. He resembled a lesser agent of Loyds of London peddling maritime insurance. The only things that disturbed the image were his frayed shirt cuffs and trouser hems stained with mud.

"Friend of yours, Perkins?"

"Not exactly, but worth knowing."

"Enough with the Perkins shite. I nabbed this Hebe for non-sanctioned boxing on the wharves."

"Chief Inspector Abberline pinched me for costing him a month's wages. His bloke went down in the first round."

The man brayed like a donkey in what passed for a laugh. "I got two passions in life. Losing money on horses and fights and putting away villains. Especially men who prey on Judies."

"Well, Inspector, it doesn't seem like you and your bloodhounds have done much of anything to catch the madman butchering women on the other side of the bridge."

Abberline jabbed his finger into Bryson's chest. "Ezra didn't bring me here to have you, a pretender, lecture me on what I have or have not been doing." He lowered his head like a bull charging a red cape and stormed out of the hotel.

Perez propelled Bryson onto the street. "Inspector, he doesn't know what you've been doing, how much your ferreting for the truth has cost you. Let's go somewhere for a few pints, somewhere more conducive to conversation."

Abberline crossed his arms over his chest. "Who is springing for the holy water?"

Perez winked at Bryson. "You have your paper's expense money, so it's only fair you keep the glasses topped."

The establishment they visited on the gentry side of London was a far cry from the squalor of Whitechapel. Bryson calculated how much he was going to have to fork out. "I thought you said we were going to a pub."

Abberline grinned. "Did I say a pub? Won't find many of them around here. It's been a long day, and I'm in need of something more substantial than warm beer, mouldy cheese and stale crackers."

The restaurant smelled of cigar smoke and a hint of sandalwood. Tucked under every table draped in a white table nappe were Cordovan leather armchairs. Waiters scurried about bowing their heads as they took orders from men in Saville Row suits. At each place setting were several pieces of cutlery. Bryson picked up a small porcelain swan with a depression in its back. He held it up to Perez as if to ask what the hell is this. Perez lifted his shoulders as if to say, beats me.

"It's a spoon rest," Abberline said.

"Damn, I never knew spoons got tired." Bryson said and set it down. "You sure we're not too underdressed for this joint?"

Abberline signalled a spindly ancient waiter with silver hair and a napkin draped over his forearm to his table. “What would you like to start, Chief Inspector?” The waiter asked as if seeking alms.

“Reggie, you should know by now what I want. These two came for a beer.”

“I regret we don’t serve beer.”

“Then I guess they’ll just have to watch me dine.”

Bryson slapped the table. “Okay, Chief Inspector, now that you’ve had your fun, let me in on what you’ve uncovered in Whitechapel.”

“First, I eat, then talk. I don’t want to spoil my nor your appetites.”

Bryson crooked his finger at Perez to come closer. “I’ve seen this copper before somewhere.”

Abberline’s hearing was as sharp as the knife he used to slice the meat on his plate. “You’re right, Mr. Ward, you saw me at the site of Polly Nichols’ murder. I saw you as well, but had more urgent tasks at hand than to watch Sir Charles and Sir Richard engage in a pissing contest.” The inspector drained two full glasses of white wine, then two more to wash down his veal chop, boiled potatoes and mashed peas and carrots. “After wading through muck to inspect a young woman’s bloated person, I have to fill my belly. It reminds me that though I dance with the dead, I never dine with them.”

“Another murdered woman?”

“This one was found washed up on the banks of the river further up north of Whitechapel, where dandies and their conquests go punting along the verdant shores of a less foul tributary of the Thames. If it weren't for the belt cinched around her neck and her hands tied behind her back, she might be mistaken for yet another house servant who had done herself in finding herself with child from the lord of the manor."

"So, no relation to the happenings in Whitechapel?"

Abberline combed his fingers through his mutton chops. He pursued what looked like a bit of potato that had found a home under the gravy and licked it off his finger. "Ezra, since when is the evisceration of a woman referred to as a happening? I thought Americans eschewed euphemisms."

Bryson pulled the bread pudding the waiter brought to Abberline away from him. "You're right. I am avoiding calling it what is, the labour of a maniac."

Abberline retrieved his pudding. "Deeds of an insane man, perhaps, or perhaps not."

"Oscar Wilde met with Arthur Conan Doyle," Bryson said but was silenced by Abberline's donkey laugh.

"Let me guess, the doctor said these murders could be attributed to a man dressed as a woman or a woman dressed as a man or a man and a woman working in concert."

"How did you know?"

"I'm surprised Artie, such a self-proclaimed brilliant mind, would take seriously a baseless aside I made to him over five brandies. He fancies himself a writer and alienist of sorts. No doubt he will incorporate my musing into one of his stories for The Strand, without crediting me of course, but indicating it sprang from the deep well of his knowledge of the criminal mind."

"Chief Inspector," Bryson said. "I suppose you have a better explanation, a more precise understanding of the why and who is committing these atrocities."

"I do."

"Please, share your views."

"I did with Sir Robert Anderson. I told him that the murders started well before Polly Nichols. That the maiming and murder of the leaders of the IRB and Home Rule Movement, which is linked to the rise of the labour strikes here and elsewhere, proceeded the carnage in Whitechapel. That the crimes are not sporadic, not incoherent, but a clear bloody message to others."

"What others?"

"Others fomenting labour unrest and revolution like Annie Besant."

Perez stood up so quickly that his chair toppled over. "Enough tip-toeing around, say what you mean."

"I did, Ezra, and because I did, I am no longer assigned to the case. I retain the title of Inspector, but as of tomorrow, I am exiled to Cleveland Street. I am to ensure that the social club there remains a secret and that the Old Dame's grandson is not tainted by his frequenting it. No doubt your friend, Mr. Wilde, has met him there on some occasions."

"What has this got to do with Whitechapel?" Bryson asked.

Abberline used the edge of his spoon to scrape up the remains of his dessert. "Nothing, that is why I have been moved. I am too close to the truth. I find it perplexing that clients of establishments like the one on Cleveland Street are incarcerated for offences that are neither detrimental to society nor a threat to the security of the nation. What men, or women for that matter, choose to do in dimly lit parlours, the recesses of bathhouses and behind their own closed doors does not foment moral repugnance to my person. The complicity of so-called protectors of the realm in what has transpired on the streets of Whitechapel is what outrages me."

Bryson removed his notepad from his jacket pocket. "Go on. Tell me what you know, and I'll tell the world."

Abberline snatched the pad from Bryson. "What I know is this. Its revelation would result in me, and perhaps my wife and children, suffering the same fate as the other victims. All I will say is that whatever clues you discover, whatever tunnels you are taken down, are ruses. Please be so good as to the pay the bill and fuck off. I think I'll order a brandy as I am highly unlikely to ever dine here again."

That's all, that's all the information you have to share?"

Abberline held the brandy sifter to his nose. "Ezra, keep an eye on this one. He'll need someone to keep his head above the bog he's entering."

Perez picked up his chair and set it back at the table. "Inspector,

I tried to carry your man a couple of rounds, but his jaw was as brittle as sugar candy."

Abberline once again treated the restaurant's patrons to his braying laugh.

Chapter 31

The weaving machine rested on huge wooden blocks. Enough space existed for Darcy to slide completely under the beast. He inspected every joint, every seal, to determine the origin of the pool of oil spreading across the factory floor. He stopped working when he heard footsteps on the other side of the machine.

Fitch's reedy voice was unmistakable. "It's the gospel truth, Sirs. Stride and Eddowes have been circulating throughout Hollens, stirring up the women. That bitch, Eddowes, has made her presence known throughout Spitalfields and along Dorset Street. I even seen her visiting the building where Engels and that other Jew, Marx, hold meetings. She came out with a stack of papers as thick as a tombstone. Saw her passing them out to factory workers and a few known Irish radicals."

"What was printed on those papers?" A soft voice that lacked any hint of emotion asked.

"Can't say, Sir."

"Can't or won't?"

Another voice, only a touch more animated than the other, said, "Can't, brother. This simian struggles to mark his name with an X."

Fitch gulped down his anger at being ridiculed. "I could have made out the words if I had the time and managed to snatch a sheet away from that cunt."

Darcy recognized the unmistakable sound of a slap across naked skin.

"What's that for!" Fitch yelled.

The soft voice answered, "Though their actions are troubling, your use of vulgarities will neither be tolerated in our presence nor in this mill. Keep your eyes alert and your ears open."

Fitch mumbled angrily as he walked away.

"I abhor that toady," the soft voice said without a trace of malice.

"He serves a function Julian. I'll pass what he noted to Barnett, and he'll give the information to the council to determine the best course of action."

"I detest that one as well."

"Be grateful. Vermin like Fitch and Barnett are out there to facilitate what needs to be done and leave us free to conduct business."

Darcy continued to repair the machine. After he was certain everyone had left, he slid out from beneath the beast. His clothing was covered in oil as dark as dried blood.

*

Since the murder of Sarah Annie Chapman, Catherine Eddowes abandoned her façade of being just another gin-soaked mill worker. She tossed aside a carefully crafted false persona of one who cared less for the injustice of the system than she did for fooling around with her friends at the local pubs and moving her feet at the dances.

Mrs. Stride cautioned her to reign it in. Admonished her that calling unwanted attention to herself could endanger others seeking a resolution to the inequity and blatant hammer-and-nail threat of unemployment, imprisonment and worse. Cat would have none of it. "I have followed your lead, Bessie, and where has it gained us?"

Mrs. Stride placed her hand over Cat's mouth when she saw Fitch lurking behind a post. She pounded him on his back with such force that he fell into a cart loaded with bolts of cloth. "Do you know the tale of Peeping Tom?" She asked and pulled Fitch out of the cart with one jerk. "His eyes were put out. Should he have been eavesdropping, his ears may well have been lopped off."

Darcy appeared behind Fitch before he could reply. He dumped him back in the cart and rolled it toward the rear of the factory.

"Where are you taking me?" Fitch whined.

"To the sorting area where we decide what scraps are serviceable and which ones should be disposed of."

Mrs. Stride and Cat followed Darcy. Mary raised her head as they went past her. "Where are you taking Mr. Fitch; is he ill?"

"He's fit for the moment, but if he doesn't tell us why he's been sneaking around, he'll be in need of more care than a doctor or Jesus can provide."

Mary ran ahead of the cart and stood in front of it, blocking the way. Darcy inched the cart forward, but Mary refused to budge. Mrs. Stride and Cat came to her side and tried to move her, but she grasped the front of the cart with both hands and entered the cart beside Fitch. "Enough Mr. Darnell! Enough of this idiocy! Mrs. Stride, Cat, it is true that I loath this maggot, but I abhor the possibility that in drubbing him, we will descend to his level."

Mrs. Stride sighed and held her hands palms up in a sign of resignation. She and Catherine tipped the cart over, and Fitch and Mary rolled onto the cold floor of the factory. Mary stood up quickly. She dusted herself off and smiled at the two women who had become her sisters in more than blood. Fitch crawled on his hands and knees to escape. He did not have a chance to get to his feet and make a dash for it. Darcy slipped his hand between Fitch's waistband. He slammed him into a loom. "Divine intervention has indeed saved you from a proper beating. He tugged Fitch's ear and turned his head to look at Mary. "If it weren't for this colleen, you would be put through a shredder, and not a soul, even the soulless twins, would miss your presence. You will leave this place and never return. Tell Charlie Barnett that I know that you and him have been spying on us. To what purpose, I don't know. Be aware, if I find out, both of you will discover what the road to hell is paved with."

Fitch puffed up his chest in a false show of bravado. "You can't force me from here."

"Right, you have to leave on your own accord. But what I can decide is how you will remain, or should I say your remains will remain."

"Where will I go? What will become of me?"

"Nothing will become of you. You have become what you were

meant to be. As for where you should go, I don't care. Give my regards to Charlie Barnett when you see him."

Chapter 32

Bryson left word with Kit for Burton and Wilde to meet him at Darnell's. He was eager to relay Abberline's thinking. The inspector's theory lacked solid evidence but was delivered with such conviction that part of it, if not all of it, was as close to the truth as the fact that fleas unnumbered people in Whitechapel.

"Mary, be so good as to purchase tea at Belmont," Darcy said.

"We still have half a tin left from Markham's."

"I know, but it tastes like he cut it with sawdust. Belmont gives you an honest measure."

Darcy waited until Mary was out of earshot. He pointed at two chairs at the table fashioned from a flour barrel. "Things are not, nor were ever, safe for the likes of Mary here and are getting worse."

"Only for the time being. My reports to my paper and our friends in London pounding on the doors of the authorities to take action will improve the conditions in Whitechapel. I promise those responsible for the killings will be brought to justice."

Darcy shook his head. "I did not take you for an imbecile. Even though I cannot read, I can hear the writing on the wall."

"I have a hard time believing you're illiterate based on how well you speak."

"Yank, we Irish were masters of poetry and storytelling long before the Brits dipped a quill into an ink pot. Our words are the only things England has not been able to deprive us of."

"Is Mary your lover? You seem to be very protective of her."

"My lover? I take it you mean by that is she my whore?"

"I never assumed that."

"Listen, Scribbler. Mary Kelly is like a sister to me. No, not like a sister, a reflection of a sister I once had, my own sister."

"Where is she?"

"Who?"

"Your sister."

"Her shade I suppose is dancing on a bed of sod. Like Mary, she saw the world as a place to avoid conflict by seeing the promise of a better world elsewhere."

"The living conditions here no doubt took her from you."

"Cholera, consumption and starvation are considered the natural order here. None of those regular means of feeding the worms did her in. It was Bloody Sunday, Trafalgar Square, that took her from us. She saw herself as a sister of mercy without donning the habit. Her habit of tending to those in need is what took her. What the money pockets call the labour riots of 1887. We, on the other side, see it as a march of freedom, a call for justice and the release of William O'Brien and our fellow travellers from prison."

Darcy relived the day behind his closed eyelids. The images that surfaced were accompanied by the screams and curses of men and women as the police and soldiers charged a crowd whose only crime was to demand a fair shake in the world.

His sister had taken a vow of non-violence. She tended to the injured, friend and foe alike, sprawled on the wet pavement at the base of Lord Nelson's column. She extended a hand to a young policeman who had been taken down by one of his own in the confusion. The peeler came to his feet, his free hand clutching his nightstick. He swung it with the rage flowing through every muscle in his body. He beat her, even after she fell to the very spot she had helped him up from. Darcy barged through the mass of people to his sister. The policeman had moved on to beat other protesters. She still had enough breath to tell him to flee.

Darcy's eyelids lifted. He ran his hand over his pants as if trying to wipe away the stain of that day. "Deirdre was barely nineteen. Considered herself an unpledged sister of mercy. A Sister of Mercy in a world that showed her no mercy. Do you know what she said before she died?"

Bryson shook his head.

"She asked if there is a better life after death. She truly believed Irishmen, Jews, Catholics, Orangemen, and even those who crushed her skull could be granted peace, forgiveness and salvation. And what did I answer her? I lied. Yes, I said. Of course, there is a better life awaiting her. I did not have the heart to tell her, for those born poor and landless, there is no life after life."

Mary came back, arriving to a room of deafening silence. "Belmont is twice the price, but their quince jam was on reduction," she said.

Chapter 33

Barnett and Fitch met at the wharves. They had become so accustomed to the stench of dead fish and sewage that a whiff of fresh air disturbed the natural balance of their universe. Barnett tweaked Fitch's ear. "You're a spineless meater to let Darnell chuck you out without so much as breaking wind!" He slapped Fitch. "You bloody pigeon-livered idiot, what did you let them onto?"

"Nothing, I swear on the teat of the Holy Mother."

"Don't go spoiling the withered breast of the Virgin." Barnett slapped Fitch again. "What does they suspect?"

"No more than you and I and the whole of Whitechapel glean."

Barnett leaned against the wall behind the Ten Bells where they had chosen to meet.

Fitch slipped his hand under his shirt collar and retrieved a louse. "You know as well as I do all of the movement and the IRB know who is snitching. There are no secrets. If we are to exit this morass unscathed, we best take a powder now."

"I agree," a voice from the far end of the alley said. "Keep your eyes to the wall. To see me is to invite a premature but perhaps justifiable ending."

"Sir, we was just discussing." The tremble in Barnett's voice was matched only by the wringing of his hands as he turned his face to the wall.

"Who the devil are you to be ordering us around?" No sooner had Fitch blurted this out than another man entered the alley and laid him out with a strike of a spanner to the back of his neck. The sound of his skull being separated from his spine sounded like a walnut crushed between the jaws of a nutcracker.

"Jesus and Mary," Barnett screamed, still keeping the presence of mind to face the wall. "You just deprived us of the only man with ears to the intrigue going on in Hollens and with the outside radicals."

"You may turn around."

"I'd rather not."

"What you would rather or rather not do is of no consequence. Look at us and then look at the fuming mass of human dung at your feet."

Four men dressed in long black coats and wearing wide brimmed hats stood four abreast in the alley. Their faces were concealed under wraps from their noses to their chins.

The voice, his footsteps plodding through the piles of refuse, squished with each shiny boot he put forward. "Your friend, conspirator if you like, is of no use to us now. He is no longer an employee of Hollens, nor a denizen of the breathing world. Not to say, however, that he serves no useful purpose. A better purpose than informing on his fellow workers ever provided. We have a far more reliable, trusted source, than this pathetic specimen of humanity. A source that does not even know the role he plays."

The man lowered his scarf. He pressed so close that Barnett felt the hot steam of the man's exhalation. The man picked up Barnett's limp arm and uncurled his fingers. He placed the spanner in his hand. On the surface of the handle, etched in nitric acid, was DD, the only thing Darcy had ever committed to writing to attest to his tools ownership.

"Find a convenient place to deposit this." The man nudged the body of Fitch with his boot. "Some place conspicuous, where he will be found within a day, not a week. Drop the tool a few yards away from the body, not so close as to suggest it was left there on purpose but not so distanced and concealed that it cannot be easily discovered."

Barnett puffed up his chest in a fruitless effort to display his courage. "Right then, I'll need at least two of your mates to help me get him to the corner beyond Hollens where even a blind owl can find him."

"Mr. Barnett, how you convey the corpse of Mr. Fitch is your duty and yours alone. Find a way there or there will be two bodies for the Metropolitan police to contend with. Do I make myself clear, Charlie?"

*

Sunday morning Darcy slept soundly, so soundly that he failed to hear the footsteps outside. A hobnail boot smashed his door off its hinges. Asleep on a mat near the stove, Mary screamed when she saw a giant policeman leering at her. She recognized Hines from his presence at Hollens gate. He pulled off the thin blanket covering her. Before Darcy could spring out of bed, the second peeler, Milton, his head wrapped in a swath of bandage from his encounter at the dance, shoved him back onto the mattress. Hines reached down and pinched Mary's nipple. She retaliated by biting his hand drawing blood. He backhanded her and flung her onto Darnell's bed. "It's a bloody shame when even your pimp won't let you share his tick."

"Leave her be," Milton ordered. "We're here for this one."

"On what charge?" Darcy asked

"Pimping, being a general nuisance to society, a pain in the arse, and a loudmouth disturber of the public order."

"Let's not leave out being a stinking bogtrotter," Hines added.

"None of those things are chargeable offences."

"You got a point there, boyo." Milton wiped his sleeve across his mouth. A grin emerged. "None of those things make you a criminal. We're here to take you in for murder."

Darcy remained composed. His eyes, fixed on where his door once existed framed Sir Burton, Perez and Bryson outside on the street. "And who is it I am supposed to have done in?"

"Your old chum, Fitch. Word is you and him had several run-ins. Probably concerning the trollop next to you."

"And what proof do you have that Mr. Darnell is the murderer?" Sir Burton's enquiry caused the two policemen to turn around.

"Everyone knows he hated Fitch."

"That accounts for only one of the hundreds, who as I heard

despised him," Burton said.

"The Hollens twins were set to dismiss Darnell and give Fitch his job. Charlie Barnett heard him threaten Tobias. That's plenty reason for this one to bear ill will toward Fitch."

"Tobias," Darcy blurted out. "You mean to tell me, the bastard's mother stuck around long enough to give him a first name."

"That does provide motive, if it can be verified but a very slim one at best."

"Evidence, we have evidence, the murder weapon hidden not feet away from the deceased, a spanner with the initials DD etched into its handle."

"Oh that is a compelling piece of evidence, Constable Milton. DD definitely could stand for Darcy Darnell, or Dimples Darling, or..."

"Or Dead Duck once he goes to trial," Hines said.

"If your lordship will be so good as to step aside to allow us to escort this paddy to Newgate and later up the twelve steps to the noose, we'd be obliged. And Yank, bring your pencil to send news of this villain's drop back to the former colonies. Your reports on Whitechapel have proven to be good reading here as well as across the pond. The names of the radicals and malcontents you cite have proven most useful." Milton walked through the opening Burton and Bryson made and stopped. "Where's the other one?"

"Which other one?" Bryson asked.

"You know damn well, your skivvy, the Jew."

Bryson patted his jacket pockets. “Beats me, copper. He’s sure the hell’s not hiding on my person.”

“Don’t get smarmy with me. Sir Burton may be protected but you have no standing.”

Hines and Milton jerked Darcy off his bed. They cuffed his hands behind him and hooked their arms through his elbows. They walked down the street with Darcy sandwiched between them. They took a detour through an alley, stopped and slammed Darcy against a wall. Milton unsheathed his baton and thrust its end into Darcy’s solar plexus. The wheeze of air escaping his lungs sounded like a half deflated bagpipe.

“No sense in wasting the Crown’s coin on this one.” Milton raised his truncheon above his head. “Don’t worry about your skirt. We’ll make sure Charlie Barnett provides her with gainful employment.”

Milton took two steps back to bring full force of his club across Darcy’s neck. Perez appeared behind him. He drove his fist into Milton’s kidney then swept his feet from under him. He removed a key from Milton’s belt and uncuffed Darcy. He picked up Milton’s long baton and feigned striking him with it before tossing it away. Hines made a run to the other end of the alley but ran into Mrs. Stride. She threw him on the ground and sat on him.

“We’re officers of the law. You are interfering with our sworn duty,” Hines gasped.

“You talk too much,” Mrs. Stride said. “Don’t squirm, it causes my innards to rumble. Should I blow wind your chest might cave in."

Darcy picked up Milton's truncheon. "I'm keeping this one as a souvenir. If you want it back I'll make sure to name a place to return it to you. In the meantime, go back to your masters and tell them it's not only Matchstick girls and labour discontent they have to deal with. The IRB and International Workers Alliance are on board. We will hunt down those responsible for the slaughter of our sisters and brothers."

They left the two peelers tending to their wounds in the alley and walked back to Darcy's place. "Where did she come from?" Burton asked on seeing Mrs. Stride.

"I thought something was amiss this morning when I went to buy bread. I saw Milton and Hines walking towards Millers Court. I bumped into Perez. He told me those cocksuckers had pinched Darcy."

Bryson and Mary rushed out onto the street to help Darcy to his bed. He grabbed Bryson by his lapel and said, "Write this down. Mrs. Stride and I are the prophets of what is to come. I will tell you all we know and all we suspect."

Burton and Perez retreated into a darkened corner of the room and listened to Darcy describe the failure of the joint labour and Home Rule revolt of 1887.

"We lost, no getting around that," Darcy said. "Lost but gave birth to something bigger. A movement that sought better living for all those holding up the paving stones that the upper crust mindlessly tread upon. Sarah Anne Chapman and Annie Besant gave us a voice. But voices can be silenced and are. And that is what THEY are trying to do."

Burton took a cigar from his breast pocket and casually lit it. He stared holes in Darcy. "And who are these THEY, who want to muffle your faint cries for retribution, justice?"

"The ones you dine with Sir Richard. The ones who lay down a wager to watch Perez battle the purest exemplars of British superiority only to be disappointed by the outcome when the lesser of humanity prevail over their Percivals their Galahads."

Mrs. Stride extended her hand to Darcy. "They'll be coming after us for the dusting in the alley. We best pick up Cat as I'm sure they are on to her. Some of our group will hide us until we can slip out of London."

Mary picked up a mug and threw it against the wall. "Listen to yourselves! Running away will only make the hounds pursue you more relentlessly. You have done nothing wrong. These gentlemen will vouch for that."

Darcy addressed Bryson before leaving with Mrs. Stride. "Do as I asked you. Get Mary away from here. The mark is on her as well."

"Darcy Darnell, I am staying put or have your forgot you promised to take me dancing?"

"That is true, Mary Kelly. I'll send word to meet me to fulfill that promise when the kettle of troubles here ceases to keen. A parting gift before you leave for Canada or America."

Chapter 34

Annie Besant met Darcy and Mrs. Stride outside a shabby building off the main district of the West End theatres. "Where is Catherine?"

Mrs. Stride shrugged. "You know Cat, once she puts her mind to doing something you cannot bridle her. She's out signing up more workers to join the protest against the factory owners and government. Plans to lead a procession to 10 Downing Street itself to get them to pay heed to our demands."

"I trust you told her how dangerous it is to be pushing the cause in Spitafield. Is she aware she may well end up like the others?"

Darcy shifted his weight from foot to foot. "How long do you think we must be in hiding?"

Annie Besant snorted. She leaned so close into Darcy that he could smell the clove oil on her breath. "And why do you ask? Do you have an evening lecture at the Horticultural Society planned, Darnell?"

"I have a promise to keep, to take someone dancing."

"I smell like a Christmas ham because I put off having a rotten tooth yanked to arrange a safe place for you. Your neck is already in the noose and you're concerned about waltzing with some girl."

The door of the building opened. A tall slightly stooped man removed his hat to keep it from being dislodged by the low lintel of the doorway. His hair, as torch red as his beard, was parted in the middle. He nodded at Annie Besant and Darcy and proceeded to walk past them, all the while jotting something in large notebook.

Annie Besant slapped the notebook from his hand. “Don’t go pretending you don’t know us Shaw.”

“Of course I know you. I just thought you would have a little more discretion than to meet me on such public thoroughfare.” He waved his hand across the empty street. “Never can tell when a crowd of the Savoy goers may wander down here to take in one of the lesser known bawdy plays. There is only so much of Gilbert and Sullivan one can stomach.”

Annie Besant opened up the notebook and read aloud, “The play succeeded to fail on so many levels below the author and actors expectations that it can truly be classified as comedy of errors.”

“Bernie, you’re a bit harsh aren’t you on the bloke who wrote the play?” Darcy asked.

“I thought I was being generous, considering the fellow who wrote and produced this mess is me.” Shaw stepped closer to Darcy. “Good Lord, someone put the whole boot to you.”

“Been punched and kicked worse Bernard, but you don’t need to be reminded as you were marching alongside us at Trafalgar Square and took a few bruises yourself.”

Shaw took the notebook back from Annie Besant. “I received your message and have secured a safe location for Darcy, Mrs. Stride and Catherine until I arrange transport for them out of London.”

Shaw aimed his walking stick at the building. “The likelihood of those after you ever thinking to discover you at this wretched theatre just a few corners away from Drury Lane is so remote as to beg the question of why it has not been put to use for such a purpose earlier." He reached into his pocket and took out an old fashioned skeleton key and handed it to Darcy.

Mrs. Stride hugged the playwright so firmly that he gasped for air. "Thank you sir, I'm off to fetch Catherine, drag her back by the hair if necessary to take her here where she'll be safe."

Annie Besant slipped her arm through Shaw's. "You are a good man in so far as a man can be good."

"Is that a compliment, Annie Besant?"

"Not at all GBS, simply an observation."

Shaw glanced over his shoulder and pulled at his beard as Darcy entered the building. *"Besant, the worst sin toward our fellow creatures is not to hate them, but to be indifferent to them:that's the essence of inhumanity."*

Chapter 35

Mrs. Stride returned to Darcy's room to ask Mary to help her find Cat. The room was empty. Catherine Eddowes had arrived a few minutes before her to persuade Mary to accompany her and other women on a march to 10 Downing Street. Mary tried to dissuade Cat from bringing more unwanted attention on herself but agreed to walk with her as far as Hollens, but no further. She hoped to convince her friend that sometimes a quiet protest within leads to a better outcome without.

Catherine dismissed Mary's comment. "Stop talking gibberish."

When Catherine arrived at the meeting place of the march less than a dozen women and two men were present. She could not understand why after visiting each street corner in Whitechapel and every pub to spread the news of the march, so few people had shown up, despite her gaining a well done and we're with you from them. "Where are the others?" she asked.

"Haven't you heard? The authorities got wind of our action. The bluebottles and soldiers have orders to block the way. Word is anyone crossing the bridge will be arrested and prosecuted as seditionists," a thin women cradling an infant in her arms said. "We came to warn you and see what you think we should do."

Catherine sat on the curb and stretched her legs out in front of her. She pressed her lips together. The corners of her mouth turned downward.

Mrs. Stride's booming voice announced, "Though one road may be blocked, there are others open to those who choose to take them."

The furrows on Catherine Eddowes brow vanished. A smile stretched across her face. "I thought you had slacked off."

"Not likely gal, I've come to take you to somewhere where we can be secure and regroup. But that can wait for now." Mrs. Stride approached the thin woman. She took the child from her arms and lifted the moth eaten blanket covering its face. The withered features and yellow skin spoke more to the gathering of the injustices surrounding them than all the speeches and pamphlets together. "This is why we walk. This is why we talk. This child is why we demand to be heard."

As predicted, they were stopped short of their destination at the bridge. Rather than press the issue and give the bully boys on the pay of the government and their masters cause to charge and use their clubs, the women chose to stand linked arm-in-arm and sing a song composed by a reformed slaver who in his own words, saw the light. The phalanx of policemen, and soldiers relaxed as they listened to John Newton's confessional lyrics.

Mrs. Stride's voice rose drowning out Newton's hymn. Her passion for change infused every stanza, AND WAS THE HOLY LAMB OF GOD, ON ENGLAND'S PLEASANT PASTURES SEEN!

Mrs. Stride broke ranks and confronted the acies triplex formation of thugs, peelers and soldiers. She raised her arms above her head and faced her sisters. She sang in a voice so deep, so clear, that it could be heard at 10 Downing Street. The other women joined in and stamped their feet and clapped. AND DID THE COUNTENANCE DIVINE, SHINE FORTH UPON OUR CLOUDED HILLS? AND WAS JERUSALEM BUILDED HERE, AMONG THESE DARK SATANIC MILLS?

"Elizabeth, I never heard you so much as whistle," Catherine said when Mrs. Stride retook her place next to her.

"Never had cause to before now. Besides, it's a poem I know well."

"I'm truly perplexed. Never took you for a lover of words."

"As a young colleen I charred for this man who fed his body with bread as an engraver and nourished his soul with poetry. He taught me how to make letters and read."

"He must be famous."

"No, he is dead. Most think him mad but those who let his words penetrate them, see him as a visionary."

The formation of men facing the women parted. Sir Robert Anderson passed through them. His voice as thin and sharp as a nail scraped along a brick wall, did not bother to make a plea for the assembly of women to depart. Two wagons drove up, one on each side of him. One was a paddy wagon and the other, the morgue's black beauty. "Go home or back to whatever doss house or gin mill you crawled out of." He rapped his walking stick against the sides of both wagons. "Or choose which one of these conveyances you elect to occupy." Sir Anderson removed his hat and ran his kid skin gloved hand over his bald head. Something, perhaps a twitch or a faint smile, resulted in his lip quivering beneath his moustache.

"Come, let's not give them reason to abuse us," Mrs. Stride said. "For Sir Robert Anderson to grace us with his presence, it must mean someone is listening to us on the pristine side of London, perhaps as far as parliament."

The women departed one by one, casting angry and pained looks behind them at Sir Robert and his trolls of the royal order of the cudgel. Mrs. Stride and Catherine walked partway together. They agreed to meet at dusk at the bridge and headed to their respective rooms to gather their few belongings.

*

Elizabeth Stride on her way to meet Cat paused at the narrow entrance of Dutfield's Yard. The poem of the engraver kept repeating in her head. The time of Sir Robert Anderson and his class trampling her kind must truly be coming to an end. Her sisters had stared down those who would forever keep them nose deep in despair. They had not been intimidated. They had walked off with their chins held high, not buried in their necks and moving timidly like blind mice as not to offend the so called adjudicators of who belongs and who doesn't.

She heard the raucous voices and drunken songs of men gathered in a club inside Dutfield's Yard. A club dedicated to the welfare and eduction of working men. She wondered if Cat had knocked on their door to ask them to join her on her crusade to

Downing Street. Probably not. These men waged their own crusade behind the lyrics of Rule Britannia. They stubbornly adhered to the social hierarchy to gain an inch of progress for every yard they retreated.

"Are you the one called Long Liz?" A cheery voice called out from inside Dutfield's Yard.

Mrs. Stride moved cautiously toward the narrow entrance. A man dressed in a long black coat and wide brimmed hat stood on the edge of the yard. She was certain she had seen him or some like a harbinger of darkness before. Only he was shorter and blonde. The scarf thrown over his shoulder revealed a smiling face, somewhat worn from years of service to some weary cause, but friendly enough.

"Long Liz, right?"

Mrs. Stride let loose a burst of laughter. "I've been wider than long for many years."

The man doffed his hat. "I admire you Mrs. Stride. My companions and I witnessed you brazening Sir Robert Anderson and his mindless brutes. If England had more defenders of the downtrodden such as you, one cannot but dream of what changes would occur."

Mrs. Stride felt a rare warm glow on her cheeks at the uninvited compliment. The man extended a hand. She likewise reached out to him. His clasped her forearm and roughly pulled her into the yard. She barely had time to see the other man hidden in the shadows emerge. He pressed a cloth drenched in some sweet smelling liquid over her mouth and nose. The potion took a few minutes to take effect. She grew limp. The man jerked her head back by her hair and drew a thin blade across her carotid artery. They dragged her into the yard, away from eyes passing by on Berner Street. They smoked while waiting for her to bleed out, idly chatting about how much they hated this work.

"Loathe it or not, it is what we've been commissioned to do," the man wielding the knife said.

The charmer of Mrs. Stride crushed his cigarette under his boot heel. "I know. Ours is not to question why horse shite."

"Snuff it Uriah, old Lord Tennyson has nothing to do with this, and it's not us to do and die but ours to make others to desist or die."

"Let's get on with it Wesley. We are to meet up with the others. See how they have fared."

Wesley went behind a crate where he had hidden a black surgeon's bag. He snapped open the clasp and removed a lamb skin package. Inside were several pockets containing various surgical instruments. He removed a serrated knife, shook his head and replaced it in its pocket. He opted for a cleaver and another thin blade like the one he had severed Mrs. Stride's throat.

Uriah swallowed the bile rising in his gorge. "I hate this part."

"As do I," his companion said and knelt beside Mrs. Stride wiping off the blood on his knife on her skirt.

"Why not kill them and leave it at that?"

"A message I suppose, like distributing the body parts of

William Wallace, five or was it six centuries ago, to every rebellious corner of Scotland."

"I studied to be a surgeon, a healer not a butcher."

"Surgeon, butcher what is the difference? Dead meat is dead meat. Surely you learned that in India and Sudan."

Wesley handed Uriah the clever. The clatter of wagon wheels on the cobblestone street outside Dutfield's Yard prevented them from continuing their grim task. They quickly gathered their instruments and retreated into a coal bin. The wagon driver cursed. The left wheel of his wagon bounced him nearly off his seat when it passed over what he thought was a pile of rubbish. He climbed off his perch to inspect what had caused his horse to shy to the left. The colourless face and pebble eyes of Elizabeth Stride stared at him. Blood from the slash across her neck had pooled and turned black encircling her neck like a satin ribbon. He ran out of the yard wailing over and over, "Murder, Murder." Two bluebottles checking the locks of the local businesses gave chase when he ran past them. It took several minutes to calm the driver enough to make out what he had stumbled across. Wesley and Uriah packed away their tools. They vanished before the police and driver returned to Dutfield's Yard, leaving Mrs. Stride's corpse on the exact spot they had placed her.

*

Catherine Eddowes retraced her steps thinking perhaps Mrs. Stride on not finding her at the bridge went in search of her. "It was my fault," she thought. She had stopped at Hollens to tack up a crude manifesto on the gate, proclaiming the worker's intent to shed their chains and reap the rewards of their labour.

It was a small detour, but enough of one to put Mrs. Stride out of sorts. Especially if Mrs. Stride had been waiting long for her. Most likely Mrs. Stride had gone to search for her. It wouldn't be unlike the woman they once called Long Liz in her pub crawling days to track down those who disrespected her. This was before she found a man who steered her away from John Barley Corn and to a higher purpose. For promulgating rebellious ideas, her man was conveyed on the last prison ship to a penal colony in Tasmania. She learned he succumbed to a fever or was hung from the mast for attempting to escape one time too many, depending on who relayed the news of his fate. Though never wed officially, no banns posted at the local Church of England, she nevertheless took his surname and went to work in the factories around England, quietly trying to awaken women to join her in her fight against the horrors of the industrial monster devouring women and children alike. It was she who on seeing Catherine weaving between semi-respectable house maid and three day whore, plucked her from the flock of soiled doves. Cat heard footsteps behind her. She quickened her pace. Whoever was trailing her matched her step-for-step. At Mitre Square she stopped and surveyed which of the three passages leading off it were best to elude her stalker.

"There now girl, slow down. I'm winded trying to keep up with you."

Cat whirled around and faced Charlie Barnett. "What does it take to make you know I am done with you?"

"You made that quite clear darling. I am a reformed man. Have only come to tell you I accept and respect the path you have taken. I am onto joining the movement myself."

"Come off it, Charlie, you have never carried a penny that someone else did suffer to earn."

Barnett removed his pork pie hat, pressing it to his chest. "Ashamed as I am to own it, what you say is true."

"Charlie I've never seen you so glum, so remorseful. Perhaps reflecting on your sins has sobered you."

"Oh it has. May I walk with you a bit? I promise to mind my tongue and keep two arms lengths between us."

"Sure Charlie, but only until I find Mrs. Stride. You know how the mere sight of your hat sets her on a rant that lasts a month."

"Oh it's Mrs. Stride you are looking for. Not half an hour ago I saw her not far off Mitre Square, walking through Church Passage calling out your name."

He backtracked to a narrow passage off Mitre Square. He pointed his finger at someone in the narrow channel that led to a larger street on the other side. "Cat, come closer, I see Mrs. Stride standing under the street lamp."

"Are you certain?"

"Not likely many women cast a shadow as full as Mrs. Stride."

Catherine Eddowes followed Charlie Barnett. She could touch

the walls of the narrow corridor with her arms stretched out.

"Charlie, don't go putting me on. There's no one at the other end."

Four arms lashed out of the darkness, pulling her into the passageway. A third man wearing a white expressionless mask poured a sweet smelling liquid on a cloth and held it over her nose and mouth. She struggled to break free. It was no use. The cloth was so saturated that she not only inhaled the mind deadening fumes but droplets of the liquid as well. He drew a thin knife blade across her throat with the same precision as Uriah had done to Mrs. Stride. Only his cut was deeper. Catherine Eddowes did not crash ungracefully to the dirty pavement. Her assailants held her close and laid her down like a princess awaiting a hundred year sleep. No prince charming would appear to awaken her with a kiss.

Charlie Barnett remained at the lip of the passageway. "Delivered as promised." He held out his hand for payment. None was forthcoming. Not wishing to press the issue, he started to walk away. The white masked man said, "Your job is not done." He tossed a small bag near the body of Catherine Eddowes. To Charlie Barnetts's ears, the clink of coin against coin sounded like a choral recital.

Barnett entered the tight passageway. He stooped to pick up the sack. One of the dark men pressed his boot heel on Barnett's hand preventing him from retrieving his coin.

The masked man snapped his fingers and his companions

pulled Barnett to his feet. "Silas, give him this." He held out a bone saw. "It's messy but will dislodge the rumour that these kills are the mark of skilled hand."

"As you say Joshua. But not sure I can stomach such amateurish butchery."

"After what we've seen in battle fields soaked in blood and littered with severed limbs and gutted soldiers, this is a stroll through the daisies."

Barnett refused to take the saw. "Okay, you've had your chuckle. Pay me and I'll go."

"You're not done. You cannot avoid being a full member of our union. Your hand must be as bloody as ours. Your nights as plagued with nightmares that will never recede until death overtakes you, if even then, as ours." Joshua pointed at Catherine and motioned his men to throw Barnett on the ground next to her.

"I can't do it. It ain't human!"

"Catherine Eddowes was simply a package for you to deliver a few moments ago. Now get to work."

"I don't know where to start." Barnett's tears fell on Catherine Eddowes' apron.

Silas leaned over and whispered in Barnett's ear, "Commence at the nose then work your way down. Once the face is gone, you will no longer see her as someone you knew or something at all."

Barnett closed his eyes and hacked at her face. Catherine's nose flew up into the air, landing on his lap. He keeled over and shat his pants.

“Have some dignity man.” Silas stripped off Eddowes’s apron. “Go wipe yourself and finish the job.”

“You’d think the man had never field dressed a deer.”

“That is what I like about you Edward, even spitting out dung you made us laugh.”

“It is a calling Joshua. I doubt if this fellow ever saw an field much less a deer in a dress.”

“I do not find it appropriate to be making light of this business,” Silas said.

“Is that what you call it? Business? I can hear the laughter from hell where we stand.”

Joshua tossed a piece of chalk on the ground. “Eddie, when he’s done, tell him what to write on the wall.”

Chapter 36

Darcy paced back in forth in a cramped prop room where Shaw had made space for his three fugitives. It was past eight and the lamp lighter had passed by two hours earlier. Mrs. Stride was not one to dally. Surely she must have located Catherine by now. No longer able to count on their return, Darcy set off to find them. Mary, feeling a surge of guilt for dismissing Catherine, set off on her own to locate her friend.

Darcy and Mary by chance encountered each other near Dutfield's Yard. "Girl, have you lost your wits? You're as branded as one of us. You should neither be wandering the streets in the fading light nor full sun."

An infestation of bluebottles outside the yard made them veer off to avoid being pinched under whatever flimsy pretext the authorities could manufacture. They headed in the direction of Mitre Square.

"Thank you for your concern Mr. Darnell. Your disappearance confirmed you cared not a twitch about me."

Darcy held back the urge to gather her in his arms. She was too close to a painful memory to open his heart to her. "Be that it is," he strangled on the words he was about to say. "Be that it is Mary Kelly, you are mine to protect and ensure you take leave of this hellish place before it takes leave of you."

Mary dusted off his concern. "Perhaps they met at Cat's lodgings. We may encounter them should they travel the same route as us."

Darcy stopped when he heard uninterrupted maniacal laughter coming from Mitre Square. He looked inside the sliver of a passage to the street beyond. He whirled Mary twenty feet away from the scene he had witnessed. Charlie Barnett rocked back and forth on his haunches. A smile, that only cadavers in rictus claimed, spanned his face, The unrecognizable mangled corpse of a woman lay at his side. He held a bone saw in one hand. A blood and feces soaked apron was pressed against his face like a baby blanket. He glanced at the crescent moon. He jumped to his feet and knocked Darcy down and sprinted toward a canal once used by tanners to soak the urine out of the hides they cured.

"Stay here Mary," Darcy yelled and pursued Barnett.

"Yes, stay here." A voice from further inside the passageway ordered. "He will return for you soon. For now you are safe enough."

"I know your voice," Mary said.

"Do not come further. Forget that you ever heard my voice."

Silas stepped out of the cover of darkness and struck a match, momentarily illuminating his face. "Listen to him Miss. Best forget you know that voice or have ever laid eyes on me or him."

Darcy located Barnett balanced precariously on the edge of the canal. It was swollen with years of debris and human waste. Barnett tossed the apron and bag of coins aside. He emitted a screech so piercing that it scattered even the crows.

"It is not God who punishes, but the devil who rewards." Barnett still clutching the bone saw in one hand, ripped it across his throat. It cut so deep that the blade embedded itself in his neck. He tumbled into the motionless sludge. He did not float, did not drift. There was no current to move him. He sank beneath the thick muck. Only his pork pie hat remained on top of the sludge.

Men arguing from inside the passageway held Mary fixed to the pavement. One man after another debated what should be done with her. "We have no choice, Wesley," one of the men said.

"Not so," a familiar voice from someone she trusted, thought she knew well replied.

"Your neck belongs to you Joshua but you have no claim on ours," Silas said.

Darcy appeared next to Mary and uprooted her from where she stood. "Run, run until we can run no longer."

They fled through the labyrinth of streets and alleys, never pausing to catch their breath. They did not stop running until they arrived at Shaw's safe haven. Darcy pointed at a second story window. "This is where I'll stay until I can be spirited away. Before that time comes, I'll collect you."

"I mean to remain with you."

"You will not. All it takes is for one unwanted glance by some upright citizen or peeler passing by to expose this place and we will be flushed us out like grouse at a country estate shooting. I'll take you somewhere that I doubt anyone will think you'd go or be accepted."

*

Bryson completed the latest instalment of his correspondence on Whitechapel. He handed it to Perez who stood by the washstand as still and expressionless as the Queen's Palace guards. Perez took the six pages of foolscap and slipped it into his satchel without so much as looking at the first sentence.

"No interest Perez, on the butchery of women in Whitechapel I'm relaying to my readers back home, and the authorities' obvious disinterest in apprehending whoever is responsible?"

"Bryson, all you're doing is feeding your countrymen prurient tales of a maniac slaughtering women. You leave it up to your semi-literate readers to determine if the victims are virgins or whores. By the same token, I admit, it is no better here. America's propensity to lynch anyone of darker complexion daring to walk down the wrong side of a country road or God forbid smile at a Southern Belle is followed with the same morbid curiosity and salacious appeal by the subscribers of our tabloids masquerading as legitimate newspapers."

Perez opened the door to leave and nearly fell over Kit who had raised his hand to knock. Perez hooked his hands under the boy's jacket and pulled him into Bryson's room. "How long have you been spying on us boy? Who is paying you?"

Kit touched the ornate hilt of his Kirpan. "No one sir, I am here to tell Mr. Ward that a man and young woman are at the service entrance."

"Relax Kit, my friend means you no harm."

The boy led them through a hallway hidden behind the walnut panelling that the help travelled through as not to offend the hotel's patrons. They negotiated a dimly lit set of stairs. At the bottom of the stairs was at a metal door secured by a thick iron rod. A cool breeze greeted them when they stepped into an alley behind the hotel.

Darcy pushed Mary toward Perez and Bryson. "See to it she's safe," he said and left.

"Darcy Darnell come back. I am not a China doll."

"When the time's right I will take you dancing across the waves. Until then, boys take care of her."

Bryson unsure of what to do said, "I can't very well hide her in my room. Someone is sure to discover her and we'll both be sent packing."

Kit held out both palms as if to receive a gift. The gesture did not go unnoticed by Perez. He dipped into his satchel and took out two bills and placed them on Kit's left palm. The boy closed his hand around the money and dropped his arm. The right hand remained palm up facing Bryson. "Okay I get it. I grease your palm and you'll grease mine."

"Mr. Ward it is necessary to give me more money so I can pay the chambermaids to turn a blind eye while I sneak her into your room. She can hide in your wardrobe if someone knocks on your door."

Perez asked when Kit led them back to Bryson's room. "Do you still have your pistol?"

"Why?"

"We will need it if we continue on the road we're travelling."

Bryson lifted the bed mattress and removed the holstered colt.

"Put that away," Mary protested.

Someone knocked on the room's door so hard that the key in the keyhole fell to the floor. Bryson clamped his hand over Mary's mouth and shoved her into the closet. Perez cracked the door. Wilde and Burton were standing in the hall.

Bryson handed the pistol to Perez who placed it inside the satchel. Burton parted his jacket to reveal his own weapon. Wilde likewise opened his long purple evening coat and displayed the garment's flora silk lining. From a well concealed pocket in the lining he withdrew a two shot pearl handled derringer. Anticipating their question he said, "Oh, this toy? On tour in a remote village in Colorado a gambler wagered I could not keep pace with several renowned tipplers of Leadville. He placed a bet, five hundred American dollars, and his little pop gun. I left ten silver barons under the table and returned to deliver my best performance at the Tabor Opera House."

Bryson opened the wardrobe door. Mary Kelly flew out waving her arms over head. "If you ever shove me in there again without warning I'll send your bollocks so far inside your body that their whereabouts will never be discovered."

Chapter 37

Before the sun rose Sir Richard returned. He did not bother knocking. Mary was asleep. She had created a cozy nest in a corner of the apartment under the window, leaving the bed to Bryson. Burton tossed a newspaper on Bryson's chest. "Don't know how Purkess does it. He beat all the other scandal mongers to the punch." The headline in The Illustrated Police News screamed TWO MORE MURDERS IN WHITECHAPEL: CALL FOR SIR CHARLES WARREN TO TAKE ACTION OR RESIGN. The normally barely restrained illustrations of victims' of violence were absent.

"I am to meet Oscar and Ezra in Whitechapel."

"I'll come with you."

Burton pointed at Mary. "You'll stay put. Darnell entrusted this woman's safety to you. He made it clear that it's not safe for her on the streets. Don't pout. I'll keep you informed. Your readers will not be deprived of the gruesome details."

When Burton arrived at Mitre Square he understood the reluctance of The Illustrated Police News to provide a graphic presentation of crime scene.

A young policeman was arguing with Sir Robert Anderson. "It is a disgrace to leave her lying there like scraps in a butcher's bucket."

"What is your name young man?"

"Constable Watkins."

"Watkins, it is not your place to presume to know better than your superiors what is to be done or not done. When the medical examiner arrives he will take this away." Anderson pointed his cane at the barely recognizable remains of Catherine Eddowes.

Watkins turned his back on Anderson and stormed off muttering, "Between him and Warren this shite storm will never be resolved." He turned the corner and bumped into Oscar Wilde and his companions.

"Wattie, how nice to see you in uniform." Wilde reached out to embrace the young policeman.

"Keep your distance Ozzie, unless you're intent on ruining both of us."

Oscar, Perez and Burton followed Watkins to a lamppost bleeding out its last portion of light. "Dark things are going on. We found another murdered woman a few streets from here not to mention that the body of a man popped up out of the muck in the old tanners' canal."

Burton held out a flask to Watkins and Oscar gave him a machine rolled cigarette. Watkins drew in a lungful of Turkish tobacco and a cheek full of brandy. "Two streets that way the floater chalked a message on a wall for everyone to notice on Goulston Street."

"How do you know he left the message?" Burton asked.

"Because in his hand he had the tie end of the woman's apron and in his pocket a piece of chalk matching that on the wall."

Perez asked. "What did it say?"

"Go see for yourself, provided Warren hasn't scrubbed it away already. One thing is certain, it ain't going to make the Yid's life very secure around here."

The three men quickened their pace toward Goulston Street. They came upon Sir Charles supervising the erasure of the message scrawled on a wall. Warren berated the policemen tasked with the removal. "You dullards, do a proper job. Pull up a crate and stand on it. Put your back into the task at hand."

Oscar Wilde slipped past Sir Charles. He craned his neck to read the smudge words before Warren's men obliterated them. He read aloud, ***"The JUWES are not the men that will be blamed for nothing."***

Perez bumped aside a policeman who was scrubbing at the message.

Burton interceded before two peelers battered Ezra. "Goodness old boy, of all people I thought you would want that wiped off this wall before your tribe becomes targets for every Jew hater in London."

Wilde, seemingly oblivious to the events around him, asked one of the other policemen removing the words if he could take his place.

Sir Charles ordered Wilde to immediately vacate the site. "I find it distasteful that you take such perverse interest in the words of a mad man, a butcher. This is not a tawdry theatrical production. It is a crime scene."

Wilde was unfazed by Sir Charle's command. "This has nothing to do with Jews. It's an acronym. Notice how each letter is capitalized and if you look closely, you'll notice there are periods, very faint ones thanks to the admirable work of these constables, but still visible. It reads **J.U.W.E.S.** not what our eyes first interpreted."

Burton slapped Perez on his back. "Looks like that takes you chaps off the hook doesn't it?"

Perez clenched his teeth. "I suppose you have a point, Richard. But I wouldn't be shocked if there are still those bearing torches just as their ancestors did at Clifford's Tower."

"For the love of God get back to work. Expunge every trace of this before someone walks by and sees it," Sir Charles Warren bellowed at his men. "Acronym or not, very few if any Londoners have the grammatical skills to distinguish J.U.W.E.S. from Jews however it is spelt."

*

Burton left his companions at Goulston Street and revisited the murder scene of Catherine Eddowes. He sniffed the air. His nose lead him to a rubbish bin. He reached inside and removed a rag soaked with a sweet smelling liquid. He approached Catherine's partially nude body, where it lay spread eagle on the ground. He passed the rag to Sir Robert Anderson. "Don't inhale too deeply, Sir Robert, or you may end up napping next to her." Burton inspected the face, or rather what face remained, of Catherine Eddowes. "This is not the work of a stark raving lunatic. This woman, and I dare say the other victims, did not feel so much as a slight tickle. The killer or killers held this cloth saturated with ether over her mouth and nose before executing a precise slice across her throat severing her carotid artery."

"Are you now an expert on anatomy as well as everything else in the world?" A gruff voice announced the presence of the chief coroner who had arrived in a black wagon to cart off the body.

"Little tardy, aren't you Doctor Brown," Burton said.

"Try picking up three corpses in one night and tell me how Johnny on the spot you'd be."

"Gordon, the hacking, as you will probably record after a thorough autopsy, was done post mortem. He spared her the agony, but made sure the missive would be understood on every street of Whitechapel and beyond."

"Oh you're also an expert on the mind of murderers. How many men have you killed Burton?"

"Quite a few, but none recently. And you my good doctor, how many have you killed under your care?"

"Enough of this," Anderson shouted. "A dead woman lies at our feet and you two insist on playing Punch and Judy over her corpse."

"I apologize for my callousness." Burton cleared his throat. "But take heed, this is not the work of a crazed demon masquerading as a man. These murders have been meticulosity orchestrated to deliver an unambiguous declaration. Stop now or more are to come. In my experience, spree killers prefer to do their work in private and dispose of their prey where it is least likely to be discovered."

Chapter 38

Sunlight poured in through the circular window. It lit up the writing table so well that the gas lamp remained off. The man dipped the nib of a pen in an inkwell and pulled the small lever to charge the barrel. Before starting he held up a tumbler filled to the rim with an amber coloured liquid. He swirled the contents around, admiring how the sunlight captured the various hues of the liquor. “Best get started before it congeals,” he remarked prior to taking a dainty sip. He placed the nib to paper and wrote, Dear Sir, then crumpled the sheet of paper. He created numerous salutations before deciding on one. He scrutinized his calligraphy and shook his head in disgust at the too perfect handwriting and grammar. He started over and scrawled in a pig blood substitute for ink, *From Hell.* He went over to a clay wine amphora on a shelf. He reached in and removed a kidney that had turned to a grey mass, the result of being preserved in alcohol for a more than a week. He wrapped it in a cloth, patted it dry and placed in a box. Satisfied, he went back to his desk and continued to write his message, taking special care to avoid giving the impression he was anything but a semi-literate madman. He bit his thumb and pondered an appropriate ending to the letter. Finally, for lack of better valediction, he wrote, *Catch me if you can.* He sighed and held the tumbler up to the light to see if his sins were trapped in the amber liquid. The package and letter found its way to George Lusk, the Chairman of The Whitechapel Vigilance Committee.

Chapter 39

The meeting place was leagues beyond the coal smudged skies of London. Sir Burton had chosen the spot carefully. The pastoral field was an ideal location for a clandestine rendezvous to discuss the butchery and potential political mayhem set to boil over in London and perhaps the entire island. It was a spot so far off the path of weekend wanderers that only precise directions could guide his confidant to this destination.

A diligence stopped at the field stone wall where Burton sat. The right side shade of the coach opened. Sir Robert Anderson popped his head out. It took a few seconds for his eyes, used to the dark interior of the coach, to be accustomed to the assault of the full sun. Sir Richard waited until Anderson exited the coach to stand. He offered a cigarette in one hand and a flask of brandy in the other.

"You well know from our days at Trinity Richard, that I neither smoke nor imbibe."

"Pity, it's just the medicine to cleanse one of his transgressions and guilt." Burton uncapped the flask and took a leisurely swallow of brandy. "When the Yank and Jew approached me to gain entrance in the RGS you asked me to keep you informed of the writer's true intent concerning Stanley's search of the Emin Pasha."

"I did. Our government fears that not only our European competitors desire to carve out a steak out of Africa and the Middle

East but our American cousins may join the feast as well. The New York journalist may be a spy bent on discovering our weak joints there and elsewhere."

Burton clapped his hands. "Bravo Robbie, you truly have the makings of a first rate thespian. You and I know most American politicians couldn't pick out Sweden or Egypt on a globe if you gave it a spin. Besides their interest is in exploiting what lies south of their border and in exterminating the last native warriors who resist being herded into pens like sheep on what was once their land."

Anderson glanced across the field and pointed at a deer. "Lovely spot you picked here, very tranquil."

Burton swung his legs over the field stone wall and stood on the other side. "The Emperor Hadrian built a similar barrier to keep out the Picts. It failed."

"Only because he failed to dedicate the resources to defend it," Sir Anderson said.

Burton took another sip from the flask and held it out to Anderson who averted looking at it as though it were some unholy object.

"Robbie, when Ward dropped the pursuit of the Pasha story, why did you commission me to keep you informed of his investigation of the troubles in East London?"

"For the protection of the realm. Labour activists, communists and Irish insurrectionists are undermining the sandy foundation upon which the Empire is built. Worst of all, members of our own class have thrown their support behind this lot. Fabian evangelists of change, like Shaw and Annie Besant, are hypocrites. They attack the very caste to which they belong. Yet when dinner arrives, they shudder at the thought of drinking from the same glass or touching the same knife and fork as the downtrodden they so fervently champion."

"Why is it Sir Robert, that only women and not your Irish radicals and Social Democratic Federationist and Marxist are being slaughtered?"

"Women are the ones who give birth to those who may very well topple the order. Unlike men, their commitment to rights cannot be purchased for a fistful of coins and a promise of change to come but soon forgotten over a pint of ale or beaker of gin. The death of these women was never sanctioned. We never granted those responsible the permission to do what they did. We merely asked them to send a message, put the fear of the Almighty in them to desist in their rabble rousing."

"Who are the We?"

"Ones with the most to lose should revolution set the streets ablaze."

"I thought as much. A Star Chamber directed by industrialists and their government hand puppets. I suppose Charles Warren is complicit as well."

"No, Warren is a well meaning officer of the law. Well meaning, but incompetent," someone said from inside the coach.

Burton hopped over the wall and went to other side of the coach and flung the door open. Inside sat the Hollens twins. "We deplore the wanton killings of women in Whitechapel," Julian said. He blew his nose in a hankie the same time as his brother.

"Especially the ones who were employed by our factory," Archibald added.

"No doubt your remorse over these deaths is motivated by true Christian benevolence and not the fear that one might conclude that the blood trail leads back to your very factory gates."

Sir Robert nudged Burton aside and slammed shut the coach's door. "Like it or not Richard, you are as much a part of this as Judas was in Gethsemane. It was you who provided us with the names of the women and the Irish seditionists and labour radicals." He reached inside his inner coat pocket and removed a sheet of paper folded in three parts and held it out to Burton.

Burton unfolded the paper. He read the names appearing on the paper. "So these are the J.U.W.E.S who will be blamed for nothing."

Chapter 40

Perez and Wilde tossed pebbles at the darkened window of Darnell's hideaway. He cracked the window and tossed the rolled-up Police News to the pavement below. "Shaw read it to me," Darnell said in a low voice reserved for the confessional of disinterested priests.

"I fear for Mary. She recognized the voice of one the men in the passageway and caught a glimpse of another she saw somewhere else."

"And what does this lead to?" Wilde asked.

"The ears of those who are paid to protect all must be tweaked to protect us," Darnell said.

*

Darcy roamed East London to enlist men and women of like minds to march with him to the Leman Street Police Station. His call to action was direct and incited his compatriots more than all the bombastic words of social reformers and reading room radicals. "If they won't hear us on the street, we will make them listen to us in their drey even if we have to tear it down twig by twig."

Word soon spread about the protest march. Every block Darcy and his followers advanced ten more people joined them. At the police station they were confronted by a line of bluebottles wielding batons and soldiers armed with rifles and fixed bayonets. They were commanded to prevent the gathering from entering the building. If necessary to bash a few heads and cripple members of the march in the defence of the police station, absolution was granted beforehand.

Sir Robert Anderson parted the column of defenders and descended the twelve steps of his citadel. “What is this all about?”

Darcey shouted, “It’s about what’s being done, rather not being done, about the women butchered on the streets your men are supposed to patrol.”

“So you think the way to make your point is by assembling a mob to storm an official Metropolitan Police Station?”

“Only if all else fails.” Darcy looked behind him at his followers. “You are an Oxford man no doubt, so you can see you are outnumbered.”

“Indeed, I see your insurrectionists are armed with clubs, shovels, knifes and perhaps one or two illegal pistols.” Anderson smiled so widely that it looked as if his cheeks would split. He removed a whistle from his suit pocket and gave it one shrill blast. The second story windows of the police station flew open from where more soldiers aimed their rifles. “Outnumbered but definitely not out gunned, would you not agree?”

Darcy heard the sound of retreating feet. His army of supporters had dwindled to less than twenty.

“I know of you Mr. Darnell,” Sir Robert said. “I know the part you play in maintaining order and protecting your community. I am aware of your association with various, let us say, questionable political and rebel factions. Do not lead the fools who stand with you to misery. Tell them to disperse. You and your most trusted comrades may come inside unmolested and express your grievances."

Two men with rising sun green patches sewed onto their jacket sleeves stepped toward. Two others wearing heart shaped SDF buttons joined them. Darcy faced the remainder of men and women who had not deserted. "Go back home. Spread the word that Sir Robert Anderson will hear our grievances and has promised us no harm."

The crowd voiced its concern about trusting a man they knew despised their caste. A man who regarded the inhabitants of East London as little more than fodder to satiate the insatiable appetite of industry. Its men only of value to the government when called upon to die on unpronounceable battlefields far from home.

Sir Anderson snapped his fingers. The formation of peelers and soldiers parted. Darcy and his companions climbed the steps of the police station. They had entered no further than a yard into the building when the massive oak doors slammed behind them. A dozen peelers pushed them to the floor.

"You lying bastard," Darcy cursed. "You promised we were not be harmed."

A policeman provided Sir Anderson a chair. "I kept my word. You entered unmolested but once inside the rules changed." He sat down and tapped the end of his brass tipped cane on the wall beside him. "Your friends are to be charged with participating in an action that endangered the safety of appointed peace keepers and by extension the security of the state."

Darcy attempted to rise to his knees. "Hardly hanging offences, you prissy mutton shunter."

Sir Anderson struck Darcy so hard with his cane that it snapped in half. "Granted these are not capital offences but murder is." He took a deep breath then trumpeted, "Darcy Darnell, you are charged with the murder of Tobias Fitch and the assault of two police constables."

"That would be us." Milton and Hines pushed through the peelers standing in their way. "Kiss the floor darling." Milton raised his leg and brought the heel of his boot down so violently that Darcy's jaw shattered. The sight caused even the most hardened constables to cringe.

"For the love of Saint Jude, the lad so feared the drop that he made a break for it and tumbled down the stairs and broke his neck," Milton jibed.

Sir Anderson stepped over the lifeless body of Darcy Darnell. "Very wry observation PC Milton. Proceed to his dwelling and gather up all evidence of his involvement in fomenting insurrection and that of Annie Besant."

Chapter 41

IRB LEADER FEARS NOOSE! BREAKS OWN NECK DURING FAILED ESCAPE ATTEMPT. The Police News announced the death of Darcy before the medical examiner received the body. Darnell's corpse did not remain in the morgue for long. Almost immediately his body was shipped to the Royal College of Surgeons for dissection.

*

"Mary it's okay to come out of the wardrobe," Bryson said when Perez entered his room. Perez's face was drained of colour. He was not there to deliver glad tidings.

"Your Darcy was a stand up fellow. Like Samson, he took on the Philistines in their own arena. Was someone you, we all, are proud to have known."

"What do you mean, to have known?" Mary covered the distance from the closet to Perez in three steps. "What do you mean?" She pushed Bryson on the bed when he tried to intercept her.

Perez sat down next to Bryson. He held out he the Police News. Under the caption **Good Riddance to Irish Rebel and Murderer** was an illustration of Darcy at the bottom of the Leman Street Police Station's stairs. Mary threw open the window. She let the wind carry off her wail then turned to face Perez and Bryson. "And where did they take him?"

Perez did not hide the truth from her.

"Then that is where I will go."

"No, it isn't safe for you," Bryson said.

"Darcy Darnell is owed a proper burial. He's not a hog to be split open again and again for the amusement of medical students until they can no loner tolerate the smell of his decaying body." She opened the door. "If I have to go to the Lord Mayor of London, I will have him released."

Kit Singh dropped a tray of tray of tea and biscuits when Mary came down the stairs into the lobby. Bryson raced after her. Outside the Parthenon she turned east in the direction of Whitechapel. "Where do you think you're going?"

"I aim to be dressed appropriately before I go pleading to whatever Pilate has the authority to give Darcy back."

Bryson felt Perez's hand on his shoulder. "You can't stop her, so you best go with her."

*

Before they crossed the bridge that demarcated the boundaries of the tree-lined boulevards of London from its seething underbelly, Mary paused and looked up at an ornate building. Pink marble covered its façade. Beside the brass doors depicting Orpheus' descent into the underworld to recover Eurydice stood two men dressed as footmen in purple jackets trimmed in silver brocade, knee breeches and white stockings. Through the oval window above the doors, a chandelier's crystal teardrops reflected the light of the hundreds of candles on the multicoloured stained glass. Women in formal gowns accompanied by men in evening wear ascended the stairs. The doormen bowed and opened the doors. Energetic waltz music escaped onto the streets, outside only to be reinterred when the doors closed.

"He promised to take me dancing."

When they passed by Mother Cantons, Mary saw three men standing in the yard with Farrow. One of the men lit a cigarette. His eyes widened when he noticed her.

Mary squeezed Bryson's arm and pulled him past Mother Cantons. The man stepped outside and watched them hurry away. Once they were out of view Mary said, "I know him."

"From where?"

"From the night Darcy delivered me to your hotel."

The sputtering gas lamps cast barely enough light for Bryson and Mary to see their shoes. Bryson heard a cough from somewhere behind them. He stopped and walked back to the corner. He saw no one. Propped against the outside wall of Darnell's room was his door. Bryson slotted it inside the broken frame to give the impression of security. He searched his pockets for matches and lit the coal oil lantern on the table. Mary knelt and slid her carpet bag from under the bed. She took out a tortoise shell hair brush and placed it on the bed.

"My inheritance from my Ma, worth more to me than all the precious stones on the Queen's crown." She removed the blue dress wrapped in crepe and ordered Bryson to face the wall. She looked at her feet. "Pity. I must have left my new lace up boots at Mother Cantons. No matter, I'll be pleading on my knees to whatever potentate has the power to release Darcy to me."

"She is not part of this. She can do us no harm. Leave her alone." A voice from the street pleaded.

"Mr. Farrow is that you?"

Bryson reached inside his jacket for his pistol, He cursed when he recalled giving it to Perez. He pressed his ear against the door to hear what was being argued beyond it.

"Don't be a fool. The bitch recognizes your voice as well as mine and perhaps all of our faces."

"You will not touch her. That is an order."

"You no longer hold rank over us. We took a vote and what needs to done will be done."

"Silas is right. Loose ends lead to a tight hangman's noose."

"I'll have none of it."

"Then walk away Joshua. One less on your conscience to plague you."

Bryson braced himself against the door. The intruders pushed it free from the frame with little effort. The door collapsed on top of him. The men trod over it, crushing Bryson beneath it. He used his knees to push the door off him. He leapt to his feet but was quickly wrestled to the floor.

A cloth saturated with ether shrouded his entire face. He struggled to fight the man holding it. The fumes stung his eyes. His arms and legs felt as though they had turned to liquid and flowed away from his body. He resisted inhaling but ended up gasping, no longer able to hold his breath.

Fading into oblivion, he heard Mary implore, "Mr. Farrow, don't leave me to them," then a wail of agony. As darkness entombed Bryson, a man answered her plea from the street. "It is too late, Mary Kelly. Your Irish fool should have taken the money and spirited you as far away from here as a ship can sail."

Chapter 42

It took hours for Bryson to regain consciousness. He raised his right arm and let it fall to his side. It landed on something wet and soft. The screams that followed seemed to escape from someone other than himself. He turned to see what he had touched. The Banshee screeches were his. The sound was so piercing that a cat lapping up a pool of black liquid on the floor joined in. It was impossible to accept that the mangled corpse that lay next to him was once that of a young woman named Mary Kelly.

The residual effects of the ether blurred Bryson's eyesight. Two men dressed in blue coats and wielding batons came into a hazy focus. One of the men pointed at the bed and then the floor. Four serrated knifes, plus a cleaver, were on the rough planks. Bryson wiped his face with his gloved hands and smeared something viscous on his cheeks. The same black muck as on the floor saturated his clothing and his flesh.

"Dainty one, ain't he Milton? Must wear those gloves to keep his fingernails clean."

"PC Hines, we're in for a commendation or at least a tin foil medal and a bottle of proper whiskey. We've nicked old Saucy Jack next to his latest plaything."

They rolled Bryson off the bed and onto the floor. He stared at their hobnail boots. Too dazed to protest his innocence, he winced when Milton knelt on his back. The peeler pulled Bryson's arms behind him and cuffed him. He jerked him to his feet by the chain linking the shackles. The metal bit into Bryson's wrists. The peelers prodded him out the room with their batons. They steered him to an alley behind the row of hovels and shoved him inside a 6 by 6 shoddy coal shed and closed the door. Through the finger wide open slats of the shed Bryson heard them discuss what should be done with him.

"Do we bring him to the station standing or cold and bundled for transport in a meat wagon?" Hines asked.

"Alive he contributes to the hangman's salary. But dead is less trouble." Milton rapped his night stick against the shed's door. "Quit your earwigging Yank. This is a private discussion."

"Let's go for a pint and debate the merits of one over the other."

"A capital suggestion Constable Hines. He ain't likely to abscond while were gone." Milton snapped a rusty a padlock he found on the ground through the hasp of the shed's door.

Bryson waited for them to depart, their voices to fade. He used his thumb and index finger of his right hand to pull at the thumb of his left glove. Though tight, it eased off his hand thanks to the slick of blood on his wrists. He folded the stub of his thumb into his palm. He backed against a shelf and positioned his left cuff on its edge. He bore all his weight down it. The cuff dragged across to his wrist and knuckles shearing off a layer of skin before it fell to his side, dangling from the chain attached to its mate. "I owe that Coffeyville hound a bone," he thought.

More than an hour had passed since the peelers locked Bryson in the shed. He knew that they had voted to save the Old Bailey the cost of a trial and the hangman his fee. He searched the shack for something to use as a weapon when they came for him.

"There is no way those jackasses are going to take me without a fight."

He primed himself. On the shelf was an ancient coal scuttle. The handle detached from the scoop when he picked it up. "Maybe no way without a little scuffle," he said in a more subdued voice.

"Give me your manacles key," someone demanded from outside the shed.

"Don't do it Hines." Bryson recognized Milton's voice then heard a thud and a gush of air mingled with a groan.

"That is a belly slap compared to what's owed to you if you don't shut up."

"Is such brutality really necessary Ezra?"

"Maybe not Oscar, but it calms my nerves."

Milton's head burst through the shed's door. Oscar Wilde hurled Hines into the shack next to Milton. "If you would be so good as to hand me the key to your manacles I would be most grateful."

Wilde unlocked the bracelet on Bryson's right hand. He cuffed Milton's right hand with one manacle and snapped the other on his left ankle. Perez repeated the process on Hines with the peeler's own set of handcuffs."

"Release us immediately," Milton demanded. "You won't get

away with assaulting two sworn officers of the law."

Perez held his finger to his lips. "Shush, be a good lad and take a nap." He knocked Milton out with a single blow and smiled at Hines. "You can choose to join him or close your eyes on your own." Hines scooted to back corner of the shed and curled into fetus position.

Perez and Wilde supported Bryson between them and led him out of the shed. Wilde hailed a coach on the street corner. He took a flask from his pocket and held it out to Bryson who drained it with his eyes closed.

"There, there old boy, it's over. From all the blood on you, they must have given you quite a thrashing."

"When you didn't return to your hotel with Mary I grew anxious," Perez said. "I sought out Wilde. We decided to go to Darnell's to see if you and Mary were there."

Wilde peeled Bryson's fingers from around the empty flask. "Before we arrived at Darnell's we saw those two leading you into the alley. We followed them to the Princess Alice. When they had thrown back a half dozen pints we grabbed them."

Behind Bryson's shuttered eyelids he saw Mary's mutilated body lying on the bed next to him and heard her agonized screams. He buried his face in his palms and wailed, "It is not my blood!"

Perez grabbed Bryson by his lapels and shook him. "What do you mean, it's not your blood?" He ran down the street to Darnell's. He tripped over the door lying inside the room. Despite the scene of carnage that met his eyes, his mind denied the reality of what confronted him. The cat sitting on the chest of the enviscerated corpse hissed when Perez grabbed a broom and batted it away.

He forced one foot to move in front of the other as though dragging an anchor behind him. He halted before Wilde and Bryson. His eyes were fixed unblinking on the wall beyond them.

"What in God's name?" Wilde asked.

Perez clutched a tortoise shell hair brush in his hand. He held it up. A hollow reply originated from a pit far inside him. "Mary."

*

Wilde covered Bryson with a blanket and told him to lay flat on the floor of the cab to avoid detection. The coach drew up to the front of the Parthenon. The scent of freshly mowed grass and lilacs replaced the stench of Whitechapel. Oscar partially lifted the blanket off of Bryson. Dried blood and viscera had plastered his clothing in a kind of grotesque patina. Wilde banged on the roof of the cab and ordered the driver to go to the hotel's service entrance. Perez exited first to ensure no unwanted eyes were on them.

"Mother Cantons. I know that voice. Mr. Farrow please don't leave me to them," Bryson muttered over and over as Wilde assisted him out of the coach.

Perez rapped on the metal clad door of the service entrance until his knuckles were raw. The bar securing the door from inside lifted and the door slowly opened. The towering Sikh and Kit prevented them from crossing the threshold. "You must go," Kit's uncle commanded.

Bryson snapped out of his stupor. “My notes, my filings on what is happening in Whitechapel are in my room. I need them. The truth needs be revealed,” he raged.

Kit stepped around his uncle and handed Bryson his tobacco pouch. Inside were twenty perfectly hand rolled cigarettes. “This is all that is left. The investigators from Scotland Yard tossed your room. They carried away your bag and papers. Your American friend arrived shortly after they departed. He handed me his card and gave instructions for you to go to this address.”

Wilde plucked the card from Kit’s hand. He held the card up to the driver. “Crack the whip and take us here without delay.”

*

The coach rolled to a stop outside a spiked wrought iron fence. A two story white brick house was at the end of the walkway. The unadorned oak door of the house opened. Bret Harte and Sir Richard Burton walked out to meet them. Wilde and Perez helped Bryson from the cab. His vacant eyes provided little evidence of the tortured images infesting his mind. Perez and Wilde draped the coach blanket over Bryson, tossing a few extra coins to the driver for the loss of his afghan.

They ushered Bryson through the gates into the courtyard. “Farrow, Mother Cantons, Wesley, Uriah, Silas, Farrow, Mother Cantons, Wesley, Uriah, Silas,” he kept repeating like an echo.

*

Bryson passed three nights in-and-out of lucidity between brief intervals of fitful sleep. His arms were restrained by straps attached the bed frame. On the fourth day he lifted his head and looked at the straps securing him. He struggled to break free. The bed nearly toppled over. "Remove these damn things before I gnaw my hands off like a coyote in a leg trap."

"Relax, it was for your own safety." Bret Harte uncinched the straps.

Bryson slipped his hand out, wiggled his fingers, and sat up. He looked at his naked legs dangling over the edge of the bed. "Where are my clothes? I have to go to Mother Cantons."

Bret Harte nodded at a chair next to a window overlooking a garden. A severe black jacket, matching pants and white shirt with a cellulose collar were on it.

"Are you joking? If I go out in those duds, every florist on every corner will be on the lookout for the hearse following me."

Bret Harte went to a liquor cabinet and filled a snifter to the rim with whiskey and a spoonful of laudanum. "This should bring you some relief."

Without forethought Bryson drank it.

"The day after you were poured into my house like a pitcher of guilt, Perez and Wilde went to claim the body of Mary before the College of Surgeons took possession of her. They returned this morning to see how you are holding up and to ask Sir Richard something. But he was gone before they arrived. Sir Richard said he was off to Mother Cantons to locate this Farrow fellow and his piglets. Somewhat strange considering."

"Considering what?" Bryson slurred as the potent elixir began to work.

Bret Harte glanced at the wall clock and remarked to himself. "It shouldn't take much longer."

To Bryson Ward, Harte's voice sounded like a river sloshing against its bank.

Harte continued. "Considering Perkins, I mean Perez, noted the only time you mentioned this Farrow individual and the rooming house was when you stumbled out of the coach. Oscar agreed you were far too away and garbled for Sir Richard to hear your ravings."

Chapter 43

Perez placed his ever present letter satchel on Oscar's lamp table and took out Bryson's revolver. He spun the cylinder and noted bullets were missing and took two from the cartridge belt and inserted them in the empty chambers.

"What in blazes are you doing," Wilde asked.

"Off to see Sir Richard to ascertain what role he plays in this business."

*

The sun penetrated the carbon smudged sky of Whitechapel. Every recess of Whitechapel found itself bathed in a few rare hours of sunshine. Unafraid of interference, Perez marched like Daniel entering the lions' den toward Mother Cantons. He stopped outside its courtyard and pressed himself against a wall as not to be seen.

Sir Richard's unmistakable baritone sang out, "Imagine, I've found you heroes of the realm on the same unhallowed ground. Saved me a bit of foot leather tracking you down individually."

Three men in the yard dressed in upper crust civilian clothes were flinging their black long coats and wide brimmed hats onto a blazing bonfire. Silas grinned as he faced Burton. "Ah, Sir Richard, thought you'd gone native. What do I owe the pleasure of your company?"

Burton held out a tube sealed shut by a wax impression of the

Crown. "Inside there are five releases from your—" Burton strangled a note of disdain in his throat. "—duties. No more action is called upon for you to perform. A sizeable cheque awaits you in Amsterdam, drawn on the Bank of England. You will remove yourselves from Britain and pledge never to return. If I had my way, you would be slit open from the navels to your necks and thrown into that sty to be devoured by the mother sow and her brood." He stooped and used the barrel of his pistol to count the men around the fire. "Two are missing."

Silas inched forward but halted when Burton levelled his revolver at him. "Don't be so sanctimonious Richard. After all, to some degree or another we are in the same cauldron."

Burton cocked the hammer of the revolver. "I only count three here."

Silas shrugged. "Eddie seems to have taken a liking to this vocation. He's gone north to tick off a few more troublesome bitches from the list. If that harpy Annie Besant is still around when he returns, he'll do her for a plum pudding."

"And Major Joshua Cyrus?"

Silas pointed at a stain glass window of a room above the stable. "Major Cyrus? Around here he's known as Farrow. He is probably composing a lamentation." Silas winked before dropping to his knees. He pulled out a four chambered pepper box pistol and took aim at Burton. At the same moment Lucky dashed out of Mother Cantons bearing an ancient carbine.

“I’ll have none of this near my place. It’s a respectable business of sorts.” The bullet from Silas’ pistol passed through Lucky’s eye socket.

“If this is luck I’ll have none of it.” Lucky may have felt Burton’s bullet whizz over him before his head exploded.

The other two conspirators ran to the gate to escape but were met by Perez. He shot Wesley in the stomach and Uriah in the groin. As they lay on the on the earth twitching, he calmly stepped between them and fired two rounds each into their chests.

Burton and Perez looked at the open doorway of the room above the stable. A masked man dressed in a British Officer’s parade uniform descended the stairs. “So this is where it ends,” he said and parted his jacket. He withdrew a midnight black Enfield revolver. Perez raised his Colt. He pulled the trigger but the hammer fell on a dead cartridge.

“That is one of the drawbacks of that model of Colt.” Farrow bounded down the last steps. His polished knee high boots stirred the dust underfoot. “If the hammer falls just a tad off centre, it misfires.”

Burton stood sideways and aimed his Webley at the man. “Be advised, my revolver does not have that same defect. Lieutenant Silas played the wrong card. If my Hebrew acquaintance had not appeared out of the whirlwind acting the vengeful role of a modern day Gideon, those two inside the gate were free to go. I counted three when I entered. You are number four. One man is missing. Do you know where I might find him?"

"You mean, Edward. When I learned he intended to carry on, I informed Sir Anderson. He in turn relayed his concerns about poor Eddie's mental state to his Royal Auntie. He is now a resident of a comfortable asylum for relatives of the throne. No doubt the memories of his foul deeds in Whitechapel will lull him to sleep at night. During daylight he will master Whist and for fresh air play croquette on the estate's manicured lawn."

Perez plucked out the dead cartridge and replaced it with one from the holster belt. "Cease the chatter. Let me kill him."

Burton sighed. "As much as that would please me, my instructions are to resort to that when all else fails."

"He's right, kill me." Farrow ripped off the expressionless white mask revealing his mangled face. A spray of mist issued through the hole that nose once occupied. "It is frightfully difficult to breath through this and dreadfully uncomfortable."

Perez rushed toward Major Joshua Cyrus. "Only fitting that the leader of monsters should be the most monstrous of the lot." He did not have a chance to fire his pistol. Burton tripped him. The Colt flew out of Perez's hand and Burton kicked it across the yard.

"Sir Richard, if we are monsters then what are those who feed us?" Major Joshua Cyrus cocked the hammer of the Enfield and held the barrel under his chin. "I know you from somewhere else. Ah yes, your limp, I do believe I saved your leg. Perhaps in India, Crimea?" The recoil of the pistol flung him onto the last rung of the stairs. The cavernous remains of his head was less hideous than the face it once wore.

Burton caressed the side of cheek. "No Major Joshua Cyrus, my limp is from Africa, as is this scar."

Perez crawled across the yard past the body of not so Lucky to retrieve his pistol. He kipped to his feet and spun the cylinder of the pistol and blew out the dirt in each chamber. Burton shifted his weight and aimed his revolver at Perez. "Whatever is in your mind. Put it away."

Perez holstered the Colt. "Are you player in this Theatre du Grand-Guignol? Or are you more likely a spineless collaborator?" He kept his arms to his sides as he closed the distance between himself and Sir Richard.

"Neither," Burton began but stopped mid-sentence when Perez delivered a blow to his kidney and a vicious upper cut.

Burton did not budge. "Well timed my Zealot friend but even you cannot evade a gift from my Webley at this distance."

"Why?" Perez asked.

"Not why, but when? As soon as I knew what my intelligence gathering was leading to, I approached the Home Secretary. He asked me if burning the wick in the middle of the candle would snuff out the fanatics at either end. When one after another, leaders in the Home Rule faction and labour movement died, I knew my reports were used as warrants of summary execution."

"Executed!" Perez interrupted. "They were sacrificed with less compassion than those on Templo Teocalli." He backed away when Burton pointed his pistol at his head.

"Bloody Dick, Ruffian Dick aren't those the sobriquets you carry with you like the scar on your cheek? What nickname will you bear to the grave?" Perez asked.

"Leave, my friend." Burton implored. "Forget what you have learned and seen in this shit layered yard."

"Sir Richard, you and I were never friends. Certainly you never consider me an equal but I truly believed that you had a stream of honour coursing through your veins. Discharge your pistol if you must. I am off to share what I have learned with our American journalist."

"Turn around," Burton shouted. "Every man I have ever killed has seen the blackness in my eyes."

Burton did not hear the approach of Oscar Wilde but most assuredly he felt the cold snub of a two shot derringer pressed against his temple. "Richard, you have no more intention of shooting Perez than perhaps I have of shooting you. As for you Ezra, I nearly collapsed from over exertion chasing after you."

"Ozzie lower that cap pistol. We'll have a go at one another Marquis of Queensbury Rules."

"Not likely, Burton; I am thirty years younger and far fitter than you were, old man, of the same age."

Burton tossed his Webley away. "I have no intention of doing more harm than I have already done."

The anger Perez had held so dearly inside dissipated. “Where will you go that your role in this horrid affair will not pursue you?”

Oscar Wilde removed the snout of his derringer from the temple of Burton. “Then we part as witnesses if no longer friends.”

Burton stooped to pick up his pistol. He opened the flap of his coat and slipped the revolver into its shoulder holster. “I shall retire to Germany. Put this affair and my oh too saintly wife behind me. I have left in her possession my journals and confession of all the commandments I have violated and those I have invented. All except my role in Whitechapel. She, no doubt, will allow her piety to overrule truth and history and consign my writings to a bonfire to protect my name, this foul kingdom and her misbegotten faith in a merciful saviour.”

Wilde and Perez left Burton standing in the yard among the dead. They made their way through the quickly darkening streets of Whitechapel to the glowing light of the other side of London to inform their American cousin why five, maybe more, women were butchered and by whom for an inexplicable reason.

Chapter 44

Wilde and Perez arrived at Bret Harte's to expose what had transpired at Farrow's yard. With the exactitude of cartographers, they laid out the map of what they had learned. Sir Richard's role in the affair lifted Bryson from his whiskey and tincture of opium brain fog. He went to Bret Harte's study and sat at a roll top desk. He scribbled away madly, recording Perez and Wilde's every word.

"More paper. I need more paper to write all this down. I'll drag those responsible out of the shadows for the world to see." A clean shaven man entered the study with Bret Harte. With an unmistakable air of authority he said, "Not now, not ever."

Vanilla scented pomade pasted the man's thinning hair above his prominent forehead. He adjusted his shirt cuffs to protrude slightly below his suit sleeves. The intruder put his arms behind his back. "Laudable, but not permissible. What you have learned or let us say fabricated will never be published."

"Who the devil are you to tell me what I am allowed to write?"

Wilde extended his hand to shake but the man kept his arms behind his back. "Come now Sir Henry, surely you don't still bear me ill will because of a little quip I made."

"To say there is no need to separate the monarchy from the mob and that all authority is bad is to slander the very institution upon which this nation is built and to encourage anarchy. But that is not why I am here. I have come to grant amnesty to this American mudslinger and to Mr. Perez provided they leave Britain and never write or speak about what they have discovered."

Bryson rose unsteadily, brandishing his pen like a knife. "Who the devil are you?"

Wilde laughed. "Mr. Ward, you know less about the ruling order of England than I know of the dark side of the moon. Allow me to introduce Sir Henry Matthews, 1st Viscount Landaff and Home Secretary. He oversees the security of the realm and all law enforcement in England."

"I don't give a sparrow's fart if he is the Pope. No one tells me what I can and cannot publish."

Bret Harte snatched the pen from Bryson and pushed him down onto the chair. "Shut up, hear Sir Henry out."

"You should be grateful to Mr. Harte. Because of his appeal to the American Ambassador and the Ambassador's appeal to me you are being deported and not arrested and tried for the murder and mutilation of a young woman named Mary Jeanette Kelly. As for you Mr. Perez, or Perkins or by what other name you like to hide your true identity behind, no charges have been laid for the brutal assault you made on two former police constables."

"Former?" Perez questioned.

"Apparently they discovered that police work did not suit them and disappeared."

The young constable from Mitre Square came into the room

along with an older police man. Sir Henry stepped aside.

"Wattie how delightful to see you again," Wilde said.

"You know this Molly?" the older peeler asked and threw Brysons's valise on the floor.

Watkins felt the blush rising on his cheeks. "Only from the theatre."

"Where the hell are my journals and notes?"

"There are no such items. This is what you brought to London Mr. Ward and this is what you will return with to America," Sir Henry said. "Watkins and Hobbs will stay with you and will escort you to the docks."

"And as for me?"

"As for you Mr. Perez, your presence here is no longer desirable. I have arranged your relocation to—" A flicker of a smile crossed Sir Henry's face. "To Winnipeg, the Empire's version of Siberia."

*

Watkins and Hobbs stood outside Bret Harte's house for three days to ensure their charge did not take a run. Perez went back to his flat and discovered it had been ransacked. The Tallit he had not worn since abandoning his grandfather's tradition to make his mark as a boxer and later join the army was on the floor, trampled underfoot by the vandals' dirty boots. He received word from Wilde that Bryson was to be escorted to his ship at dawn. Wilde wished to see him off and would appreciate it if Perez met him at the docks.

Perez arrived before Wilde. He pushed his way through the

throng of passengers waiting for the gangway to be lowered. Bryson was sandwiched between Hobbs and Watkins. When he saw Perez he spread his elbows out moving the peelers aside.

"I failed Mary. I failed all of them. I should have found some way to stop it instead of just writing about what was happening."

Perez placed his hand on Bryson's shoulder. "How?"

"I could have gone to the authorities, to Scotland Yard, the House of Lords to get their attention. They would have to listen."

"Who are these They? Do you think They have remorse or pity? They existed in the past and They still exist. It is They who burned my people at the stake. It is They who are plundering the Congo and murdering its people. In America, it is They who justify exterminating all traces of the original inhabitants, lynching people of different complexions from telegraph poles, street lamps and trees like obscene Christmas ornaments."

"What are you saying?"

"They exist because we let Them." Perez reached into his pouch. He took out the Colt Revolver and opening Brysons's jacket slipped it between his waistband. "Go home Mr. Ward. Go home." Perez walked away disappearing into the mist settling over London, past Oscar Wilde who was on his way to wish the American bon voyage.

Hobbs struck Bryson on his back. "If I had my way you'd be lashed to the anchor of that vessel and dropped over the side. As for that dirty little Jew, for what I heard he done to Milton and Hines, he should be in Reading where the boys can give him a dandy welcome on the hour."

Watkins pulled Hobbs away. "Leave off. Our order is to make certain he departs on that ship and is never seen here again."

Hobbs rapped his baton against a dock pole. "Wouldn't it be a crying shame if he was to accidentally slip on the ramp and break his neck."

Wilde quickened his approach and held Bryson's arm. "Listen to your mate, Constable. Allow this Yank to return to New York and write about the hospitality of Albion, the New Jerusalem. Then you can and go back to shivering and pounding the pavement in the delightful damp of Jolly Old London."

Bryson leaned nose-to-nose with Hobbs. "Copper, once I'm gone maybe your masters will loosen your leash and send you and your fellow peelers out to capture the maniacs who sanctioned the slaughter of five, maybe more women."

"That's enough from you," Hobbs bared his teeth. "Weren't no five blessed virgins done in. They might be worth the ink in today's paper. Maybe a memory, but tomorrow I'll wager the interest in five whores, five cunts who gladly spread their legs for any bloke with a penny and a pint to spare, will fade. Those tarts and this Jack the Ripper won't even be a whisper by month's end."

Watkins pulled Hobbs away from Bryson. "I told you to leave off. Once he is on that boat we will have no part in this."

Hobbs shoved Watkins to the dock floor and charged Bryson. Wilde easily intercepted him. With a graceful arch of one hand he flattened the bluebottle's nose. He knelt and dabbed away the blood pouring out of Hobbs' nose with a monogrammed handkerchief. "How many fingers Constable?"

"Five," Hobbs slurred.

Wilde propped Hobbs against a crate. "Good fellow, five it is. Should Sir Anderson ever visit this part of town again, tell him I am truly pleased that he recruits fine men such as yourself who can count."

The steamer ships horn sounded, notifying passengers it was time to board.

Chapter 45

Bryson remained in his cabin for three days without venturing onto the deck of the SS Montrose. The voyage would take two weeks, fourteen days, not nearly long enough to put distance between his nightmares and Dorset Street. He rested his arms on the railing and leaned as far over as possible without tumbling into the ocean to observe the wake the liner left behind. A stranger accompanied by a young boy wearing a newsies cap and clothes two sizes too large tapped Bryson and held out an unlit cigar. "Would you possibly have a match? I seem to have left mine in my cabin."

Bryson fumbled in his jacket pocket for his match box. He cupped his hands over a lit match. The man circled the end of his cigar in the flame. He inhaled deeply and blew out a perfect smoke ring.

"Nothing like a good Cuban after a pleasant dinner and a glass of Port to set the world right." The man pocketed Bryson's box of matches. "Do you mind?"

"Keep them," Bryson said.

"What is you destination?"

"New York."

"You do know this ship is going to Quebec City. You'll have to take a train from there. It only runs once a week."

"So I was informed by the gentleman who booked my passage."

The young boy slipped his arm around the man's waste and leaned his head against him.

"New York, a little too busy for my taste but a good city. I intend to stay in Canada for a spell to see what opportunities exist for a man with my talents. Spur of the moment decision. My son and I were in Belgium and boarded this ship in Antwerp."

"Daddy you are more talented than all the men on this boat," the boy purred. "He is a doctor of sorts."

The man gave the boy a stern look and nudged him away. "Sh-he, gives me too much credit. I am a Homeopathic Doctor and compounder. What's your game?"

"I was in London, Whitechapel, covering a couple of stories for my paper."

"Isn't that is where a few chippies who plied their trade were murdered?"

Bryson felt the bile rise into his throat. He suppressed the urge to knock the man silly. "They were not whores."

No matter how much Bryson wanted to reveal the truth, he knew that the narrative dominating every newspaper from London to San Francisco had become the gospel to the people smudging their fingers with printers ink.

The man and his son walked away. Bryson observed how the boy's hips swayed. He made a point of avoiding them the rest of the trip.

Upon entering the mouth of the Saint Lawrence River a pilot

boat sounded its horn. Bryson felt it strange that the ocean liner cut its engines to permit the boat to pull along side. A Bosun's chair was lowered and two men from the pilot boat came on board. They were greeted by the Captain of the Montrose. They entered the hallway of the first class accommodations together. Twenty minutes later the men and the Captain returned with the Homeopath and his son.

The doctor curled his shoulders into his body and avoided looking at anyone. The boy was a different story. He took off his hat and shook his head. Long blonde hair tumbled over his shoulders. He removed his bulky coat and oversized vest and flung them into the river. The unmistakable mounds of a woman's breast pushed against the fabric of the shirt.

The Captain stopped next to Bryson. "Now there's a story for your paper. I thought I recognized him at dinner and wired the British authorities. I knew for certain that he was Hawley Crippen, a murderer. Killed and dismembered his wife and only the Good Lord knows how many other women. Might even be that Ripper maniac the police are beating the bushes to locate."

"He may be guilty or innocent of the killing of his wife but I assure you he is not the Fiend of Whitechapel," Bryson said.

"You must admit Mr. Ward, it would put everyone's mind at ease to know someone with a name and a face was responsible."

As Bryson took the stairs to the lounge, he paused to say, "Or faces."

Epilogue

Bryson positioned himself in front of the large window illuminating Morris Breck's office. He held up a paper and read aloud.

Indulge me while I tell you about five butchered martyrs, five women who possessed more courage and fight than the entire British Empire or, for that matter, our own not-so-Grand Old Republic. Like all martyrs who challenge the orthodoxy of social and religious order, their reputations have been besmirched by those who feared them, pursued them and killed them. Before we bask in our own pretence of moral superiority, let us walk the impoverished streets of the Five Points, follow the sluggish currents of the fetid bayous of New Orleans where the bloated bodies of black men drift into the Gulf of Mexico for the crime of wanting to be seen as equals. If this is not enough to open your eyes, then visit Appalachia company towns where miners who never see the sun come home each night to the gaunt consumptive faces of their families to share a crust of bread and field greens for supper. The women's names I have unwisely mentioned in past dispatches. To recount them now would serve no purpose.

Morris rolled his chair away from his desk and leaned back against the wall. "Punchy, but it's not going to sell newspapers."

"You're right. It isn't going to."

Morris removed a bottle of whiskey from the bottom drawer of his desk. Alcohol no doubt distilled in a Brooklyn cellar and tinted with a touch of brown shoe polish and a thimble of kerosene for colour and bite.

"Rough one over there," Morris said and used his handkerchief to clean the inside of two dusty glasses on his desk. He poured a three-knuckle measure into each glass. "This Mary what's-her-name really touched you. As a newshound, you should have known better than to get too attached. Here, like most other papers, the job is to make the public want more, not morals."

Bryson threw back his hooch in one gulp. "Her name is Mary Jeannette Kelly."

"Who?"

"The last sacrifice to the darkness. The one I was entrusted to save. The one I didn't."

Morris poured another drink. "Bryson, what's done is done. What can't be helped can't be helped."

"What the fuck is that supposed to mean? It doesn't make sense."

"Wasn't meant to. Very few things make sense about life or death."

"Jesus Morris, I never took you for a penny-a-word philosopher. Pour me another dose of your death of choice."

"Ward, before you go back to your squat and wallow in the what-ifs of the world, I have an assignment that may take your mind off Whitechapel. At least might blur the memory during daylight. An all-expense trip to cover the Chicago World's Fair. I've even arranged a place for you to stay. A new hotel looks like a castle, built by some guy named H.H. Holmes, like that detective fellow Arthur Conan Doyle created. Think he might have been in London roughly the same time you were. Your paths might have crossed."

Bryson turned his glass upside down and trapped a spider crawling across the desk. The fumes of alcohol caused it to shrivel up. He crossed the room and opened the office door. "All expenses paid?"

"Within reason. I want receipts."

"To the nickel boss."

"Ward, what was she like?"

"Who?"

"Mary Kelly."

"She liked to dance." The glass on the door shattered when Bryson slammed it behind him.

The End

Acknowledgements

I thank the many people who have read and suffered through several drafts of The Last Dance of Mary Kelly. Their comments and observations have helped immensely in shaping this novel. Special and long overdue thanks goes to my wife, Terry Ades, an accomplished writer in her own right, whose criticism, though biting, is always valid.

Author's Biography

E. David Brown arrived in Canada in 1976 to attend the University of British Columbia. His career incarnations have included freelance writer, bartender, store manager, Human Resource Director, and CEGEP professor. He received a BA in English with a minor in History from the University of Houston, an MFA in Creative Writing from the University of British Columbia, and an MA in Administration and Policy Studies in Education from McGill University. While at UBC, David was awarded the CBC award for screenplay and documentary work. His novel, *Tell You All*, is a black humour retelling of the story of Lazarus. He is the author of *Nothing is US: A Memoir*. The story spans the globe, starting in 1951 and ending in 2001. *Nothing is Us* deals with racism in the U.S. South, Kennedy's assassination, the Cuban missile crisis, Martin Luther King's murder, student response to the war in Viet Nam, the harmful effects of the military culture on families and the destructive cult of red-blooded American Texas patriotism, as well as the aftermath of his getting kicked out high school and the Navy.